7/04

"May I join you

An accented voice

She glanced at the m___ ___ a double take.
"Ross? What are you doing—?"

"I do not know this Ross person. My name is
Miguel. I am a stranger here in your city and I am,
sadly, alone."

"You're what?" She couldn't believe what she was
seeing. Ross had smoothed back his hair, bought a
stylish suit and now was pretending not to know
her. He looked so hot, so sexy, and he wasn't
teasing.

"How is it that a woman so beautiful is alone on such
a night as this?"

"I was waiting," she said, then paused for effect.
"For you."

She almost laughed at the B-movie line, but then
Ross—Miguel—looked into her eyes and said,
"I'm so happy."

At that, she did the most amazing thing. She took
him by the lapels, pulled him close and planted her
lips on him. He made a sound low in his throat and
kissed her back, a hot, steamy kiss.

She broke off the kiss and gasped, "Is there
somewhere we could go?"

Blaze™

Dear Reader,

Falling in love too fast—that's Kara's trouble, along with thinking that sex equals love. What better way to overcome the problem than having sex with an incredible lover she couldn't possibly fall in love with? Her best male friend, Ross Gabriel, fits the bill perfectly. He's the opposite of the steady, responsible, appropriate man she knows she'll eventually settle down with. With Ross, she'll learn to enjoy sex without complicating it with all that love stuff, right?

Wrong. The heart doesn't care about steady and responsible and appropriate. The heart just chooses. And Kara's heart chooses Ross. It takes the rest of her a while to catch up....

This was my first Harlequin Blaze novel, and I had fun describing the sexy games Ross and Kara played. I loved seeing her explore and take charge of her erotic nature, with Ross's eager help.

And Ross...whew, what a honey—a dream lover—imaginative and energetic and sensitive. This poor boy took a while to realize this was the best sex of his life not because of the fantasies but because he was in love. Duh. The man was so dedicated to having fun, he was afraid to notice he'd outgrown his old life until Kara pointed it out to him.

I hope you find Ross and Kara's story as fun and sexy and tender as it seemed to me.

All my best,

Dawn Atkins

Books by Dawn Atkins

HARLEQUIN TEMPTATION	HARLEQUIN DUETS
871—THE COWBOY FLING	77—ANCHOR THAT MAN!
895—LIPSTICK ON HIS COLLAR	91—WEDDING FOR ONE
	TATTOO FOR TWO

FRIENDLY PERSUASION

Dawn Atkins

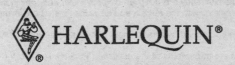

HARLEQUIN®

TORONTO • NEW YORK • LONDON
AMSTERDAM • PARIS • SYDNEY • HAMBURG
STOCKHOLM • ATHENS • TOKYO • MILAN • MADRID
PRAGUE • WARSAW • BUDAPEST • AUCKLAND

For my husband, David…
my own perfect stranger and best friend

ISBN 0-373-79097-X

FRIENDLY PERSUASION

This edition published by arrangement with Harlequin Books S.A.

® and TM are trademarks of the publisher. Trademarks indicated with
® are registered in the United States Patent and Trademark Office, the
Canadian Trade Marks Office and in other countries.

Visit us at www.eHarlequin.com

Printed in U.S.A.

1

"JUST BECAUSE YOU'RE SLEEPING with a guy doesn't mean you have to pick out china patterns," Kara's best friend said, pointing her nearly drained Fuzzy Navel in Kara's direction. "Stop channeling your mother. Sex does not equal love."

Kara Collier sighed at the lecture. "I can't help it. I'm a serious person. I want a serious relationship." She downed the last dollop of her frozen prickly-pear margarita and licked the rim of the glass—salty as tears.

"You always rush things," Tina continued. "You did the same thing with Brian. And a year ago it was Paul. What happened this time with Scott?"

"I just asked him if he'd like a drawer—for convenience, you know, to keep a change of clothes when he stays over—and he accused me of trying to smother him."

"Affection-miser," Tina declared. "I was afraid of that."

"Not another *Cosmo* quiz."

"Experts write those surveys."

"Did you really think Scott and I wouldn't have worked out?" Kara asked, filled with gloom.

Tina nodded. "Sorry. I might have been wrong. Sometimes I am."

"I didn't see it. Once I sleep with a guy everything

changes. My mind starts running with plans and dreams. Maybe I should just stay away from men.''

"Celibacy's a possibility, I guess," Tina said, her expression doubtful. She tipped her glass to collect a mouthful of ice. Kara braced for the crunching. What did they say about ice crunchers being sexually repressed? That couldn't be the reason in Tina's case. She was the most sexually liberated woman Kara knew.

"The only problem," Kara said, "is that after a while without a man I get kind of—" she squirmed in her seat and leaned closer to finish "—*itchy*. You know?"

"You mean horny, Kara. Just say it. *Horny*."

"That's such a crude word."

"Crude but accurate." Tina shrugged, her spaghetti strap sagging over her pretty shoulder. Tina wore her dark hair curved close to her face. She had petite features and a bow of a mouth—Betty Boop with a smart-ass answer for everything.

"Can I get you ladies something?" Tom, their favorite bartender at the Upside, shot them his darling half smile—Mona Lisa if she'd been a man.

"Yes, you can, Tom," Tina said. "You can get my friend here a new attitude about sex."

Kara's face heated. "Tina," she warned, knowing it was pointless to try to get Tina to hold back.

"Not my specialty," Tom said. "I can, however, get you another prickly-pear margarita and a Fuzzy Navel, double ice." Tom always remembered what they were drinking, even though they made a point of trying different things during their weekly wind-down happy hour. They went Tuesdays or Fridays, depending on how hectic things were at work. Today was Tuesday.

"Not his specialty, my ass," Tina muttered. "That man has sex god written all over him...from that gorgeous head of hair to those size-twelve feet. And you know what they say about the size of a man's feet.''

"Everything isn't about size, Tina. Or sex.''

"Prove it,'' she said, then glanced at her watch. "Where's Ross? I want to ask him about the Emerson campaign.''

"He was finishing the sketches for the beer company pitch.'' Ross was a graphic artist who worked as an art director at Siegel and Sampson Marketing, the ad agency where Kara was an account manager and Tina a copywriter. He joined them for a drink most Upside nights and was due any minute. He was also Kara's best male friend.

"You should take lessons from Ross and me and have sex for sex's sake,'' Tina continued, "instead of wearing your heart on your parts.''

"You have such a way with words,'' Kara said. "And that's not fair. I try to take it slow, but when the guy seems right, I can't help but think ahead. I don't want to invest emotional energy in something that's going nowhere.''

Kara lived by her goals—in every aspect of her life. Added to that was her parents' divorce when she was sixteen. She'd concluded her mother had married the wrong man and the lesson seemed clear—choose men with care...and with your future in mind.

"You're either picking the wrong men or rushing the right ones,'' Tina concluded, her eyes on Tom, who was bending to get something from a low shelf. "What a great butt,'' she mused wistfully. "The quiet ones are deep, you know. And Tom's so alert. Think of all that attention in bed. Mmm-mmm-mmm.'' She drummed her highly decorated nails on the bar.

"Could we focus on my problem here?'' Kara said.

"Oh, right." Tina shook herself, then turned her big eyes on Kara, crossing her curvy legs with a quick movement. "Sorry. Talking about sex gets me thinking about sex. Like looking in a bakery window discussing the éclairs. You gotta have one."

"I may choose the wrong men," Kara said, "but at least I choose. Don't you ever want to settle down?"

"Someday, maybe. Maybe not. I see no point in gluing myself to a guy. When he rips away, you're a blob of jelly at his feet. I'm not doing that."

"Why are you so sure he'll rip away?"

"Because that's how it works. I tried clinging once. In high school I fell hard and it was a disaster."

"High school is Hurt Central."

"It's a proving ground. Lessons for life." Tina frowned. The topic seemed to bother her. "But that's me. Let's get back to you." Tina tapped her lip. "Okay. Without a man, you get horny, right? Then handle your horniness. Buy a vibrator. When you itch, you scratch. Simple."

Kara shook her head. "It doesn't work that way with me. I need another person for my, um, equipment, to work. I never know where the guy's going to touch me next, so it's always a surprise. When it's just me, it's boring."

"You're missing out on a good time," Tina said. "It's the electronics age, baby." She pretended to smoke a cigar and wiggle her brows à la Groucho Marx. "At least check out that naughty lingerie store by the doughnut shop."

"I don't think a gadget's the answer."

"So maybe it's lack of experience. How many men have you slept with, anyway?"

"Not that many," she admitted. There'd been two

relationships in college, and in the eight years since, just four men, including the three Tina had mentioned. Kara had dated other men, but not long enough for sex to happen...and complicate things.

She'd chosen stable men with relationship potential, but somehow they weren't quite ready or they had commitment issues or mother issues or just plain issues. "I tried to go slow—I waited six months this time—but I just got too..."

"Itchy?"

"Yeah. And Scott was there and he seemed so perfect." He was the attorney for one of their clients.

"He only *seemed* perfect. You were itchy when you met him. That's like going to a grocery store when you're hungry. You bring home all kinds of nasty things you'd normally never look at twice."

"Maybe you're right," Kara said. "So what should I do about it?"

"Change your thinking," Tina said. "Having sex simply means two people care enough about each other to share physical pleasure. Period. Sex is a healthy release, not an engagement party."

Tina made sense. Kara wanted to be sexually liberated, but in her heart of hearts, she was a traditionalist. You got close to someone, had sex, fell in love and got married—or at least moved in together—in quick order. "But I want it to be more than that."

"When you're ready, it can mean happily ever after, I guess. But you're not ready, Kara. You just think you should be. Do you even miss Scott?"

"Not exactly." Especially not sexually. He liked things in a certain order and almost timed—five minutes of kissing, five minutes of breast and penis work, two minutes of thrusting, then bingo. She wasn't exactly a tigress in bed and she preferred the man to take the lead, but she'd tried different things—climbing on top, doing a little striptease—and Scott seemed more annoyed than titillated, so she figured she wasn't doing it right. She wasn't that experienced in the variety department...and, okay, maybe a little inhibited.

Tina looked past Kara's shoulder. "Here comes Tom with our drinks. I think he and I, rubbed together, would make nice sparks. Let me show you how it's done."

Tom set their drinks on napkins and smoothly slid them forward. "Need anything else?"

"Funny you should ask," Tina said, leaning forward, deepening her cleavage. "I was wondering what you do after work. For fun, I mean."

"Usually I go home and go to bed."

"Sounds interesting. Alone?"

He gave her that mysterious smile. Kara could see his appeal. He was clean-cut and gently handsome with a broad, solid frame.

"That doesn't sound like much fun," Tina said.

He shrugged. "If you mean what do I do on my days off, I like quiet things."

"Me, too," Tina said, which was a lie, Kara knew.

"I find that hard to believe."

"Well, what quiet things are we talking about?" Tina stirred her drink very slowly, her eyes glued to Tom.

"For me, it's sailing. I have a small boat I take to the lake."

"Sounds nice. Water and waves and rocking." She lifted a straw full of drink and let it slide into the side of her mouth, a gesture just this side of suggestive. "I always wanted to learn to sail."

He shook his head. "Your nails are too nice." He

patted her hand, then moved away, leaving Tina open-mouthed, her straw poised in midair.

"So that's how it's done, huh?" Kara teased.

"He blew me off." She sounded more mystified than wounded. "I swear there were definite vibes."

They watched Tom pour bourbon into a glass for someone at the other end of the bar, completely ignoring them.

"Maybe I'm not his type," Tina continued. "Maybe he goes for blond bombshells with exotic eyes like you."

"Please." Tina had convinced Kara to ditch her glasses for contacts because her uptilted eyes were "unique." Kara knew her figure was decent, but she was far from a bombshell, and she had to watch what she ate to keep her hips under control. As for her hair, it was blond, but so unmanageable she often pulled it back into a ponytail or a twist in the librarian look Tina never failed to malign.

"Why don't you go for it?" Tina urged.

"Because he's not my type. We'd have nothing in common."

"That's the whole point. You need to sleep with someone you can't possibly fall in love with. Someone sexy as hell but all wrong for you."

"Oh, yeah?"

"Yeah. If not Tom—and I have first dibs on him—someone like… I don't know. Let me see." She looked around the bar, which held a number of attractive men, since it was a popular singles watering hole. "These guys are all business types. You need somebody less responsible, more of a bad boy. Someone like…"

The bar door opened and, as if on cue, Ross Gabriel walked in.

"Ross!" Tina declared. "He'd be perfect!"

"Ross? He's my friend. My good friend." Kara loved nothing better than to hang out in the art department exchanging cheap shots and jokes with Ross. They were known to finish each other's sentences. She couldn't have sex with him.

He was cute, though, she noted, watching him swagger in, blinking at the sudden dimness. Kara had been instantly attracted to him when she'd started work at S&S, until she discovered he was just an overgrown boy—Peter Pan with a sex life. He was her age—twenty-nine—but he lived in a funky apartment in a dangerous part of town, his only transportation an ancient motorcycle and a battered bike. He considered a kegger in the desert to be high entertainment, and, despite talent, intelligence and a terrific way with clients, he was perfectly content to remain an art director at S&S, designing ads, not overseeing anything or anyone, until they closed shop.

But it was more than his lifestyle. He was a babe magnet. And Kara was too ordinary to be considered a babe. Ross would never say that, but she'd read it in his face and that took care of any desire to flirt she'd had.

Right now, he'd barely gotten inside the bar and was already talking to a woman. He had an easygoing, bad-boy-who-brings-his-mom-flowers way about him that women warmed to. He made you feel really seen, and he was an excellent listener. It was a routine, probably, since Ross looked after Ross and never went far beneath the surface, but the blonde on the bar stool was interested, Kara could see by her open body language.

"So what if he's a friend?" Tina asked. "He's hot.

He's experienced. And you could never fall in love with him.''

"You got that right," she said, watching the woman write something—her number, no doubt—and hand the paper to Ross, with an extra touch of his sleeve. How did he do it? He was indifferent about fashion and tended not to comb his dark, longish hair, though he always managed to look arty. On him, stubble looked charming.

Could she sleep with him? The idea gave her a sharp charge. This is *Ross,* she reminded herself. The brother she'd longed for as an only child. He was like Tina, but better in some ways. Tina told her what to do; Ross mostly listened. He gave her the male perspective on her breakups, until she ended up laughingly philosophical instead of morose.

He was also the guy who'd held her forehead in the S&S bathroom when she'd gotten sick on fish tacos, then driven her home and watched over her all night. Of course, he'd kept her awake with Three Stooges movies at top volume and consumed all her imported beer and impress-your-date pâté, but it was the thought that counted.

Meanwhile, Ross had caught sight of them and was headed their way with his great affable smile, which faded as he got closer. "What'd I do?" he asked, and Kara realized she and Tina had stared at him during his entire approach. "Is my fly down?" He checked his zipper.

"You're fine," Tina said. "We were just noticing how cute you are."

Kara jabbed her in the ribs. *Don't you dare.*

"Uh-uh. No way," Ross said. "You can kiss up to me all night, but I'm not doing that Emerson project,

not even with overtime. I save my nights for romance.''
He waggled his brow.

"You are so lazy,'' Tina said. "If you'd show a little
initiative you could manage the whole art department.''

"All that responsibility, with a mortgage and an ulcer
to match? No thanks. I want my options open. Who
knows when I might decide to hike the Andes?''

"Think about it. I'm taking off,'' Tina said, sliding
down from the stool. "We can talk about Emerson Faucets and Stoppers tomorrow. I'll let you two make your
plans.'' She winked at Kara.

"Tina,'' Kara said between gritted teeth, but her
friend had wiggled off on her impossibly high heels and
ultratight skirt.

"What plans are we making?'' Ross asked Kara.

"Nothing,'' she said, quickly changing the subject.
"I noticed you're in trolling mode.''

He feigned innocence. "You mean Lisa?'' He tilted
his head toward the blonde at the end of the bar. "Don't
give me that 'Ross has hooked himself another bimbo'
look. She's an accountant with Smith Barney.''

"I'm pleased to see you've raised your standards.''
Ross tended to share his conquests with her—blow-by-
blow once he'd had a couple beers—and the last few
women he'd dated had needed Cliffs Notes for their
driver's tests.

"You know too much. Now I'll have to kill you,''
he said, pretending to go for her throat.

"What can I get you?'' Tom said, interrupting Kara's
strangulation.

"Just practicing for the next agency meeting,'' Ross
explained to Tom.

"Looks like you need a beer with some guts,'' Tom
mused. "How about a black and tan?''

"Exactamundo."

"Your friend left?" Tom asked Kara. "Tina?"

"She wanted to get home."

"I hope I didn't hurt her feelings. I just didn't expect her to do that. Hit on me." He sounded surprisingly shy.

"I'm sure she's fine," she said. Kara didn't dare explain that Tina had him in mind for a demonstration of meaningless sex, but she added, "She thinks you're quite attractive."

"Really?" He quickly frowned out his eagerness. "She's just lonely." He left to get Ross's drink.

"What was that about?" Ross asked.

"Tina was flirting with Tom."

"He doesn't seem her type—too humble and lovable."

"I guess that makes him a challenge."

"And God knows our Tina loves a challenge. So, where was I? Oh, yes." He put his hands loosely around her neck again.

She noticed how warm and strong his fingers were. She wished Tina hadn't suggested sleeping with him. She couldn't get the idea out of her head. "I give," she said, leaning away from his grip. "I was just keeping you on your toes."

"If you can't do something right, don't do it…in front of Kara."

"You think I'm uptight?"

Her tone caught him and he searched her face. "What happened? You're upset. Didn't Miller like the presentation? I'm sorry I couldn't make it."

Ross liked to present the creative concepts to clients. Kara preferred to have him at those meetings—his energy was infectious and he inspired confidence.

"No, he was pleased. You were right that he'd like the ads in that order. And he worshiped your print ad with the dancing beagles."

"Worshiped? The only thing Miller worships is his bottom line. You're my biggest fan at the salt mines."

"No. Tina's right. You're very talented. I heard Lancer is heading to L.A., which means the creative department manager spot will open up. You should apply."

"Stop shoving me up the ladder of success. I'm happy hanging here on this bottom rung, thank you." He paused and looked at her closely. "So if it's not the Miller thing, what is it? Your eyes are sad."

"It's just…Scott broke up with me."

"Damn. You want me to beat him up?" He took a boxing posture and jabbed, his biceps swelling nicely under his black T-shirt. The shirt looked great with the peace sign on a collar-length leather strap around his neck.

"No need. He was very considerate about it."

"Figures," he said, dropping the pose. "You go for those Fortune 500 types, who consider a snappy game of squash to be a test of their manhood. I know how to fix him—restring his squash racquet with low-test catgut. That'll destroy him."

"Scott's a good guy. And since when have you been so Neanderthal?"

"Good point. I'm a lover, not a fighter."

A lover. She felt that charge again. Looking at him made her feel even worse. The stud in one ear complemented his smart-ass half grin, faint stubble and tousled hair, black as his shirt.

"Anyway, he can't be that good if he was bad to you." He squeezed her upper arm.

Great hands. She felt a tickle between her legs. "You're sweet."

"It's just an act." He winked at her.

But it wasn't. Not when it came to her, she knew. They looked out for each other.

"You're too good for those jokers," he said. "Too smart. When you flash your intellect, their little willies just shrivel up."

"Oh, please." But she felt better all the same. Because he was a man, she guessed, with a man's view. And he was a friend, which made him safe—and absolutely *not* a viable sex object.

Ross accepted the mug of two-toned ale from Tom, saluted Kara with it, then took a drink. She watched his Adam's apple go up and down, noticing how his neck muscles slid. He was in great shape for someone too lazy to go to the gym. He must do something athletic despite his claims to the contrary. It couldn't just be sex, could it?

"So what happened?" He licked the foam off his upper lip in a way that made her insides clutch. "Not too many gory details, though. Nothing about how big he is, or any of that. I might be intimidated."

"Oh, stop it. Women don't care about size. It's only men who always want to whip it out and compare. It's not the boat, it's the ocean, or the motion, or whatever the hell that saying is."

He chuckled, low and sexy, and leaned forward. "Pretty lusty talk for the mistress of sedate. What's up? Did he make you feel unattractive? Because you're hot. Never forget that."

She blushed. "No. It just didn't work out." She watched, transfixed, as he slid his fingers along the mug's surface. He had long artist fingers. Fingers that knew what they were doing everywhere they went.

"Come on. Give me the scoop. I tell you about all my women."

"Like I have to pry those stories out of you. You can't wait to spill. I can't believe you broke up with that woman—Heather, wasn't it?—because she sounded like Minnie Mouse when she climaxed."

"It was more than that. She didn't like Otis Redding."

"Now that's unforgivable."

"Come on. Tell me," he said, his voice so kind and full of affection her throat tightened.

So she told him about the drawer and the smothering, and Ross frowned and studied her face, made that "mmm-hmm" sound like a doctor with a troubling diagnosis, and finally said, "You were wasting yourself on him."

She smiled. "You always make me feel better."

"My pleasure." He patted her hand, the gesture soothing as a hot bath.

"Tina thinks my problem is that I get too serious too fast," she continued. "From lack of, um, experience." She blushed. Here she was revealing how sexually limited she was to a man who'd provided fireworks for dozens of women.

"With sex, the issue is quality, not quantity… Take it from someone with the Gold Seal of Approval." He winked, teasing.

"Lord, you're arrogant. So, you're saying I'm picking bad lovers?"

He shrugged. "Could be the Teeny Peenie Syndrome."

"Enough with the penis stuff, Ross."

"I mean that figuratively. Feelings of inadequacy. Ask any shrink."

"Oh, you," she said, pushing his arm—more muscular than it looked, she noticed. Things about Ross tended to sneak up on you. He acted more casual about work than he was, for example. She'd seen the satisfaction on his face when a client loved his work, and he listened hard for the bottom-line results of their campaigns.

He had delicious eyes, she noticed—a liquid gold-green, with sexy crinkles at the edges. "Anyway, Tina thinks I need to learn to have sex for the sake of sex, so I don't get hung up on the wrong guy because I think I have to fall in love with him to sleep with him."

"Makes sense, I guess, in Tina's world view. She's a girl after my own heart."

"How come you never slept with her, anyway?"

"Who says I haven't?" He winked. "Nah. We're friends. Sex is sex and friends are friends."

Now they were getting closer to the delicate subject she couldn't stop thinking about. "Could you ever, um, have sex with a friend?"

"Depends on the friend." He picked up his mug and began a long, slow drink.

"How about me?"

Ross choked on his beer, set it down hard. "You're kidding, right?" He laughed.

"It was Tina's idea," she said, wounded that he found it so hilarious. "She thought I should sleep with someone completely unsuitable, and of course you were the first person we thought of."

"Ouch," he said, wincing in pretend pain. "That's not very nice." He studied her, then seemed to sense her hurt. "It would be weird. We're friends."

"I know," she said. "I feel the same way." Except for the electric jolts she'd been getting since he sat down.

Being around Ross was so much fun, it made up for any bruise to her feminine ego his treating her like a buddy had given her. She loved watching a new idea hit him—like a pinball striking every bell and bar, making him light up and zing. And whenever she got upset about a client, she went straight to him and he'd have her blowing off steam playing darts or Nerf basketball or running up and down the fire escape singing Queen songs.

"I wouldn't want to mess up our friendship," Ross said.

"Right. And sex messes things up."

"Not always," he said. "It can be absolutely simple and carnal." He gave her that look.

She faltered. "But we'd make a terrible couple. We're opposites."

"They say opposites attract." Was he just teasing? "But there's sexual incompatibility to consider, of course."

"Wait a minute. Am I being insulted here?"

"Not at all." He grinned. "You're fine. We're just different. You're sort of buttoned up and pressed down. And I'm, well, never buttoned."

"That's because you're always in a T-shirt. And I'm not always buttoned up."

"Oh, yeah?" He gave her a mischievous look. "Twenty bucks says you're wearing granny panties."

To her chagrin, she remembered she did indeed have on her stretched-out elastic, full-size cotton undies today. "That's not fair. All my fancy ones happen to be in the laundry right now."

"My point exactly. *My* women don't *wear* panties— fancy or otherwise."

The thought of Ross contemplating her decidedly un- sexy underwear mortified her, so she teased back. "Be- sides, I would never sleep with someone with so many notches on his headboard it probably looks like a saw blade."

"Oh, no. The notches are from the handcuffs."

She blushed again. Ross was definitely out of her sexual league, but he'd aroused her competitive in- stincts. Along with some others she'd rather not name. "Maybe you've underestimated me. I might be a ma- niac in bed. You never know about the librarian types." Was she trying to talk him into this?

"I wouldn't want to risk breaking your heart," he teased.

"Get over yourself. I fall in love with likely pros- pects. And you're the least likely prospect I know."

"But I may have unplumbed depths."

"That's not the kind of plumbing I'm interested in, baby," she said, affecting a sexy tone that came off stiffly.

"You're trying too hard."

She sighed. She hated that she wasn't free and easy about sex.

"You always try too hard. That's why I'm good for you. I help you ease up on yourself—and everybody else."

"Well, *you* don't try hard *enough*," she argued. "If it wasn't for me, you'd have—"

"Lost my job through tardiness alone, I know. We're good for each other." He saluted her with his ale.

"Yeah."

"Just not sexually."

"Right." Another twinge of disappointment. "Besides, there's no way I could do it," she said. "Kissing you would be like, I don't know, kissing…my brother."

"You think so?" he said and then, with no warning whatsoever, he leaned forward and kissed her.

A jolt shot straight to her toes and back again, making everything in between tingle. Oh…my…God. She started to tremble and was afraid she might faint.

Ross broke off the kiss. "I know for a fact you don't have a brother, but if you did, would he kiss like that?"

"I—I'm not sure." Their eyes locked.

Then Ross smacked his lips. "Mmm, strawberry lip gloss."

That killed the mood. To Ross, that had been just a kiss.

"Decent technique," she said, covering for how overwhelmed she felt.

"Decent?" He lifted a brow. "Give me another chance. Maybe I was nervous." He leaned in, beckoning with a crooked finger.

She shook her head. "You made your point." Even as she said no, her entire body wailed for more. "The main thing is that we're friends and we have to protect that. I'll find some other unsuitable man to *not* fall in love with."

He looked at her, his eyes full of wicked mischief. If anyone could teach her how to have fun with sex, Ross could.

Uh-uh. No matter what Ross said, sex made things complicated. Ross was her friend and that was better than sex any day—even sex with him. Besides, if one kiss could turn her into a quivery mass of need, just think what the whole experience would do. She might never be the same.

2

ROSS HAD ANOTHER black and tan after Kara left, but it didn't wash away the strawberry kiss that had coated his mouth and lips with sweet promise. He tasted it all the way back to his apartment.

She'd actually quivered when he'd kissed her. *Quivered.* What responsiveness. Those crisp designer suits were wrapped around one sensuous woman.

He'd had thoughts about Kara when she'd first marched her serious little butt in the door at S&S, but she'd been so intent and dogged—and repressed—that he didn't pursue her. Before long he'd gotten to know her and found her warm and open and funny and smart and they'd become friends. And friendship was a way bigger deal than sex.

He'd seen she was the type who put her heart on the line. And he'd never allow himself to hurt her. He couldn't put pain in those eager, vulnerable eyes.

But Tina thought he could teach Kara how to separate lust from love.... Interesting. Could he? When he thought about that strawberry kiss, it seemed worth a try. On a purely physical level. Simple sex might be just what Kara needed. Could she keep it simple, though? Seemed unlikely. She was an intense woman. He, on the other hand, had simple sex down to a science.

Ever since college. Ever since Beth. That was when

he'd learned it wasn't a good idea to get attached. People changed. Or, more importantly, he changed. Beth had wanted someone stable and dependable. He'd tried to be that—taking the job her dad had lined up for him at a big graphics studio. But the work had been mere production—the replication of someone else's creativity. He hated the daily routine, the repetitiveness, the tedium. He'd felt trapped. Then he'd started to get bored with Beth. He'd fought it, tried to hide it, but eventually all he saw was her anxious face, pale as pearlescent ink. *What's wrong, Ross? Is it me? What am I doing wrong?*

It's not you, it's me. It's me, really. A tired excuse, but, in his case, so true. He was a restless guy. He'd been young at the time and didn't know himself well. Now he knew to stay away from women whose hearts he could break. Serious women looking for The One. Women like Kara.

His tongue found more strawberry at the roof of his mouth. Mmm. Some sack time with Kara would be amazing. She sounded like she was really interested in exploring sex with someone. Why couldn't that someone be him? He knew her and cared about her. Some other guy might take advantage of her good nature. Could he make it safe for her? Show her how to keep sex in perspective? That was the only way it would work...if she could handle it.

He loped up the steps to his apartment, trying to remember whether or not he should avoid Lionel and Lucy, his landlords, who lived just below him. It wasn't that he didn't set aside the rent money, but he sometimes forgot when exactly it was due or where he'd hidden it so he wouldn't spend it.

He'd paid, he remembered. Early, too, and thrown in a little extra for next month, since Lionel had been worrying about affording his daughter's gymnastics day camp. Rental income tanked in the summer. Confident he was in his landlord's good graces, Ross paused to wave through the window at Lucy.

He unlocked his door and took in the chaos with a grin. He could pick up a little, but he was more interested in working on that guitar riff he'd learned from a guy at a blues bar the night before.

Even as he tuned up, he found he was still thinking about Kara and that kiss. She'd pretended it had been nothing more than a peck, but there was fire there. Possibly total combustion.

She'd seemed certain she couldn't fall in love with him. That was a good sign. And probably true. They were so different. She drove him nuts at work with her checklists and protocols. Of course, that was her job. Account execs stayed on top of the details, herded everyone and schmoozed the clients. The artist's job was to be creative. At work, Kara and he were in perfect sync, but in a relationship there would be war.

He started with an easy chord progression. She'd looked so down about Scott. Why she picked those lame-asses he'd never know. He'd like to help her if he could—give her the confidence she needed to not lock on to the next corporate clone who caught on to how great she was.

She was always helping him, covering for him when he overslept, giving him pep talks when his mind seemed to have squeezed out its last creative juice. He liked to look after her, too—calm her down when she got herself wound too tight.

He moved into the licks the guitarist had shown him over one too many brewskis. If they set up some ground rules maybe... *Ground rules?* Lord, he sounded like Kara.

But she was going to do this, one way or the other. He recognized that determined Kara look. He couldn't stand watching her get hurt by another jerk. And he knew what to watch out for with her...and if they had no expectations beyond the sex...they could have a damn fine time together.

The more he thought about it, the better it sounded. With ground rules in place, and good intentions all around, what was the worst that could happen?

"I CAN'T DO IT," Kara said to Tina the minute Tina came into the office kitchen for coffee Wednesday morning. Kara had already been at work for an hour. She sipped her decaf Lemon Alert tea, but she was so preoccupied it seemed tasteless.

"Hold that thought," Tina said, raising a hand to stop Kara's words. Tina claimed she couldn't think until she'd downed some caffeine and she didn't see in color until ten o'clock.

Kara waited while Tina took two fast swallows. "Better," she announced. "Now, what is it you can't do?"

Kara made sure no one was heading into the kitchen, then she whispered, "Have sex with Ross." In fact, she dreaded their noon spades game. The idea of gazing at him over her usually wretched hand made her break out in a sweat.

"Why not?" Tina asked.

"It's complicated." She'd lain awake half the night contemplating the idea, but every time she got around to reliving that kiss she freaked out. "Something happened...we kissed...."

"No!" Tina's grin filled her face. "Dish, girl. How was it?"

"Intense."

"Perfect! Hot sex, good times, no hassles. Just what you need."

"No. It feels risky."

"Risky? You couldn't fall in love with Ross. Talk about the odd couple. You two would make Oscar and Felix look like the Bobbsey Twins...no, wait, were the Bobbsey Twins both girls? You know what I mean. It's too early for similes." She opened the refrigerator and began looking around, searching out leftover pastries from a client meeting, no doubt.

"I'm worried about our friendship," Kara said. "We could end up acting strange around each other."

Tina pulled out a bear claw and took a bite. "Mmm, this one isn't even stale."

"And what if I did fall for him, as insane as that is? It just feels too wrong."

"I'd say it feels too right. You're such a puritan about pleasure. Why can't you just relax and have a good time?"

Why couldn't she?

"Ross would never let you get serious."

"True."

"Anyway, if you're ready for lesson number two in how to have sex for sex's sake, I'm taking another crack at Tom tonight. I figure he's got some rule against dating customers, so I'm doing a damsel-in-car-trouble after hours. Watch and learn."

"Past my bedtime. You can give me the play-by-play tomorrow." Kara paused, remembering what Tom had said about Tina being lonely. "Are you sure Tom's the kind of guy you want? He seems like a pretty serious guy.''

''Not when I get through with him,'' she said, but she didn't sound as certain as usual. Maybe Tina was lonely, like Tom said. Her manhunter attitude did seem forced at times. Kara had assumed she'd just been seeing Tina through her own filters, but if even Tom had noticed...

''Just be careful, Tina. I don't want you to get...'' She started to say *hurt,* but Tina would hate that, so she said, ''too involved with a guy who might get hooked on you.''

''I'll be fine. So will he, believe me,'' she said with her characteristic confidence.

Two hours later, Kara returned to the kitchen for her usual midmorning snack—fat-free yogurt, a hard-boiled egg and five carrot sticks—the only variation being the addition of celery, when she felt festive. She opened the refrigerator and bent to get her bag from its place, thinking that her life was as predictable as her snacks, when something utterly new happened—a warm hand stroked her butt.

She yelped, bumped her head on the bottom of the ice compartment, then turned to see Ross standing too close, wearing that appraising look she'd seen him give potential female conquests. A shiver ran through her, but she masked it by rubbing the bump on her head. ''Was I in your way?''

''I thought you had a little something on your skirt— dust, maybe,'' he said, his wicked expression contradicting his innocent words. He reached past her to close the refrigerator behind her. ''I've been thinking about your proposal,'' he said, standing too close.

''Oh, that.'' She felt herself go red. In the stark light

of the office kitchen, the idea seemed ridiculous. "I think that second Fuzzy Navel gave me fuzzy *brain*." She tried to laugh.

"Tina had the Fuzzy Navel. You had a prickly-pear margarita."

"Oh, right. See what I mean?"

"I think I can help you, Kara."

"You already have. You kept my drink straight. Not to mention my skirt dusted. I'll be just fine." In fact, she'd already made a plan. She was going to stop by the naughty lingerie store Tina had recommended for something electronic, then rent a sexy video—a tasteful one. She figured the combination of video and vibrator might be complex enough that she could pretend there was someone else arousing her besides her electricity-aided self. That should cancel her sex-equals-marriage equation, or at least reduce the itch for a while. Hopefully, that would be enough.

If it wasn't, she'd think about finding someone to experiment with. Someone *not* Ross.

"You're chickening out?" Ross said, his eyes teasing. "The kiss was too much for you?"

"Not at all. We're friends, remember? We don't want to risk that."

"Yeah, but maybe being friends makes it better. I know what you're trying to accomplish, so I can help you better than some strange guy would. We could be careful. We could, say, set some ground rules."

"Ground rules?" Her ears perked at that. He'd obviously spent some time thinking about this.

"I knew you'd like the ground rules part." He grinned. "So come to my apartment tonight and we'll have some beer and figure out how to make this safe."

"I don't think so," she said. She *was* chicken. She

wasn't sure she could handle this, and losing Ross's friendship would be terrible. Not to mention the tension at work. If the gadgets and videos didn't work, she'd find someone else.

"You don't know what you're missing."

Her stomach shimmied at the look in his eyes. He was probably right. It would be wonderful to put herself in Ross's hands…so to speak. She liked him, and she knew he cared about her. There wouldn't be any of that awkwardness of being strangers.

"I'll have to take your word for it," she said. She was *definitely* chicken.

AFTER WORK, Kara entered Naughty and Nice and marched purposefully to the devices shelves, head high. She was a sexually active woman who had every right to explore new sensations. She faltered a little, though, when the most tasteful vibrator she could find was in a lurid purple box that screamed *self-pleasure toy*.

To cover her real purpose, she snatched up a few items on her walk to the register—some party napkins with suggestive jokes, a feather boa, some flavored body paints and a package of what turned out to be edible underwear. She kept her head down and prayed the bored girl behind the counter wouldn't shout out, *Price check on the Heavy Duty G-Spot Pleasure Wand*.

The clerk didn't bat an eye, thank God, and Kara rushed out of the store with her purchases in a plain brown bag, feeling as if she'd dodged a bullet.

Next stop, the video store. Pausing in the self-help section she picked out an instructional video featuring a positive-thinking guru, then slipped behind the purple curtain with the Adults Only sign over it. Ignoring the sideways glances of the men browsing—no, lurking—

at the racks, she scanned titles that made her blush to her roots, and finally grabbed a tape with a soft-focused photo and no evident body parts.

Making sure only the motivational tape showed, she clutched the tapes close to her chest, pushed through the purple curtain...and ran smack-dab into Ross. The shock made her drop her sex-shop sack, spilling her brightly colored purchases on the carpet.

She stood there frozen for a second and Ross bent to pick up, then hand the items to her one at a time, examining each one. "Looks like you have a busy evening ahead of you," he said, giving her the vibrator.

"Never you mind," she said, shoving it into her bag, blushing furiously.

"And what are you renting?" he asked, snatching the tapes from her fingers. He held them high, out of her reach. "Hmm, *Firefighters in Flames* and *Getting What You Want NOW...with Tony Rockwell*," he said, reading the covers. "I can see the firefighters—all those muscles and that big *pole*—but I had no idea you had a thing for old guys with bad dye jobs," he said, handing the tapes back.

"Oh, stop it," she said. "I'm experimenting, okay?"

"I'm kind of hurt you're going with paraphernalia when I'm offering my fleshly self."

"I'm exploring...um...options."

"Flaming firefighters? Please. You *are* chicken."

"Am not." She was so humiliated she just blurted, "Okay, smart guy. You're on. Let's go to your place and see about some rules." What else could she do? He'd dared her and she had her pride. She'd find out what he had mind, at least.

The minute they got to his place, Ross started rushing through the apartment picking up stuff.

"Don't fuss on my account," she said. She'd been to his place numerous times and he'd never batted an eye when she had to push stuff off the couch just to make a place to sit. His frantic cleanup now charmed her.

His furniture consisted of funky items he'd scored at yard sales and nostalgia shops, along with things he bought off friends who needed money. He had a fish tank made from an old-fashioned clear gas pump in one corner and a Roy Rogers lamp-end-table ensemble next to an orange Naugahyde sofa.

Only the art was decent—fabulous, actually. Art photography, original oils and several sculptures. His record albums—he collected vinyls of blues artists and had a mint condition turntable—were in orderly racks. Ross had taste, just no concern.

Cords from three video game controllers were tangled in the middle of the floor and the couch cushions were propped against the cocktail table—backrests for gamers, no doubt. "Mind if I put these back?" she asked, picking up a cushion.

"Be my guest. I'll get us a couple beers."

She sat down on the recushioned couch and thought about what she might be doing—having sex with Ross. She shivered.

She did want to learn to separate sex from love, and she'd been attracted to Ross from the day they met. She'd always envied the women who knew him as a sexual partner. Then there was the thrill of knowing he wanted her enough to plan ways to convince her to do it.

But what about their friendship?

Maybe being friends would make it easier, like he

said. It would save time, get past all those awkward getting-to-know-you moments....

Was she losing her mind, thinking of sex with Ross as an efficiency measure? Maybe the ground rules would convince her. Or scare her off.

The hand she used to take the beer from Ross shook so badly that he put the bottle on the table, sat beside her and rubbed her cold fingers between his warm ones. "Don't be nervous, Kara." He looked into her eyes. His were velvet green with brown lace. Hazel, except sexier. "We'll take it slow. Nice and slow."

A shiver crawled up her spine. "How about those ground rules?" she said, extracting her hands to go for the notepad she kept in her purse.

"Let's just talk, okay?" he said, taking away the pad and pen. "We're friends, remember? Friends talk to each other."

"Right." She took a deep breath and blew it out.

"You're blotching. You always blotch when you're nervous." He studied her a moment longer. "I do know you," he said on a sigh, and thrust the pad at her. "Go ahead and write. You'll jitter if you can't."

Relieved, she labeled the list *Sex with Ross—Ground Rules*. "Okay. Number one." Before Ross could suggest something, she said, "Friendship first."

"Absolutely," Ross agreed. "Nothing gets in the way of that."

She wrote it down. "How can we be sure?" She frowned.

"That's rule number two," he said. "The minute either of us feels weird, we quit. No questions asked, no harm, no foul."

"Maybe that will work." She wrote it down, then bit her lip.

"Rule number three," Ross continued. "Stay focused on the goal."

"Goal? I've never heard you use that word," she said.

"Let's say I'm motivated," he said with a suggestive lift of his brow. "The goal is to show you how to have fun with sex."

"But it can't just be me. You have to have fun, too."

"Oh, I'll have fun. Don't you worry about that." He gave her that look again.

She shivered again.

"Next, this can't interfere with dating other people," Ross said. When she looked at him quizzically, he shrugged. "There's a hottie I'm working on at LG Graphics."

"And who could forget Lisa, the accountant with the high IQ from the Upside? You're such a hound," she chided. But then added, "Actually, that's perfect. If I know you're seeing other people, I couldn't possibly get attached." This just might work. "Number five is we have to be honest," she said, writing the words *BE HONEST* in all caps. "No being polite just to please the other person."

"And if we're not sexually compatible, we quit. That's number six, I guess."

She stopped, her pencil in midair. "You think I'm boring, but I'm really not. The granny panties were only because—"

"Relax." He chuckled. "I just mean sex is like dancing—sometimes your rhythms don't match. No biggie."

"I guess so." She frowned, worried.

"I'm sure we'll be fine. You're hot, I'm hot, we'll be hot together." He winked. "Oh, and if there's something you want me to do—sexually—you just say it and I'm there.''

"Okay, but nothing too racy.''

"Nothing you don't want,'' he said, but his eyes said, *Or that I can't talk you into.*

She gulped. "I guess. But if it gets too, um, complicated, I can quit, no questions asked, right?''

"Rule number two, remember? No harm, no foul. Any more rules you can think of?''

"You're positive about rule number one? Friendship first?''

"Absolutely. I couldn't survive Siegel on the rampage without you keeping me from putting my foot in my mouth. Anything else?''

She pondered, taking a deep swallow of her beer. This was completely new territory for her, so she had no idea what rules she might desperately need at some point. "One more,'' she said. "If we need a new rule at any time, we can add it.''

"Oh, God. The Queen of Revision appears. Now this feels like work.''

"Being flexible is a good thing,'' she said.

"Mmm, I'll say. I know a woman who can lift her ankles way up to her—''

"Stop it, you're scaring me,'' she said, slugging him. "I'm no contortionist, so don't expect anything spectacular.''

"You might surprise yourself,'' he said, low and sexy. "We might unleash a tigress.''

A nervous giggle erupted from her. "I'd settle for a sex kitten.''

"Oh, me, too. With sweet little claws that dig in just this side of pain.''

Her insides heated up. "Anyway, I guess that's it," she said. "Shall I read them back to you?"

"I got it," he said, "and you do, too."

"Okay, then." She slid her notepad back in her purse. She'd make a copy for both of them later.

Then, there she was, sitting knee to knee with Ross, with nothing to do but look into those hot green eyes and wonder about the woman with her ankles up to her whatever. She grabbed her beer bottle to take a drink and banged it into her teeth. "Ouch."

"Careful with that thing," he said, taking the beer from her icy fingers and putting it beside his on the table. He extended his arm along the couch behind her and scooted closer. "All this talk has me in the mood. How about we get started?"

The only light in the room was the golden glow through the stretched rawhide on Ross's Roy Rogers lamp. Romantic in an adolescent kind of way. And Ross smelled good, she noticed—clean and fresh with a sporty scent. He had such a sensuous smile. And he wanted her. Would she disappoint him? Suddenly she wasn't ready. "It's getting late. Maybe we could start fresh on Saturday."

"No time like the present, Kara," he said, his eyes raking over her in eager appraisal. "Don't you always say procrastination is the enemy of progress?"

"Not fair to use my work ethic against me." He was right, though. If she waited, she'd have Thursday and Friday and all day Saturday to get nervous. She did need to learn how to keep things casual. If not Ross, then who? Someone she'd have to start fresh with. Why not now? "Okay," she said. "Let's do this thing."

"You make it sound like a project."

"No. I don't mean that. I'm just—"

"Nervous, I know. How about a little atmosphere?" He leaned past her and pushed a button on a remote. The gravelly voice of a seventies singer known affectionately as the Walrus of Love swelled into the room.

"God, you're using your warm-up move on me," she said. He'd told her of the magical effect Barry White on auto-play had on women.

"Sorry," he said. "I go with what works."

"Try to stay fresh for me," she said. "In honor of our friendship?"

"Deal." He leaned in and she braced for a replay of last night's kiss. Except he went for her neck with a soft, nuzzling motion. Mmm. *Women love you to mess with their necks*—another tidbit from Ross's repertoire. It did feel good and her body started a slow melt until she remembered the woman Ross had dated whose leg twitched just like a dog's when he hit a certain place. Kara burst out laughing.

Ross stopped, frowned. "What's so funny?"

"Sorry. I just remembered Lorraine. Wasn't she the one with the twitching leg?"

"Yeah, right. Focus, okay?"

"Sure. Sorry."

"Let's do something I know you'll like." He moved in for a kiss. It started like the Tuesday one, then got better. Everything inside her went soft and melty. She leaned in closer. Ross's hands slid up to touch her breasts. Sooo good.

Then he started patting her chest. He broke off the kiss. "Is that one of those water bra thingies?"

"What if it is? Come on." She went for his mouth again.

"You don't need that fake thing. You have perfectly good breasts."

"The darts are big on this blouse. I need some padding. Just ignore it."

"Right," he said. He shifted her body so she was lying on the sofa and he was half on top of her. Lovely, but she kept thinking this was just the next step in his usual mating ritual.

"You're so beautiful," he said.

"Is that a line?"

"Of course not. You *are* beautiful. Your contacts show off your eyes. Crystal-blue. Nice shape—kinda almond."

"Thank you." It was glorious to hear compliments like that from Ross. This situation had tremendous potential.

"Remember the time that guy licked your eyeball and swallowed the lens?" Ross said.

"Yeah," she said. "Never date a man who still lives with his mother at age thirty. They get strange."

"Enough talk. We're losing momentum here," he said.

"Right." She pulled him down for a kiss.

"Mmm," he murmured, "that's what I'm talking about."

She felt a momentary thrill, then she noticed a lump behind her head. She reached around and fished out transparent red bikini panties. She held them out. "Either you've got some explaining to do about your wardrobe or one of your ladies left a souvenir."

He shrugged. "Suzee forgot, I guess."

"How could she forget her underwear?"

"Ah, honey, I get them so hot they forget their own names."

"Pul-eeze. You may be good, but, trust me, a woman

knows where her underwear is at all times. She left this to mark her territory.''

''I don't know…Suzee's kind of scatterbrained.''

''I thought you didn't date bimbos.''

''I don't as a rule, but she can do the most amazing things with her tongue.''

''Could you stop raving about the sexual skills of other women? I feel like I'm being haunted by the ghosts of lovers past.''

He took the panties from her and tossed them over his shoulder. ''Forget other women and their clothes. Let's get you out of yours.'' He slid his fingers under her blouse, but maybe because she was nervous or because he was Ross, his fingers stimulated her tickling reflex. She jerked away, giggling. ''I'm ticklish there.''

''Oh, hell,'' he said. ''How about here?'' He pushed his fingers higher.

''That's okay, but…'' She tried to hold it in, but laughter burst out.

''Are you trying to make me feel bad?''

''You got the tickle thing going. Let me get on top.''

''Somehow I knew you'd want that.''

She ignored the dig and wiggled out from under him, but missed the edge of the sofa and fell to the floor with a squeak, dragging him with her. ''Ouch,'' she said. ''Your elbow's in my boob.''

''Sorry. How can you feel a thing with that inner tube in there?''

''Cut it out.'' She went for his ribs and he laughed and jerked away, so she tickled him in earnest. He returned the favor, and they were soon rolling on the floor laughing and tickling each other.

''This is hopeless,'' Kara said, pulling herself to a sit.

''I've just begun to fight,'' Ross said. He leaned in

and kissed her, slow and sweet. Then he moved his tongue in a way that reminded her of the eyeball licker and she laughed into his mouth.

"You're giving me a definite case of shrinkage," he said. "Lucky for me, I know I'm a stud."

"Lucky for all the women on your speed-dial, you mean." She grinned at him. He really was sweet and very sexy, with his longish dark hair tousled across his forehead. She touched his face. "This just feels too silly. Thanks for trying, Ross. You're a good friend."

He sighed with regret. "Too bad." He slid his hand across her left breast. "I'd love to get under all that water." He straightened her collar and patted it. "At least we worked some of the starch out of your blouse."

"Yeah."

"The kissing was nice, don't you think?" He rubbed his thumb over her chin sensuously and with regret.

"Very," she said. For a second, she wanted to go at it again, but she'd start giggling, no doubt. And it was a relief they wouldn't be risking their friendship, ground rules notwithstanding. "I'm just going to have to meet somebody new to figure this stuff out. A stranger I could never fall in love with." Even though it had fizzled, this preliminary trial showed her the potential of this approach. It could change her life for the better. It just wouldn't work with Ross.

"How do you plan to do that?" Ross was looking at her intently.

"I'll go to a bar, I guess."

"Not a biker bar or anyplace rough. Because I can't let you do that."

"I'm not crazy," she said, touched by his protectiveness. "I'll just find somebody who's like you. Someone not my type. A ship passing in the night. A musician. Or I could find a business traveler. Or a pilot.''

"Where will you go?" he pressed. "What bar?"

"I don't know. Maybe the downtown Hyatt. Lots of pilots and flight attendants stay there and there are always business conventions. Don't worry about me," she said, shoving at him gently. "I'll be fine. I'm a big girl."

"Okay, I guess." He looked her over again. "Don't settle for just any guy. You really are hot. I hope you don't have any doubt about that. Ditch the water bra. And make sure to use a condom or see proof of a blood test."

"Okay, okay, *Dad.* Thanks for being my friend."

"Too bad I couldn't be your stranger."

"Yeah, too bad." If she could meet a stranger who kissed like Ross... That would be too perfect to be possible.

3

ROSS SPOTTED Kara right away. She sat at one of the high round tables in the middle of the Hyatt bar, looking very hot in a black dress as tight as a second skin, with a scooped neckline that revealed lots of creamy breast. Her fair skin looked luminous in the dim light.

He ran his fingers through his moussed-back hair. She wanted to sleep with a stranger, so he was giving her one—a South American playboy, to be exact. He'd bought a European-style collarless black silk shirt and a burnt sienna linen suit, borrowed a gold bracelet from a friend, and practiced his Spanish. He'd stopped short of a fake mustache, figuring it would interfere with his kissing and what if it peeled off?

Why was he doing this? For one thing, the thought of her flashing her shy smile at strange men just about killed him. What if she got into trouble? He had to watch out for her.

There was something more, something primitive related to the night before. Holding her—even while she giggled—had reminded him how attracted he'd been when they'd first met, and if she hadn't burst out laughing, he would have gone for it. Her skin had tasted great—like vanilla and cinnamon and she'd felt delicate but sturdy. He wanted to hear how she sounded when she came, listen to her make those soft, desperate noises of pleasure. Couldn't wait for them, in fact.

She needed a stranger, so he'd be a stranger. Of course, he could just pick out a nice guy for her, set them up on a date—first threaten the guy's life if he hurt her, of course—but who better than him to help her out? They'd gone through the ground rules. He knew how to keep it simple and carnal. He just wanted to do it.

He hoped Kara would get into the game right away. He didn't want to look too closely at his motives.

There she sat, looking nervous as hell, completely oblivious to how sexy she was. He found that delightful. Plenty of men were checking her out, too. A car-salesman-looking guy at the bar had just caught her eye. He looked the guy over. *Used* cars, for sure.

She smiled tentatively, nervously wagging her crossed leg—spike heels on her feet. Mmm. She sure as hell didn't have on granny panties tonight. Probably lace—red or black? He hoped it wasn't a pair of those edible things she'd bought yesterday. Just thinking about Kara's underwear got him aroused.

The car salesman smiled at her and rose from his seat. *You can do better than him, Kara,* Ross thought. *Don't settle.* He had to act quickly before she was tempted to take this sleazeball home for a peek at her red lace panties. He rushed forward, tripped, but caught his balance on a table before anyone saw him acting uncool.

The lounge lizard noticed him heading for Kara and sat down, frowning.

Sorry, guy. The best man just won.

"May I join you, señorita?" he asked Kara in his best Spanish accent.

"Excuse me?" Kara glanced at him, then away, then back. "My God. Ross? What are you doing—?"

"*Perdóname, señorita.* I do not know this Ross person. My name is Miguel. I am from Argentina. I am a stranger here in your city. Business brings me here and I am, sadly, alone.''

''You're what?'' Kara couldn't believe what she was seeing. Ross had smoothed back his hair, bought a stylish suit and now was pretending not to know her. He wasn't grinning, so he wasn't teasing her. He looked absolutely serious, this Miguel.

He was being her stranger, she realized. Bless his heart. He certainly looked different. He'd moussed his hair back, revealing his high, elegant forehead and making his swarthy complexion seem more dramatic. He'd even worn a different cologne, something more musky than usual. Dressed this way, he seemed mature and exotic and devastatingly sexy.

''Please, sit,'' she said, patting the stool beside her. She was intrigued that he'd come—and relieved, she had to admit. A creepy guy at the bar had been about to head her way, and her heart had begun to pound. She'd been losing her nerve. Meeting a stranger just for sex seemed too chancy, too awkward. But here was Ross. Thank God.

''Es mi honor,'' Miguel said, sliding onto the chair. He leaned close to her. ''Can you tell me something?'' he asked. His eyes, gleaming in the candlelight, were gorgeous. Together with his dark hair, they made him seem mysterious and a bit dangerous. And he smelled so good.

''Anything,'' she said in her sexiest voice. She leaned forward the way Tina always did to emphasize her cleavage. Her nervousness had evaporated, she realized. If Ross could become a stranger, why couldn't she?

''How is it that a woman so beautiful is alone on such a night as this?''

"I was waiting," she said, then paused for effect. "For you." She almost laughed at the B-movie line, but then Ross—Miguel—looked into her eyes, and said, "I am so happy," and it became the perfect thing to have said. "Shall I buy you something to drink?" he asked.

"I have a better idea." And then she did the most amazing thing. She took him by the lapels of his expensive jacket and pulled him close and planted her lips on him, even pushed her tongue forward a little. She was shocked at herself, but maybe not really. This exotic stranger was also her dear friend, after all. He was exciting, but safe, too. And his being a different person gave her permission to be different, too.

Ross—Miguel—made a sound low in his throat and kissed her back, even better than last night.

She felt so weak she feared she might slide off the stool and fall to the floor. "Is there somewhere we could go?" she gasped, breaking off the kiss.

"I have a room in the hotel."

"You're kidding!" she said.

"Would I joke about a thing like that?" he said in his own voice.

"I guess not," she said. "I can't believe you're doing this for me. And you bought new clothes, too." She felt emotions rise in her—tenderness and gratitude and lust. Lots of lust.

"I'm doing this for both of us, señorita," he said, resuming his role as a Latin lover. "What may I call you?"

"Kar—no, Katherine," she said, choosing the first elegant name she could come up with. "Take me to your room, please."

"My pleasure," Ross-Miguel said, and tucked her

snugly against his waist and walked her out of the bar to the glass elevator that led to the guest rooms.

She couldn't believe she was about to make love with the same man who drank milk out of the carton in the S&S kitchen, wandered around the office barefoot, and collected Superman comic books. Now, he was an urbane cosmopolite looking down at her in a way that told her he knew exactly how to drive her mad with lust and planned on doing so.

He held the elevator door for her, the gold bracelet emphasizing his strong hands. The elevator soared, sending her already-jumpy stomach to her knees. At the seventeenth floor, Miguel held the elevator door for her, then walked her down the hall, holding her so tightly she felt each talented finger dig into her muscles.

Outside his room, he turned her against the door. "I can't wait another *momento para tus...para tus... ¿Cómo se dice...?*" He frowned, looking for the word for *lips,* she was certain.

"*Labios,*" she provided.

"*Exactamundo,*" he said, butchering the Spanish, but she didn't care because then he kissed her. Actually it was *un gran beso*—full of romance and desire and it made her weak with wanting.

Behind her back, he opened the door and they stepped into a room so sumptuous Kara was seized with worry that Ross couldn't afford it. "I'll pay half," she blurted before she realized the effect that might have on the magic of the moment.

"But, Señorita Katherine, I am a wealthy man. My only joy is to spend my money on the people I care about."

"Oh, right," she said. "Sure. But think about it."

In answer, he pulled her into his arms and stroked

her body through the silk, lifting her dress tantalizingly high on her thighs. "This is beautiful," he said. "So thin I can feel the texture of your skin." He cupped her bottom.

"No granny panties," she murmured.

"I'll say," he said, stroking her again, then moving up to the top of her zipper. He was going to strip her and she couldn't wait.

"And if I'd known I would meet you tonight, I wouldn't have worn *any*."

"Mmm," he said, slowly lowering her zipper to her waist, his eyes on her the entire time. Cool air teased her back where her dress had opened. Then he pulled the front of her dress down far enough to reveal the black lace teddy she wore underneath. His eyes gleamed with approval.

She hadn't known whether she'd actually meet a man tonight, let alone sleep with one, but she'd dressed sexy in order to feel sexy. Miguel's expression told her she'd succeeded.

Miguel pushed her dress the rest of the way down and it whispered into a silky puddle at her spike-heeled feet.

She felt surprisingly calm—not nervous like she'd normally be at a moment like this—or fearful that she looked hippy or she'd be clumsy.

"You are so beautiful, Kara.... I mean Katherine. Do you know how *bellísima* you are?"

She blushed and smiled.

"Look." He gently turned her to face the ornate full-length mirror beside a marble end table and stood behind her. "Do you see?"

Embarrassed at first, she glanced at herself in the mirror, caught a flash of black lace, then looked down.

That wasn't enough for Miguel, who lifted her chin. "Look," he murmured. "You are lovely."

So Kara looked Katherine right in the eye. And liked what she saw. The sexy lingerie was perfect on her pale skin. Her blond hair had a sexy tousled look, her cheeks were pink with excitement, and her eyes gleamed wickedly.

She reached up to cup Miguel's jaw, loving the picture they made. Miguel's body framed hers, his olive skin, dark brown suit and dark hair a delicious contrast to her fairness.

He reached under her arms to cup her breasts through the black lace, holding them completely, as if to own them. The sight was pure sex. Heat shot from her breasts to her core. She pushed her backside against him, sliding against his erection, glorying in it, feeling wicked and wanton.

Then Miguel slowly teased the teddy straps from her shoulders, his fingertips tickling her skin—an exquisite and shivery sensation. He tugged the flimsy fabric down to her waist, baring her breasts to them both in the mirror. She watched her nipples knot with arousal, feeling the sweet, tight pain of it at the same time.

Ross lifted her breasts lovingly, as if they were fragile as eggshells. His breath hissed and his eyes closed with the pleasure of touching her.

Then she had to touch *his* skin, to see him naked in the mirror, too. She turned and pushed his jacket from his shoulders and he shook it to the floor. She began to unbutton his shirt, but her fingers trembled and the second buttonhole was tight. The moment stretched.

"Allow me," Ross said, working on the button himself, smiling confidently at her as he tried to loosen it. Except he couldn't get it either. "Forget it," he muttered in Ross's voice. He crossed his arms, grabbed the shirt hem and yanked it up and over his head.

She ran her fingers across his taut pectorals, then his flat stomach. He groaned and closed his eyes.

"You must get lots of exercise in Argentina on your hacienda," she murmured.

"Enough, I guess," he said, sounding shaky with lust. He pushed her teddy down her body until it fell to the floor.

Once she was naked before him, he paused, awe in his expression. "You're beautiful," he said, sounding very Ross. He caught himself and resumed in his accent, "You are like art, Señorita Katherine. *Perfección.*" He ran his hands along the curves of her hips.

She felt so wonderful, so aroused, she didn't have her usual urge to slip under the covers and keep her partner too busy to look at her very closely. Instead, she reveled in her nakedness and wanted to enjoy his.

"Now you," she said, and unhooked his buckle and zipper, not surprised to find no underwear behind them. Miguel, like Ross seemed to be a man who would forgo any unnecessary barrier to sensation.

Ross stopped her from pushing his pants to the floor so he could take something out of his pocket—a short strip of condoms. Bless him for his thoughtfulness.

"I'm on the Pill," she said. "And healthy."

"I'm good," he said, returning the condoms to his pocket before he let his pants fall.

"I'm sure you are," she said, her gaze drawn down his body to his erection. She glanced up at his face.

"For you," he said. "I am this way for you."

She grasped him gently.

He groaned, gripping her upper arm, his fingers digging in. "You make me crazy," he said, his voice hoarse with need.

"You mean *loco*," she murmured, sliding her hand along the solid length of him, loving the way he quaked at her touch. "And that's what I want—to make you crazy in both your languages." That was a very sexy thing to say, she realized, liking Katherine a lot.

Then Ross released her arms and slid his palms slowly down her arms and across her hips, his touch so light he barely made contact with her skin. He skimmed the surface of her pubic hair, setting the nerve endings there on fire. He was teasing her, and she couldn't stand it.

"Touch me, please," she said, pushing herself toward him. His fingers slid in and oh, so lightly brushed her clitoris. Liquid gushed from her and she feared she'd climax before she got to feel him inside her.

As if he'd read her mind, he lifted her off her feet and set her gently on the table beside the mirror, the cool marble a delicious shock to her thighs, and teased her with the tip of his penis.

She automatically wrapped her legs around his waist as if this were the most natural position in the world instead of something completely new to her. She tried to pull him into her.

"Slowly, sweetheart. Let's make this last." He turned so they could see themselves in the mirror. "Look at us," he whispered.

She looked. The sight was erotic and illicit—as if they were voyeurs to their own ecstasy. As she watched, Ross lowered his mouth to suck her left nipple. The sight set her on fire and the sweet tightness made her gasp. She threw back her head, afraid she would explode or scream or pass out.

"Is this good?" he asked her. "Does this feel good?"

"Oh…it…oh…it's so…" She could only gasp single syllables.

"Good," he said, triumph in his voice. He pushed into her, millimeter by exquisite millimeter.

"Please, more," she moaned, not caring what she said as long as she got more of him.

He moved faster, his body trembling with urgency as he thrust deeper and harder.

"Oh, oh, oh," she gasped. Now and then she caught sight of them in the mirror—her knees spread, breasts swollen and tight-tipped, his buttocks rippling as he thrust into her—powerful, yet needy, too.

Then his speed quickened even more. He moaned, then slammed into her and exploded, the spasm bringing on her own climax. She cried out, writhing and twisting while he pumped into her for long, glorious seconds. When it was over, she sagged against him, tucking her face into his neck. "That was amazing," she breathed.

"Yeah," he said, then, almost as an afterthought, *"señorita."*

She smiled into his neck.

He slid out of her body, then hugged her in a familiar way. Uh-oh. She became abruptly aware that she'd just had sex with her friend Ross. She slid to the floor, embarrassed. "I'd better go," she said, and kissed him on the cheek.

She grabbed the puddle of silk and lace—her dress and teddy—from the floor and rushed into the bathroom to dress. When she came out, Ross was sitting up in the bed, beautiful and tan against the white sheets.

"Why don't you stay?" he said. "We have the room

all night.'' His expression promised even more sensual delights.

But that would spoil the illusion. Like Cinderella before the clock sounded midnight, she had to get away before reality sank in. She slipped on her shoes and shook her head. "That would be too much. You gave me exactly what I needed."

"I'm glad."

"You were perfect—a perfect stranger."

He saluted her. "I aim to please." But that was too Ross, so he added, *"Adiós, cara mía."*

"Adiós, Miguel, *mi amor,"* she said with a grin.

All the way home, she felt invigorated. She couldn't believe that was her with her legs around Ross's hips, crying out wildly for more. Just like one of Ross's women. She'd never had sex like that in her life—reveling in her body, watching herself move and moan. And sitting on a table? *Omigod.* She would have thought it would be too awkward. But *nooo.* With Ross it was graceful and perfect.

She tested herself. Did she feel she was falling in love? Not at all. She felt sensual and confident and relaxed and wonderful. It had been just the way Tina described it—two people sharing physical pleasure. It didn't have to be love.

Except, what would happen when she saw Ross at S&S for their noon game of spades? It could be really, really weird. Or really, really funny. Or really, really hot. She had no idea which.

She knew one thing—she'd split the hotel bill with him. She'd checked the rate on the way out. Three hundred dollars was too much for Ross to spend on a favor to a friend. Luckily, she knew that he was an extravagant guy without a thrifty impulse in his soul. Otherwise, she might have to wonder if there was more to this mystery date than was good for either of them.

4

"ABSO-FRIGGIN'-LUTELY amazing," Tina said after Kara had described the events at the Hyatt the night before. They were in the coffee room where Kara was drinking a double-bagger of Earl Grey because she could barely keep her eyes open. She'd lain awake all night reliving her Latin lover adventure.

"It *was* amazing," Kara said wistfully. "Only I don't know what to say to him now. He saw me...you know...like that."

"Like what? With your head thrown back, eyes rolling, sweating and moaning like a beast? Like that?"

"No, better than that. I was really, really sexy." The memory made her blush. "And today I'm going to have to ask the guy whose hips I wrapped my legs around last night to quit belching the lyrics of songs over the office intercom."

Tina opened the refrigerator for what Kara knew to be her usual morning pilfering. "God, nothing in here but Sampson's peanut-butter celery that he never eats." She emerged with a piece of it.

"Could I get some help here?" Kara said, calling her friend back to her problem.

"Just act normal," Tina answered, waving the stalk in the air. "You have a double life. Last night you were an exotic stranger and he was Don Juan. Today you're back to being a repressed account exec and he's an overgrown kid who collects comic books."

"I guess so. And last night did the trick. I can definitely see how sex without love works."

"Poof!" Tina said, pretending to tap Kara's head with her celery wand. "You're sexually liberated."

"It was nice of Ross to do that for me, don't you think?"

"He got something out of the deal, too," Tina said, then gave Kara a speculative look. "You're not making too much of this, are you? No urge to register at Macy's or anything?"

"Of course not. This was a one-time thing." Except all she'd done for the past ten hours was relive the event and long for more. "So, you say, just act like nothing happened?"

"Exactly."

She sipped her tea, clutching the warm mug with her nervously cold palms. "Speaking of nothing happening, how did it go with Tom last night?"

Tina blushed. Amazing. Tina never blushed. "It was bizarre. It started out like I planned—it's two a.m. and I tell him my car won't start and could he give me a ride home. He looks at me funny, but he says he'll do it." Tina tapped her lip with the jagged-ended celery stick.

"Then what?"

"So, I climb into his car, lean into him to free my seat belt, giving him plenty of thigh to ogle—and he ogled, all right. Good, I think, we're getting somewhere. I'll invite him in for thank-you coffee and we'll see if he's as attentive in bed as he is at the bar.

"He hardly talks in the car, but I drag out of him that he's close to his family, and he's taking classes to be an engineer. His eyes are so blue…. Anyway, we get to my place and I ask him to come in and you won't believe what he says to me." Pause. Tina was such a drama queen.

"What?"

She took a bite of celery and chewed slowly. "He says, 'You need your sleep.'"

"What?"

"*Then* he says, 'Give me your distributor cap and I'll put it back on before you pick up the car.' Can you believe it? He was on to me the whole time. Then he offers me a ride to work this morning."

"Wow. What did you do?"

"I gave him the cap, but I rode in with my neighbor."

"So, are you giving up?"

"Are you kidding? I figure he likes to make the first move. Old-fashioned, but nice. He held the door for me and walked me up to my apartment, too. A gentleman." She sighed, then tossed the stub of celery into the trash. "I'll just play it his way. Let him come to me."

"Maybe he's not your kind of guy, Tina."

"He's hot. That makes him my kind of guy."

"What if he wants to get serious?"

"No guy wants to get serious. Not if he has half a chance not to. That only happens in romance novels."

"Just be careful."

"Ditto," she said, looking past Kara's shoulder. "Miguel at twelve o'clock."

Kara whirled to find Ross leaning against the doorjamb taking a swig from a quart bottle of V8 juice.

"Ross!" she said, too bright, too nervous.

"Have fun last night, Kara?" he asked, his expression neutral. "Meet anybody?"

"I, uh, I…actually, I did." Her heart pounded in her ears at the sight and smell of him—she could still detect Miguel's spicy scent. It seemed weird to talk about it in front of Tina, but she needed some acknowledgment that she hadn't been alone in the miracle of it all.

"That's good." Nothing flickered in Ross's eyes. She almost despaired. Hadn't it meant anything to him at all?

"I hope it was all that you wanted." Then he touched her shoulder—softly, but with an intimacy that turned her to liquid. It meant something to him, all right.

"All I wanted. And more," she said. But not too much? She wasn't thinking about engagement rings or wedding cakes, right?

Tina snorted and looked from one to the other. Then she pointed at Kara. "You be careful. That's all I'm going to say." She toddled off.

"Good advice," Ross said softly. "Surprising, coming from Tina."

"I know. She's getting downright maternal."

"Are you all right?"

"Sure. Yes." Her mouth was so dry and he was standing so close.

"I mean, you're not smitten or anything?" He was trying to joke, but he looked at her very closely.

"Smitten? Ha," she joked back. "You're good, but not that good."

"I'm not known for my modesty."

"Evidently not. And I remember both my name and where my underwear is." Electricity shot through her, as the image of Miguel pushing her teddy to the floor came to her. "Talking about it feels weird," she said.

"Yeah." Ross ran his fingers through his hair. "Hard

not to, though. I can't stop thinking about it." His eyes flared again.

"I can't believe that was *me* doing *that*," she whispered, blushing madly.

"Believe it. You were hot. But I wasn't surprised. You don't seem to know how sexy you are."

"Thanks." His praise warmed her to her toes. "That was good for me, Ross. I learned a lot. Thanks."

"And you're sure you don't feel the urge to offer me a sock drawer?"

"No way. You're too much of a slob."

"Let's not get insulting now. I liked it better when you were worshiping at my feet."

"Pul-eeze," she said, shoving him playfully out of her way. "Back to work, Mr. Love Meister."

Relief filled Kara. She and Ross had had amazing sex and they were still the same joky, easy friends they'd been the day before. Later that day, feeling jaunty, she slipped a check under a straightedge on Ross's drafting table to pay for half the hotel room.

Except when she returned to her desk after a Dairy Arizona meeting, she found the check on her desk torn in half with a Post-it note that said, *My pleasure...Miguel.* Lust washed through her and her legs turned to boiled pasta.

Ah, Miguel.

At home that night, Kara felt terrible—alive with *itching.* She couldn't read and TV was boring. She even tried the firefighter video, but it looked silly and flat, not warm and sensual. How could anyone settle for video sex when there was the real thing out there? She wanted more of Miguel.

What if Miguel wanted more of Katherine?

There was only one way to find out. An hour later,

she stood in the doorway to the Hyatt bar, dressed as she had been last night, her heart in her throat, looking for a certain lonely South American playboy with an on-and-off accent. What was the worst that could happen? If Miguel showed up, perfect. If not, no one would ever know how foolish she'd been.

Unfortunately, Miguel didn't show. Probably for the best. How could a second time compete with the first? The major charm of last night had been the miraculous newness of it all. Ross must realize that. How uncharacteristically sensible of him.

Finally, when the lounge singer, an ancient-looking guy wearing a tux and a toupee in equally bad taste, started singing "Strangers in the Night," she almost laughed out loud. Strangers in the night, indeed. She slid off her stool and practically ran out of the bar.

WHEN ROSS STEPPED into the Hyatt dressed like Miguel and feeling like an idiot, the last strains of that Frank Sinatra tune about strangers exchanging glances were fading from the air. He just wanted to see if Kara—make that Katherine—was having the same thoughts he was. If not, so be it. They'd had a nice night and that should be enough.

He stayed for an entire set of the lounge singer until the guy started *doo-be-doo-be-doing* his way through "Strangers in the Night" for the second time. Ross hadn't heard that song in years. His parents had the album and when his mom was depressed she would play it and get that wistful look on her face. She never said anything, but he could hear her thinking, *If it weren't for your father and you kids, I'd be exchanging glances with a stranger right now.* He'd hated that.

So much better to make fun of the singer in his powder-blue tuxedo and bad rug, especially since Ross's stranger in the night had not shown her perky breasts in that slinky black dress.

He should have known. Kara was smart. That night had been perfect, and how could he top perfection? He was good, but not that good.

KARA GOT TO WORK early the next morning. She'd peeled off the skintight dress and kicked it into a corner—a move worthy of Ross—and slept off that stupid fantasy. If even reckless Ross knew better than to try again, something must be wrong with her. Maybe she *was* trying to fall in love with him.

She'd nipped it in time, though. Her concentration was in sharp focus this morning. One hour into the day and she'd already coaxed the Dairy Arizona CEO into getting his board of directors to sign off on the ads. Her tenacity was legendary at S&S. *If you want it done, give it to Kara.* That was the book on her and she was proud of it. By the end of hour two she'd drafted the promotion plan, and then headed into the kitchen for her mid-morning snack as a reward. She was definitely over the fantasy aftereffects.

Today she'd gone with low-fat cottage cheese with pineapple and sliced cantaloupe instead of the usual yogurt and carrots. She was a lot better off living dangerously with her snacks than her sex life. She rounded the turn to the kitchen and found Ross sitting at the table, his feet up, reading the alternative newspaper, whistling to himself.

The tune was familiar—"Strangers in the Night"— the same song the bad-haired, ruffle-shirted lounge singer had performed last night. What had put that in his head?

She'd swear his hair seemed stiff, as if he'd put mousse in it, and she thought she picked up traces of Miguel's spicy cologne. She'd proceed with caution, in case she was imagining things. "I didn't know you were a Sinatra fan," she said.

Ross looked up in surprise and she could swear he blushed. "Oh, that. I went to a bar last night."

"With a lounge singer with a robin's-egg tuxedo and a terrible toupee?"

"You were there?" he asked, lifting a brow in a cool gesture, but his tone was eager.

"Yeah," she breathed, "hoping to see someone I just met."

He rose from the chair and came to her quickly. "Miguel was there," he whispered. "Too late, it seems. *Qué lástima.*"

Her knees gave way and she leaned against the refrigerator.

"Do you want to do it again?" Ross said.

"Do you think we should?"

"It would be just sex, right? For fun?"

"Absolutely. M-maybe there's more you can, um, teach me."

"Yes, Grasshopper. You can learn the ways of the master."

"I didn't know sex was a martial art."

"Why do you think those Chou Lin warriors are always so peaceful and smiley?"

This was good. They were joking like always.

Then Ross leaned in for a kiss.

"Bad idea," she said, and slid away from him. Right now they were Ross and Kara in the S&S kitchen, not Miguel and Katherine in a hotel suite. "Not here."

"Tonight, then," he murmured in Miguel's delicious

accent, "while Miguel is still in town and dying for Katherine's mouth."

Kara had to brace herself against the counter to stay upright.

"What's the matter with you two?" Bob, a graphic artist, stood in the doorway. "Sampson figure out who's been stealing the celery?"

"Nothing," Ross said, while Kara cleared her throat.

"Don't forget you're taking me to the airport tonight," Bob said, pulling open the refrigerator and poking around. "Tina said there were bear claws in here."

Damn, Ross mouthed at Kara, pretending to bang his forehead with his palm. "Right," he said out loud. "The airport."

"Seven p.m. Desert Air," Bob said, still rummaging.

It's okay, Kara mouthed back, sick at heart. Tonight was out for Katherine and Miguel.

"Tomorrow night then," he said out loud. "Saturday."

She nodded.

"Tomorrow night, what?" Bob asked, coming out with a somewhat-shriveled peach, which he rubbed on his shirt.

"Nothing that concerns you, doofus. You'll be in Seattle."

Bob shrugged and walked out. The musky sweetness of peach nectar mingled with the sexual tension in the kitchen air.

Kara and Ross held each other's gaze. "Tomorrow night, then," she said finally, and backed slowly away. She came to her senses in her office, not quite sure how she'd gotten there. All she knew was she had a date with Miguel for Saturday night. And this was only Friday morning. So many hours to wait…

She remembered her snack and headed back to the kitchen just in time to see Tina slide the last pineapple ring onto her tongue. The empty cottage cheese and cantaloupe containers sat beside the sink.

"That was my snack," Kara said.

"Sorry."

"It's all right." She couldn't eat anyway. She was too dazed.

"I got the script for the Desert Airline ad worked out for you," Tina said, clearly trying to make up for the purloined food. "The one with the baby and the grouch in first-class?"

"Great." Kara sank into a chair.

"You look faint," Tina said. "Want me to run out for a hot dog for you?"

"It's not hunger. I have another date with Miguel."

"No! When?" Tina whisked into a chair beside her.

"Tomorrow night. He's got to take Bob to the airport tonight."

"Ooh, baby. You are *hot*." Tina licked her finger, then touched her hip and made a sizzling sound. "Tell Tina all."

Kara told the tale of Katherine and Miguel missing each other at the Hyatt bar.

"God, it's like an O'Henry short story. Only with hot sex. So what are you going to do this time?"

"We didn't talk about it. The same thing as Wednesday night, I guess. Except I'll pay for the room this time."

"You can't do the same thing. Too boring. Plus, it'll never be as good."

"What then?"

"Well, let's put on our thinking caps," Tina said, scooting closer. "We've got time to figure it out."

"Yeah," Kara sighed. "Saturday night's so far off. I don't know how I'll last."

"So make it tonight. After the airport."

":After?'"

"Yeah. How long could it take to drop Bob off? Hey, even better—" Tina got that dangerous look in her eye "—do it *at* the airport. I've got the perfect idea—and even the uniform."

ROSS CLIMBED OUT of Bob's battered Xterra into the warm spring dusk on the departure side of Terminal Four, and watched Bob remove his duffel from the back.

Ross prided himself on being a stand-up guy and a solid friend. The kind of friend who helped his buds move, took them to the airport and watched their pets when they were gone. Unfortunately, being a good friend to Bob was keeping him from the hottest sex he'd had in a long time. Maybe ever.

"Thanks, man," Bob said, tossing the strap over his arm. "You're a rock." He gave Ross a low five. "You can drive her if you want. I get back Sunday night."

"I'll be here."

"Thanks." Bob gave him the flight info and Ross watched him walk through the automatic doors. Then his eyes caught sight of a familiar figure. He did a double take. Was that Kara in a flight attendant's uniform? Maybe he wanted her so much he'd conjured her up. He blinked. The woman gave a hesitant smile. Absolutely Kara.

"Hey, traveler," she called to him, trying to sound sexy but with nervousness in her voice. So Kara—ballsy but shy. She was forcing herself to do something she thought would be good for her.

He walked down the sidewalk to her. "Traveler?" he asked.

She met him a mere kiss away. "How about before the rest of the passengers board your flight, I offer you a little coffee, tea...or me." She ran a finger—trembling, he noticed—down the middle of his chest to his waistband.

"My flight?" he repeated like an idiot. The uniform she wore was a Desert Air one. S&S was working on a promotion for the hometown airline, so Kara obviously had borrowed the suit. It was skintight and she seemed to not be wearing a blouse under the jacket, which dipped deeply between her breasts. Evidently, she had something planned. Something hot.

"Where am I headed?" he asked, tugging her by the hips against him.

"The mile-high club, I hope," she murmured, licking those plump lips of hers.

"I always wanted to sign up for that." He ran his hands down the curve of her backside.

"Park in short-term and meet me at the counter and I'll, um, bring you on *board.*"

"Can't wait," he murmured back, then watched her sashay through the automatic doors into the terminal. He was dying to go after her, but they'd tow Bob's truck if he left it in the drop-off zone, so he drove like a maniac to the parking garage and found a spot, his vision so blurred by lust he narrowly missed a concrete post. His hard-on made it tough walking, so he sort of swaggered his way to the ticket counter, where Kara waited for him with that look in her eyes.

He didn't even wonder how she'd arranged for them to get onto the tarmac—when Kara wanted something, she worked every angle until it happened—he just followed her curves toward an empty airplane in a hangar, grateful, this once, for her unstoppable nature.

The plane looked permanently stationary with a serious set of stairs to its open door. Maybe something they used for kiddie field trips or to desensitize people afraid of flying. There were a few people in the hangar—mechanics clanging away on a plane and some men in a clump at the far end of the hangar—but no one looked twice at the flight attendant and her passenger ascending the stairs.

Ross climbed behind Kara, delighted by the enticing triangle of firm thigh that appeared and disappeared as she moved upward. He wanted to touch, but restrained himself. Kara had a plan. He'd give her a chance to put it into operation.

At the entrance to the plane, she turned to him with that stewardess welcome smile. "Welcome aboard, Mr...?"

"Migue—Mike. Just call me Mike." He needed a new character for this fantasy. He noticed the air had a warm cinnamon scent, completely masking the stale smell of airplane fuel and plastic. Kara had obviously taken air freshener to the place. He wouldn't be surprised if she'd vacuumed, too.

"Mike it is," she said. "We have a first-class seat reserved just for you, Mike."

He sat in the brown-leather seat she indicated. With the armrest up, the two seats made a decent sofa. He stretched his legs. First-class leg room. And he was sure they'd find a good use for every inch of it.

"Let me make you more comfortable," Kara said. She pushed the recline button and his seat back tilted a few inches. She leaned across him to make the window seat recline as well. He noticed beads of sweat in the space between her breasts and that she wore a nearly transparent bra under the V-lapelled jacket. No blouse.

"Much better," she said. She stood up, her face flushed—nervous, he could see. "I find airplane travel lonely, don't you?" she said, but she didn't wait for an answer before she babbled on. "It seems to me that when two strangers meet each other in the air, there can be a magic connection, don't you think? As if they've created a private little world? All their own? And…"

She was anxious about this. He needed to calm her, so he slid his hand under her skirt, moving upward slowly, watching her face the entire time.

"Oh," she said. Shock flickered across her face and a shudder passed through her body. He inched a little higher on her thigh. She wobbled as if she might faint. He loved the way she reacted to the merest brush of his fingers—as though she'd never been touched before. He couldn't imagine anything more erotic.

"This isn't what I planned," she managed to say, bracing herself against the back of the seat, her fingers squeaking on the leather. "You're the passenger and I'm the attendant. I'm supposed to be taking care of you."

"Oh, you are taking care of me," he said, his fingers sliding higher. "You're taking care of my curiosity. I've always wondered what was under these tight, tight skirts.…" He brushed the thin strip of silk that stood between him and Kara's most tender flesh. She gasped.

"Shh, now," he murmured. "You'll have to be quiet so the other passengers don't realize that I'm touching you like this."

She nodded rapidly, then pretended to glance around the plane. The light coming through the plastic windows was romantically dim. He could almost imagine rows of passengers reading magazines, listening to music or dozing as the plane gently rocked through the air...and he stroked Kara's most private of places.

He wanted to watch her face while he made her come without being distracted by his own needs. It would be tough, but worth it for the pleasure it would give her.

He tugged her panties down and out of his way and grazed the curls between her legs.

"Oh, oh, oh," she said, her knees giving way.

"Steady," he said, as he ran a finger along the crease between her buttocks and thigh. She tensed. The flesh on her bottom was firm—only a thin layer of padding over taut muscle. "You feel good."

"Uhn-nn," she managed. *Thank you,* was probably what she meant.

He slid his other hand up the back of her other leg to cup her bottom, loving the moan she gave in response. Then he slid a finger very gently between the folds of her skin, not all the way to her clitoris, just enough to give her a charge.

"Oh, my," she said, sagging against the back of his seat. "Oh, oh, oh." She grabbed his hair and tugged— a measure of her excitement that aroused him, too.

"Careful," he reminded her. "If the other passengers know I'm touching you like this, they'll want to touch you, too. I could never allow that. You're all mine."

"Ross—I mean Mike," she said, her eyes flying open.

The mistake set off a little alarm in his head. She needed to think of him as Mike, not Ross. And he'd better not be thinking of her as Kara. "Tell me your name, beautiful sky angel," he said, slowly stroking her.

"A-a-angel," she stuttered, barely able to speak, it seemed. "Angel sounds good."

"Perfect," he said, carefully separating the folds of her flesh, thin as paper and slick with wetness, going for her core. "You're my angel on this flight. Now, let me make you fly."

"You are," she gasped, trying to play along, he could tell, but distracted by what his finger was doing.

"You're so wet," he murmured.

She clutched his face against her stomach, and he kissed her through the stiff fabric, wishing the skirt were gone so he could put his mouth on her soft, warm belly and then lower to taste her sweetness. But both his hands were happily busy.

Besides, they had the pretend passengers to think of. Seeing real people out the window and imagining passengers envying him made him even more aroused. His right hand kneaded her bottom, his left slid gently along the path she'd made wet for him.

Now Angel's fingers moved down the sides of his face, memorizing his features as if she were blind and wanted to know him. Her fingers bore her light floral scent. So Kara—innocently erotic. How he wanted those sweet fingers on him where he was swollen with blood, nearly exploding with the ache to be inside her, pushing in as far as he could reach. No. This was for her. He had to make a sacrifice for the greater good. He smiled at his bogus nobility.

Her fingers traced his lips, which he parted to suck her finger into his mouth.

"Oh. Oh-oh-oh. *Oh*," she said. "That feels so... I feel so... Your mouth is...your fingers are..." It wasn't like Kara to struggle for words. He smiled as he continued to stroke and suck her into mindlessness. He licked the space between two of her fingers, nipping with his teeth. She moaned and collapsed against the seat.

A shudder coursed through her. Then very deliberately, he slid one of his fingers inside her to discover the slick wetness, smooth corrugations and delicious warmth of her interior.

She stilled at the contact, then began to push herself against his finger. He picked up her rhythm, his erection aching to move exactly that way inside her.

"Oh, oh, yes, yes," she said, moving faster. He sucked and nipped her fingers, squeezed her bottom with the other hand while his finger pushed in and out keeping up with her rhythm. He could feel her orgasm rising in her, almost as if he were part of it, part of her.

"Oh, I can't stop," she cried out. "I can't… help…it." He looked up and watched her face as her body began to shudder with a climax. Her eyes clouded, she bit her lovely lip, and flush fingered up her neck. The walls of muscle around his finger squeezed sweetly.

And then she fell against him, shuddering and quaking. He kept his finger inside her long enough for the quivering to stop, then slowly withdrew it.

"Oh, my good— Oh dear…oh, oh. I've never felt anything so…it was so concentrated, so…just…big."

"Come here." He leaned back against the plane window and pulled her into his arms, brushing her hair out of her face. "So, that's the mile-high club, huh?"

Kara lay across Ross in the seat, panting and trembling from the pleasure that had hit her like a Mack truck. This hadn't gone according to plan. Ross was supposed to be a lonely traveler who hadn't been with a woman in a long time, and she would be a geisha of the air who would fill his empty heart. Except Ross had reached under her skirt, set her on fire and sent her seduction plans right out the plastic window.

"That was supposed to be for you," she said, fighting for breath.

"Ladies first." Ross grinned, not the least disappointed, it seemed.

"So now it's your turn," she said, determined to make him feel as good as he'd made her feel. She pushed up to her knees, then straddled his thighs, looking down at him.

"What will the other passengers think about you climbing on me like this?" he said, grinning in languorous anticipation.

"That they should be so lucky," she said, unhooking his belt with nervous fingers. She lowered his zipper and found him. "Did I do that?" she said, trying to be playful, no matter how her heart pounded.

"I'm afraid so." He sounded anything but afraid.

"It looks painful." She tightened her fingers around him—velvet and steel and lovely against her palm. She slid her hand upward, stalling at the crown.

"But it's a sweet pain," he said, pushing into her grip.

"You know, we stewardesses are taught first aid," she said, and rose onto her knees over him. "Let me see if I can make it all better." She guided him to her wet opening, then inside just a little way.

He looked relieved, but she lifted herself off him.

"Where are you going?" he said, grabbing her hips.

"Not far," she said. She lowered herself onto him just a little, then rose, then slid down, then up, then down, bringing him slowly and deliciously deeper into her, the way he'd entered her the night before. None of the usual questions plagued her. *Is this too fast? Too rough? Am I jiggling?* Ross's face told her she was doing great.

"You feel so good," he said. He slid his hands under her jacket to cup her breasts through her bra, watching her face as he squeezed her nipples between thumb and forefinger.

"Oh," she said, alive with the heat of it. Now she rocked and moaned and he groaned and thrust, paying no mind to the "passengers" watching from behind. The fantasy was fading as she became absorbed in sensation, so she fought to stay in character. "We try to make our first-class passengers feel special," she said, feeling as if she might faint.

Ross went deep inside her, pushing upward hard, making her ache deliciously. One of his hands left her breasts, slid under her hiked-up skirt and found her spot.

"Oh," she said, freezing for a second. That felt so good. As though he knew exactly what she needed. She leaned down to kiss him in gratitude, but it turned hungry and she sucked his tongue into her mouth. She felt another climax approaching. She'd never been one for two at a time—why be greedy? And the second one took work. But not this time. This was easy as breathing.

The pressure built and built until she exploded. Ross's spasms began, too, and they rocked together. Light flashed behind her lids and she lost control of her movements for a few seconds.

When it was over, she dropped her cheek onto the top of Ross's head, holding his face against her chest, loving the smell of his hair and its texture, his hot breath on her breasts, the way he was a stranger and someone she knew at the same time.

"That was great," Ross said, gasping for breath.

"It was, wasn't it?" She'd been worried the fantasy would fall flat, seem silly, but it had worked magnificently, even better with Ross's improvisation. It had been different than Miguel and Katherine, but equally good. Maybe even more intense because they'd gone at it deliberately, both of them with the eager intent to please the other. "I couldn't wait for Saturday, so I made it tonight."

"I love it when you get impatient. When I saw you in that uniform, I thought I was hallucinating," Ross said. "Where did you get it?"

She sat up and leaned back so she could see his face. "I borrowed it from a Desert Airline agent."

"Did she know what you had in mind?"

"I said it was a practical joke."

"That was no joke." He winked at her affectionately. Very Ross.

And just like that, Angel disappeared, leaving Kara straddling Ross with no underwear on.

Quickly she slid off his lap and into the aisle. Ross zipped up while she pulled up her panties and straightened her suit. Then she resumed her Angel role. "We know you have a choice when you fly, Mike. Thank you for choosing Desert Air. Enjoy your stay in the Phoenix area, or wherever your ultimate destination may be."

"You've spoiled me forever for coach," he said, climbing into the aisle. "From now on, it's first-class or stay at home."

"I'm so glad," she said.

He patted her bottom as he passed her and headed down the stairs. She watched him head off across the hangar. From the top step, she took a deep breath of the

spring air, enjoying the strings of yellow and blue run-
way lights with their glowing halos. A departing plane
roared overhead, making everything seem to vibrate.
The airport had always been an exciting place to her,
but now it would never be the same.

It wasn't until Ross turned and blew her a kiss from
the door to the terminal that she realized they hadn't
talked about what this meant. Were they done? Was it
over? It should be, but oh, how she longed for more.

5

BRIGHT AND EARLY Monday morning, Kara put the plastic airline wings on Ross's drafting table with "Fly united—Angela" on a note—pleased at how coolly casual it sounded. She'd managed to put the fantasy in its place. She had turned to scoot out of his work area before Ross arrived and ran smack into his chest. "Oops!" She backed up, the heat of his body staying on her palms and forearms.

"Kara," he said, grinning. He caught sight of her memento and picked it up. "Fly united, huh? Good advice." His eyes heated. "I thought about you in that uniform all weekend long."

"Did you?" She'd sounded too eager, but it was a relief to know she wasn't insane to keep reliving their "flight."

"Oh, yeah. Any chance S&S will get Amtrak as a client? I'd love to try that in a train."

"Don't think so," she said, fighting to stay flip, even as her pulse raced. "Now I always thought it would be really hot to do it in a taxi."

"A taxi, huh?" He lifted a brow, impressed. "As a matter of fact, I do know a guy with a cab." But now he didn't seem to be kidding.

She raised her hand in a T. "Time out," she said. "I was joking. I think we should leave well enough alone."

"Oh. Sure," he said, but disappointment flickered across his face. "It's getting weird?"

She nodded.

"I can fix that," he said, and snatched his dolphin water pistol off a shelf and shot a stream of water at her. "Take that."

"You rat," she said, looking around the room for another play weapon. By the time she'd found his Nerf machine gun, he was far down the hall. "Don't miss the meeting at ten!" she shouted after him. She sighed, deeply relieved to be just friends again.

But he knew a cabdriver...

"ROSS? HELLO?" Ross's date, Amy from LG Graphics, waved her hand in front of his face. "Did you hear what I just asked you?"

"Sorry. Sure. What?" The truth was he'd noticed a woman in a beige suit who reminded him of Kara in her stewardess outfit and he'd had a flashback of her rocking above him while his hands held her breasts under her jacket. That had been six days ago and he couldn't stop thinking about it.

"I asked you if you always knew you wanted to be a graphic artist," Amy repeated with the indulgent smile women tended to give him—why did they forgive him so easily?

She had every reason to be irritated with him. It was their first date and he was fantasizing about another woman. Not like him at all. He was great on first dates. Second and third ones, too. After that it got dicey. But he never pretended differently and he chose women who liked it that way.

"Not always," he answered her, trying to get in the mood to play. "I liked art. Kind of fell into design. I enjoy it, so I stayed with it. For now, anyway. How about you?''

''My high school counselor steered me this way and I had a gift...'' She went on talking about design and her company and he tried to listen. What was his problem? Amy was completely his type—great breasts, good mouth, funny and smart—see, Kara, no bimbo—but he couldn't stop thinking about Kara-Katherine-Angel and what they'd done together. It had been mind-blowing, even for him, and he was no stranger to sex games.

With Kara it was different. Maybe because she was so innocent and wide-eyed about it, and working so hard—with dogged gusto. That's how she was at work, too. Determined, driven, never-say-never. He shouldn't be surprised she'd apply those traits to her sex life. He was just grateful to be on the scene. He looked at his fingers. What pleasure they'd given and received Friday night. God bless Bob for needing a ride to Sky Harbor.

''You seem a little preoccupied,'' Amy said, her annoyance finally showing.

''I know. I'm sorry. I guess I'm just tired.''

''While I'm in the ladies' room, perk up, would you?'' she said, standing. ''Get a cup of coffee. Maybe espresso.''

He watched her go, curiously disinterested in the provocative sway of her hips. He kept seeing Kara's self-conscious but firm strides. He loved the way she tried to hide how sensual she was.

What the hell was wrong with him? He had a perfect playmate in his sights and he was thinking about a fantasy that was over.

Did it have to be? Kara wanted it to be. But he had an idea that would be good for her control-queen tendencies. He'd love to show her more about the glory of giving herself over to physical pleasure. Another lesson, right?

But this was her game, not his, and she had to want it. Since Monday, when they'd joked about the plane flight and doing it on a train, she'd been elusive—actually congratulated him on this date with Amy and made him promise not to use a Spanish accent on her. Wasn't that proof she could handle more? They were still friends. They'd pushed past the awkwardness at work with ease.

Watching Amy return from the john, he decided to at least see what Kara thought of his idea. Nothing ventured, nothing gained. He'd take Amy home early, and he wasn't going to give himself a bad time about it, either.

"GREAT IDEA, ROSS," Saul Siegel said in the account meeting on Friday, sending a pointed look at Dan Lancer. *Why didn't you think of that, Mr. Big Shot Creative Department Manager?*

"Absolutely," Kara added, proud of his suggestion of giveaways at hardware stores for Emerson Faucets and Stoppers. "Mr. Emerson loves tangible stuff—key chains and little tape measures—something customers can hold."

At the praise, Ross promptly shot Kara with a rubber band. The minute anyone took him seriously, he had to act like a kid. That annoyed her, but it was so Ross.

She fought a smile. Everything was normal since the mile-high club fantasy of last Friday. They had a firm grip on ground rule number one: friendship first. In fact, Ross had had a date last night with the woman from LG Graphics. When he'd mentioned it, Kara had gotten a twinge of jealousy—like the hint of a toothache—but handled it. Ross went through women like T-shirts. That was part of his charm and what made him safe for her sexual exploration. Which was *over now*. Except she couldn't stop thinking about his alter egos—remembering Miguel's tan fingers on her breast and how Mike had taken possession of her body on the plane...and especially how he'd tenderly held her during the aftershocks of the skull-rattling orgasm he'd given her.

"Sounds great," Lancer said. He'd hardly been working since he'd decided to take the job in L.A. Ross would be a great replacement, if he weren't so committed to underachievement. Maybe she would say something to Ross. Again.

She watched him fold the meeting agenda into an elaborate paper airplane. Normally she would have kicked him under the table so he'd stop annoying Siegel. This time she could only stare at his nimble fingers, remembering how they'd slid up her thighs as if her body had called them there. *Right there. Yes. Now there. Oh yes, and at just that speed—*

"Kara? Hello?"

She ripped her gaze from Ross's fingers to Saul, whose raised brow told her he'd asked her a question.

"The client's concerned about the budget," Tina said, jumping to her rescue. "But the marketing director wants to expand. Didn't you tell me that, Kara?"

"Oh, uh, yes. Absolutely. Baylor Jones is our ally in this. I'll cost out the option for him long-term."

"Good." Siegel seemed satisfied. "And I would appreciate it if you and Ross would play your games on your own time."

She gulped. Saul meant rubber bands and paper airplanes. If he only knew...

Ross shot her an expressive wink and she flamed with blush.

Tina shook her head at her. *You wild kids.*

"Moving on," Siegel said. "Plain Jane Bakery..."

Kara vowed to exercise more self-control. She wiggled in her seat, the movement giving her a twinge of arousal. Her senses had been heightened by the sex lessons. Smells seemed stronger, sounds louder, textures more intense. Cool air from the AC vent lifted the hairs of her arm like a lover's fingertips. The leather chair was cool and smooth against her thighs, since she'd stopped wearing panty hose as a buffer. The fabric of her bra brushed and squeezed her nipples.

She looked at Ross, with his the-world-is-my-skate-park smile, and felt proud that she'd taken this chance. She'd done something completely out of character and it had worked fine. She'd learned from it. Love or marriage or settling down was the last thing on her mind.

The only problem was she kind of wished they could continue their game. She had a feeling that was a bad sign.

The meeting broke up and Tina caught her by the elbow. "I can't believe you two sat there having sex with your eyes the whole time."

"You think anyone noticed?"

"Uh, no. They thought the puddle of drool under your chin was condensation from your water glass."

"No one would believe it, anyway. I hardly believe it myself."

Tina gave her a motherly look. "Don't forget who you are, Kara. One walk on the wild side does not a wild woman make."

"And I should take advice from a woman who'd take apart her car to get a bartender into bed?"

"That's me, not you. Speaking of that, can you skate early for the Upside?"

"Not early. I'm behind on the Emerson stuff."

"That's because you spent the week staring into space. Come on, girl." Tina shook her gently by the shoulders. "Get it in perspective. You'll make me think I've created a monster."

BY THE TIME Kara eased into the cool dimness of the Upside for the happy-hour confab, Tina was already working her plan. Since Tom was an old-fashioned guy, she'd opted for an old-fashioned approach—naked jealousy. She was talking to a blond guy about three feet from where Tom stood behind the bar. Judging from the way Tom was glancing at her, then violently rinsing the same glass over and over, her plan was working.

Kara slid onto the stool directly in front of Tom—within eavesdropping range of Tina and her prey—and surveyed the drink selections in neon marker on the blackboard above Tom's head.

"So, rock climbing, huh?" Tina was saying.

"Yeah. That's my gig," the blonde answered. He was very cute, but too young for Tina. "We're hitting South Mountain on Saturday morning. Wanna come with? I could show you the moves."

"I just bet you can," Tina purred.

Tom rolled his eyes—he was listening in, too—his expression morose.

"How about a Silver Scorpion?" Kara said to him.

"Why does she do that?" Tom asked. "Overdo herself that way?"

Her first reaction was to bristle at the double standard. Men could have all the sex they wanted and it just made them more virile. Women who were direct about their needs were sluts. Then she saw how miserable Tom was and realized he was more interested in Tina than he wanted to admit.

"I thought bartenders were supposed to understand human nature. You have a ringside seat at the human circus."

"Huh?"

"Tom," she said patiently, "can't you tell she's trying to impress you?"

"She is?" He looked lost for a second, his hand frozen on the martini glass, a drip of water catching the light in a dazzling prism as it fell to the drain below.

She looked at Tina, resting her chin on her palm, pretending to be transfixed by Cliff Climber. She was completely bored with the guy, and kept glancing at Tom. "Yeah, she is."

Color raced from Tom's forehead to his face and neck and probably everywhere else in a terrific blush. Just darling. Maybe Tom would be good for Tina. He was a solid guy with a big heart. But what if Tina hurt him? She'd hate that.

"Let me get you that drink," Tom said, coming to himself. "Kama Sutra, right?"

"No. Silver Scorpion. You're losing your touch." Tom never forgot a drink order. In fact, he was so good she often just asked him what she looked like she needed. Not tonight, though. He was too flummoxed over Tina to know club soda from tonic.

Kara was halfway through her drink—a concoction of crème de menthe and lighter fluid so nasty she vowed to cross it off her repeater list and trust Tom, even when his drink radar seemed wonky—and Tina had moved on to a computer salesman who was a taxidermist in his spare time, when Ross walked in the door.

She actually *sensed* him first, and looked up only to confirm her prickling awareness that he'd entered the same room she was in. Her heart thudded and she put her drink down so hard some of the poisonous liquid spilled onto the bar, probably etching it.

She'd been hoping Ross wouldn't join them tonight. In the romantic light of the Upside, she was afraid she'd confuse him with one of his sexy alter egos. It wouldn't take much, after the airline flight, to send her lunging across the barstool for more. And she was pretty sure that was a bad idea.

Ross didn't take his usual meandering route to the bar, either. Admiring women looked his way, but he headed straight for Kara, catching her gaze and holding it, as if he saw only her. That meant too much to her, so she zipped her eyes away and pretended to wipe up the drink she'd spilled.

"Hello," he said softly, leaning in.

"Hi. Gotta hit the ladies' room." She jumped off her stool so fast she lost her balance. Ross caught her by the elbow. "Easy there. Don't run away." His hazel eyes searched her face, dug deep. "We're friends, remember? Ross and Kara, the tickle twins? I shoot rubber bands at you in meetings and you tell me I can't be Peter Pan all my life."

"Yeah," she said, relief rushing through her. "I remember. Thanks." She had the urge to brush that lock of loose hair from his forehead, but something told her not to.

"Go to the bathroom," he said, patting her playfully on the butt. "I plan on making you laugh and I don't want you peeing yourself."

"I have complete control over my bladder, Funny

Man.'' Her bladder, yes, but the rest of her was another matter.

Ross was watching for her, Kara saw as she returned to him. She found the words *How about another date?* on the tip of her tongue, so she changed the subject as soon as she sat down. ''I think Siegel wants you for Lancer's job.''

The light in Ross's eyes went out. She was both relieved and sad. ''Are you nuts?'' he said.

''You heard him. And he gave Lancer that look.''

''The look was *Quit tanking, Lancer. I'm having to listen to lazy-ass Gabriel.*''

''What do you have against success anyway?''

''Who says that's success?''

''Taking a promotion when you're good is not a cop-out.''

''I'm not like you, Kara. I don't work for approval or to get ahead. It has to be fun. When it stops being fun, I leave.''

For some reason, his attitude bothered her more than usual. She had the urge to push him. For his own good, of course. ''But you're the best person for the job. Bob's a complete flake. And Julie…well, Julie's young and moody. And Ray's too abrasive. No one else is experienced enough. And if they bring in someone from the outside there's a learning curve. You've got great rapport with our clients. This is exactly what you need.''

''What *you* need is another drink,'' Ross said, waving at Tom. ''Another one of these.'' He pointed at her glass. ''Double it.''

''Just a single and skip the lighter fluid,'' she said to Tom, then continued with Ross. ''I just don't want to see you lose out because of a false view of yourself.''

"Thanks, sis, but I'm fine."

"Okay," she said, defeated but pleased she'd steered the conversation away from anything remotely sexual. Proof positive she had her head on straight about Ross. Tom brought their drinks and she'd just taken a swallow when Ross said, "So, how about a fantasy date tomorrow night?"

She choked. Flaming crème de menthe shot up her nose.

Ross slapped her back while she coughed. "You okay?"

"Fine," she said hoarsely as the liquid carved new sinus cavities in her head. "What did you say?" She'd heard him, of course. She just needed a second to cope with the desire that poured through the rest of her body, competing with the heat from the misdirected liquor.

"I was hoping you'd be free. I mean, in case someone stopped by...say at seven?" He spoke slowly.

"Do you think we should do this?" Her voice wobbled.

"I have an idea for a new lesson. It would be good for you."

"Well, if it's a lesson...and it would be good for me." She grinned at him, her heart beating double time.

"Good. Leave the door unlocked. Be in the kitchen doing something—making tea or something."

"Okay."

"And wear something easy to get out of—buttons down the front."

Buttons down the front? Ooh. "Okay," she breathed. She had a blue dress with fabric buttons down its length that would work fine. She felt herself tighten between her squeezed-together legs. Ross wanted to play another game. *Hooray.*

"Sounds like a plan," Ross said, tilting his mug in her direction. A plan? Ross hated plans. Maybe they would both gain something out of this—she'd learn about sex and Ross would learn about...planning?

Okay, that was a stretch. She was practicing having just sex, right? And practice makes perfect.

6

FROM HER SPOT at the bar, Tina could see the sparks flying between Ross and Kara at a nearby table. Those two were playing with fire, all right. Meanwhile, even though she'd planted herself within his earshot while she collected men's phone numbers and got bored to death, she wasn't sure Tom had even noticed her. The things she did for sex. Right now she was pretending to be fascinated by a guy named Bart who sold wood for a living.

"People don't understand pressboard," Bart was saying. "They think it's a garbage wood, but it's really quite versatile."

"One more," she called to Tom, holding up her empty melon martini glass. Sickeningly sweet, but she needed something to amuse herself while talking to this dimwit.

"Isn't that about enough?" Tom asked her gently.

"Hardly," she said, annoyed at the judgment in his tone. She'd need a gallon of the stuff to get through this conversation. All she really wanted to do was to go home to Comedy Central on cable. *Friday Night Stand-Up* was her favorite. But she'd set herself a goal and she wasn't about to give up now.

"You like comedy?" she asked Bart.

"I like a joke now and then. Do you know the one about the Jew, the Catholic and the Methodist?"

"Hit me." She let him tell it—badly—and downed her drink too fast. Tom had watered it. He'd better not charge her full price.

Bart said something to her that she didn't quite catch. "Huh?" she asked.

He leaned in. "You want to get out of here?" he repeated, taking the opportunity to let his wet lips touch the edge of her ear.

That was *it*. Enough. "Yeah, I do want to get out of here," she said, drying her ear with a napkin. "See ya." She stood up, but felt a little woozy and leaned into Bart.

"Relax, sweetheart. I'll take you home," he said, standing with her. He slapped some money on the bar.

"I got it," she said, pushing his money away and fumbling for her wallet.

He tightened his grip and began leading her away.

Uh-oh. This joker was holding on too tight. She tried to yank away, but the floor swayed and she couldn't quite get her feet to cooperate. She seemed to be holding on to the doofus for balance. They moved toward the door.

Then someone blocked their exit. "Let go of the lady." Tom's voice was low and no-nonsense.

Bart went pale. "I'm helping her home."

"She said no, pal. I heard her. Now let go."

"Okay, okay," Bart said, lifting his hands. He shifted his neck in his collar, then straightened his jacket. "Take it easy on the booze," he said to her. "Not every guy will put up with a tease."

"You thought I was teasing you?" she said. "I was barely tolerating you. And you can't tell a joke worth sh—"

"Tina," Tom warned.

"I'm not kidding," she said to Tom, then shouted after Bart. "It was a *Buddhist,* a Jew and a Christian, you dolt. That was the point of the joke."

She turned back to Tom, then felt her stomach lunge.

Reading her face, Tom helped her run to the ladies' room, where, to her utter humiliation, she threw up the last two melon martinis, while he held her around the waist.

Finished, she rinsed her mouth at the sink. When she lifted her face, Tom wiped it with a paper towel. "Better?" he asked, looking at her with that above-it-all expression. He pitied her. God.

"Good as new," she said, pulling away from him. She only drank out of nervousness, and something about this seduce-Tom thing made her anxious. "I was bored and I drank too much, okay? Strategic error to go with a froufrou drink." She didn't mean to sound snotty, but she didn't like being rescued.

"You should be careful about the guys you drink with."

"I can take care of myself, believe you me," she said, slurring slightly. "Tha' guy would have been missin' a testicle in about a minna ana half."

"How about if I drive you home?" he said, hiding a smile.

"Just call me a cab. And, for your information, none of this woulda happened if you had just gone out with me like any normal guy." Oh, dear. She hadn't meant to say that out loud.

He looked at her for a long minute with his seriously blue, absolutely clear eyes. "Let me make it up to you by driving you home."

She was too tired to fight, and before she knew it her head was lolling on the seat of Tom's Volvo sedan—it figured he'd drive the dullest car on the planet—but then she felt queasy again and had to ask him to pull over so she could throw up in an oleander bush. How had she let this happen?

They reached her apartment building, and before she could drag her sorry butt out of the car, he was at the passenger side helping her out and off her feet and up into his arms.

"I can walk," she said weakly, wagging her legs to get down.

"Just let me do this for you."

She stopped kicking—it made her stomach roil—and Tom loped effortlessly up the walk with her. It might have been sexy—kind of Rhett Butler and Scarlett O'Hara—if she weren't annoyed at being helpless and pitiable.

At the door, she managed to find her keys and unlock the door, and Tom carried her down the hall and into her bedroom, where he lowered her onto the bed, then disappeared without a word.

Good riddance. She would put this awful incident right out her mind. Though she should have thanked him. She'd do it next time she was in the bar. She sat up to remove her clothes, and had her blouse and bra off when she was surprised to see Tom in her doorway holding a glass of water and something in the other palm.

"I'm sorry," he said. He had that deer-in-the-headlights look at the sight of her breasts. He put what he was carrying on the bureau and backed out of the room. "Aspirin," he called to her from outside the door. "Take them now and you'll feel less awful tomorrow."

She listened to him leave, heard his car pull away,

then flopped back onto the bed. Forget the aspirin, she thought, sliding one foot to the floor to keep the room from spinning. She'd be happy just to *make* it to tomorrow.

ON SATURDAY NIGHT, Kara stood in the middle of her kitchen in her front-buttoning blue dress, front-clasp bra and matching lace underwear—she'd considered the edible panties, but nixed the idea because Ross might laugh—and watched the clock tick.

Seven - oh - five…seven - oh - six…seven - ten. Damn. Couldn't he be punctual for this? She felt stupid standing here, drinking glass after glass of water—she was too nervous to make tea—waiting for the door to open.

The longer he made her wait, the more time she had for doubts about the wisdom of another fantasy date with him. She had to keep this in perspective. This was a learning experience. With a clear goal. A goal she was pretty sure they'd reached. But maybe this one more time to be sure…

Seven-fifteen…seven-eighteen. She decided to give him a call. She headed for the bedroom phone and ran straight into Ross, who yelled, "Jeez!"

"Sorry," she said. She had time enough to notice he was all in black—tight black T-shirt and tight black jeans—before he whirled her around and grabbed her by the waist from behind and covered her mouth. "You were supposed to be in the kitchen," he muttered.

"Muhfhmfph."

He freed her mouth so she could explain. "You were late. I was going to call you."

"Okay. We'll start over. You look great, by the way. That dress is perfect." He slid one hand up her thigh and low, across her belly. "Mmm." He seemed about to kiss her.

"Ross? You were attacking me, remember?"

"Oh, right." He slammed his hand over her mouth again and held her tightly around the waist. "Don't scream and you won't get hurt."

"Mfphfmmph."

"You promise not to scream?"

She nodded, so he released her mouth.

"What do you want with me?" she asked, feeling aroused, excited and a little scared.

"Everything. Your body. Your mind. Your senses. I want full control over everything you feel." Then a blindfold went across her eyes and he tied it tightly.

"Oh." A thrill coursed through her. This could be good.

With that, he hefted her up and over his shoulder like a sack of potatoes. His shoulder jammed her diaphragm, making it hard to breathe or talk.

"What are you doing?" she managed, groaning, her head pounding with blood rushing there.

"What does it look like? I'm kidnapping you," he said, and walked toward the door.

"What will my neighbors think?"

"Good point." He stopped.

"How about if I keep my eyes closed and just walk with you?"

"That'll work," he said, setting her on her feet, and removing her blindfold. "I only kidnap very smart women. Now shut your eyes."

She did—well, except for a narrow slit so she could see where he was marching her. They reached what she recognized as Bob's Xterra. Ross must have borrowed it. Thank God he wasn't trying to kidnap her on his motorcycle, which she'd refused to ride. Too scary.

"Lie down on your side," he commanded, helping her onto the back seat.

After she lay down, he pulled her hands behind her back and tied them together with a smooth, cool cloth. She peeked through her lashes and saw it was a colorful necktie and it still bore a price tag. He'd had to buy a tie just for this. That made her smile. She squeezed her eyes tight before he tied the blindfold back on.

Then Ross fumbled with something—her seat belt, she could tell by the click. How responsible, she thought, until he started driving wildly and she began rolling around the seat. With her hands tied and eyes covered, she couldn't brace herself or see what was going on. That made her feel helpless and a little scared. "What will you do to me when we get there?" She tried not to sound frightened.

"Nothing you won't enjoy," he said in his Ross voice, obviously picking up her tension. "Ground rule number three, remember? Nothing you're not into?"

"Okay." She relaxed. This was Ross, after all. He'd take care of her. "But I think that was number four."

"Don't get technical. You'll spoil all the fun."

She smiled, feeling much better.

They drove a little farther, then Ross jerked them into a sharp turn and braked hard. Only her seat belt kept her from tumbling face-first to the floorboard. When he opened the car, she felt a light spring breeze and caught the mossy scent of water. They were near a pond? A lake?

Ross undid her seat belt and helped her climb out. Now she smelled eucalyptus and heard a merry-go-round. The combination of carousel, eucalyptus and water was a dead giveaway. They were at Encanto Park, which had a kiddieland and a lagoon. She remembered that Ross knew people who worked at the golf course there.

"Don't make a sound," he warned, then grabbed her by the waist and quick-walked her into a building. It was cool and smelled of concrete and, of all things, roses. They must be in the little caretaker's house beside the rose garden.

He guided her a few steps inside. Then he moved away. He wouldn't leave her, would he?

"Ross?"

"I'm right here," he said, startling her by being just inches in front of her face. "And call me the Love Thief."

The Love Thief. Intriguing…

"Let's get you out of this dress," he said, and slowly began to unbutton the big cloth buttons. This was why he'd requested front opening. "You are my prisoner," he said, moving slowly from button to button. "All you can do is feel what I want you to feel—what I let you feel."

He was right. With her hands behind her back, she couldn't do anything but wait for his next move, his next touch. Air cooled her damp skin as her dress fell more and more open.

The Love Thief ran a finger along the line of her bra and she shivered. "Front clasp," he said. "Good." He moved behind her and untied her hands just long enough to slide her dress off her arms. Then he clasped her hands together at the wrist in front of her body.

She felt so exposed in just her bra, panties and high heels. And he was looking at her. She couldn't see his face or gauge his reaction except through his ragged breathing, which meant he was aroused, and that pleased her.

"Back up," he commanded.

She took two backward steps and hit something.

"Now lie down on the bed."

She did what he told her and he stretched out her arms, one at a time, then tied them to something metal—the headboard probably.

Blind, with her arms spread wide and her hands bound, she felt as exposed as if she'd been completely nude, held open for him to do what he would with her. She had that itchy, fearful tickle of helplessness and made a halfhearted attempt to tug her hands free of their restraints.

"There's no point in struggling," he said. "I have you. You're all mine."

Again she felt the twinge of arousal and powerlessness.

"Do you like this?" The Love Thief asked hoarsely. "Being at my mercy? Not knowing where and how I'll touch you?" The mattress lifted as he got up and she felt him sit at the foot of the bed. "Only knowing that whatever it is, you'll want more and more?" He took her foot in his warm hand, tugged off her heel, and gently stroked the sole of her foot with the pad of one finger.

"Ooh," she moaned, the sensation so good she held really, really still. "Yes. I like that. All that."

"Good. I want you to trust me with your body. You do trust me, don't you? You know I won't hurt you?"

"Y-yes," she stammered.

"The only thing the Love Thief will steal from you is your pleasure…" he whispered, removing her other shoe to tease its sole, "until you can't surrender a single moan more."

She shivered violently at the possibilities.

He ran his finger up her shin, barely skimmed the edge of her panties, then shifted to stroke the line where her leg met the mattress. "Does that sound good to you?"

"Yes," she gasped, desperate for more contact.

"Good." He stopped touching her. "So, what should I touch first?" he mused.

She held her breath. What would it be? Her mouth? Her breasts? Her core? The possibilities were riveting and frustrating because she could only wait in the helpless dark for him to decide.

"I think this." He flicked the clasp and her bra fell open.

She gasped and felt instantly vulnerable. She imagined his eyes on her breasts watching her nipples tighten. The thought made moisture trickle into her panties. She wanted more. *Touch me. Kiss me. Suck, squeeze, nibble, lick, anything, everything. Just do something.* She lifted her body off the bed to try to reach him.

"Uh-uh-uh. I'm in charge here," he said.

She collapsed onto the mattress in exasperation.

Fabric rustled, cloth brushed her thigh and she realized Ross had taken off his shirt. There was no rattle of buckle or slide of zipper, so his pants were still on.

She felt him move in, felt his heat. Now what? *Please, something.* Her heart battered her chest, she held her breath. Something hot and wet touched the hollow of her neck, electrifying her. His tongue, that sweet muscle.

"Ooh," she said, fairly gushing into her panties.

He'd barely touched his lips to her neck and she was ready to climax.

"Do you like that?" he asked softly.

"What do you think?"

In answer, his tongue moved to her collarbone, then lower to the very top of her breast. "How about this?"

"Y-yes."

Lazily, with mind-bending stealth, his lips made their way lower on her breasts. She couldn't help pushing up for more, but each time she did, he pulled away. *The nipple. Please, my nipple, I'm begging you,* she wanted to scream. But she knew he'd deny the request if she made it.

Luckily she held her tongue, because he soon found that precious nub, which fairly pulsed with heat. He circled it with moisture, then pulled it into his mouth with a sucking sound.

Electricity rushed through her, lighting up places all over her body—places aching for Ross's touch, aching to touch *him,* but her hands were tied. She pushed her breast farther into his mouth. This time he accepted it and groaned. He was getting carried away, too. Thank goodness. She hated being in this frantic, hungry place alone.

He moved to suckle her lonely other breast. *So good.* She pushed up into his mouth, but he released her breast, shifted more fully on the bed, then kissed beneath her breast, then lower to her stomach, then lower, until at last she felt the blessed pressure on her cleft. His tongue pushed against the thin fabric of her panties, wetting her clear through to the tender spot beneath. She thought she might melt from there upward, like so much granulated sugar in water.

She couldn't let him stop now, no matter what. She

lifted her hips and locked his head in place with her knees. She made a helpless, stuttering sound and wiggled against his mouth. She wanted more—more tongue, more direct contact.

Stubbornly he pulled his mouth from dead center and began to lick along the leg edge of her panties, sending her already tightened clitoris into a harder knot. She shifted to try to force his mouth to the hot spot, but he gripped her hips and held her maddeningly in place.

"You keep forgetting who's in charge," he murmured. He removed his mouth altogether, so that all she felt were his hands holding her and the cooling moisture he'd left.

"Please," she cried out, hoarse with need. This was agony.

"Let go," he commanded. "Give yourself to me."

"I am. I will…please."

Thankfully he didn't wait for her to stop wiggling— she couldn't have—before easing his tongue under the edge of the thin material of her panties, close to where she wanted him, but not…quite…there.

"Please, please, pleeease," she moaned, sweat breaking out all over her body, which felt chafed with unmet desire. She yanked at the ties around her wrist, wanting her hands *now*. Wanting to grab his hair and push his mouth right *there. Cool the burn. Put it out. Now.*

"I can see you're suffering," he said in pretend sympathy. "I guess I'll have to help you." He slowly teased her panties downward and off her feet. Then he lifted her knees, opened her legs and finally, finally pressed his mouth where she was frantic for him.

His tongue was on her, strong, but soft, offering glorious relief. She groaned and panted and tried to lunge for him with her restrained hands, now almost raw with the effort of trying to touch, to control, to move. She was in his power, completely unable to guide his lips and mouth, tongue and teeth and hands.

Like it or not, she'd given herself over to him.

And that, she learned, wasn't half-bad. The Love Thief's tongue found her again and again, flicking the spot just so. Now his fingers joined the action, moving into her and out, while his mouth applied pressure above in a sweet agony of sensation. He wasn't teasing her now, he was moving unerringly to her pleasure point.

"Oh…" She almost added *Ross,* but at the last second managed to be conscious enough to say instead, "Oh…good."

"Mmm." He nuzzled her in a way that told her he loved being there. She was never sure about men and this most intimate act. Was it a burden? Did they get bored? Dislike the sensation, the taste? Ross seemed at home.

Her hips lifted shamelessly up at his mouth. *More, more, faster,* her body was saying. He obliged, his tongue doing magic things—swirls and swipes and pushes that escalated the sensation to a throbbing clamor for release. She was moving frantically and somehow he managed to stay with her, keeping his mouth in position despite how she writhed and twisted and bounced.

She was terrified he would stop, pull away, leave her unsatisfied, but as she swelled closer to climax, she could feel that he wanted her to get there, too. His movements were as frantic as hers.

The feeling intensified, tighter, tighter, tighter, until it became that white-hot sting and ache, and then she shot free, rocketing over the cliff, surfing the rare space of it. She fought the urge to say Ross's name, ending up with garbled syllables, aware all the time of his hands holding her in place, his mouth stilled, his finger quiet, absorbing her pleasure, her joy.

Then it was over. Slowly the jerks and quivers subsided. If only she could free her hands so she could thank him physically, touch him, give him release. She twisted her right hand and found the tie had loosened and she could get free.

She started to reach for Ross, then she remembered this was a fantasy—the Love Thief and his Prisoner of Love—so she decided to stay in character. Surreptitiously, she freed her other hand, but held on to the bars of the headboard, pretending she was still restrained.

"That was nice," he said, kissing her stomach and slowly sliding up her body.

"Very nice," she said, but the minute his lips reached hers, she heaved herself over onto him, pinned his legs with her knees and his upper body with her chest. She paused to shake off her dangling bra and yank the blindfold from her eyes. Then she pinned his wrists. "Now you're *my* prisoner."

He grinned and pretended to struggle while she used the neckties to bind him where she had been.

Ross tested the knots. "Not bad," he said, adding hopefully, "I suppose you'll have your way with me now?"

"Don't sound so happy about it." She bent forward and nipped his neck, letting her teeth dig in a little, sucking, wanting to mark him with a love bite.

"*Please* don't stop."

So of course she did. "I'm in charge here," she said sternly, straddling his hips, rising on her knees.

He was so handsome lying there naked to the waist,

his upstretched arms revealing taut, delineated muscles. Tied down though he was and under her power, he seemed completely in charge, willing her to touch him. She wanted to, but first, she had to tease him—on general principles.

"Let's get you out of these clothes." She attacked his belt and zipper and he lifted his hips so she could pull off his jeans and toss them away.

Her heart jumped at the sight of the swollen length of him, reaching up, eager for her touch. "Hmm, now what?" she said, putting a finger to her lip in pretend consternation.

"Touch me, for God's sake," he growled.

"Oh, I don't think so," she said. "Not quite yet."

He groaned. "You're going to torture me, aren't you?" His eyes flared with heat and desperation.

"Oh, absolutely." She thought of something one of the vixens in the firefighter video had done, and decided to try it. She took her breasts in her hands, pushed them together, then leaned forward and brushed her nipples over the tip of his penis. So delicious. Her nipples felt charged by the sensation of firm velvet on their sensitive tips. And Ross went nuts, lunging up for more. Much better than the video—this was real and raw, not staged.

She sat up.

"Lord, don't stop," he said.

"You liked that?"

"Oh, yeah," he said. "Keep it up."

"Nope." She was amazed at herself. Here she was, inviting Ross to look at her bare breasts, welcoming his hungry stare.

He groaned, his face showing agonized yearning. "Come on. I didn't torture you this long."

"But you kidnapped me. And I wasn't all that happy

about the way you drove, either.'' This was fun. The blindfold lying on the bed caught her eye—it was a black silk handkerchief. She picked it up and rubbed it sensuously against her cheek, then slowly slid it over her breasts, tickling herself, then lower, between her legs and back and forth.

Ross groaned as if the sight caused him pain.

She dragged the cloth over his chest, then his thighs. She let it just brush his erection before whipping it away.

''You're killing me,'' he moaned.

''That's the general idea.'' She leaned forward, teasing his chest with her nipples, then grazing his mouth with her lips. He lunged up at her, but she pulled away.

''So, are you suffering?'' she asked.

''Yeah. Now give me your mouth.''

''I've got a better idea,'' she said, and took his penis in one hand and lowered her mouth to its soft, firm surface, cupping his testicles in her other hand.

A shudder went through him and the rest of his body went limp. ''Thank God,'' he said.

She let her tongue and lips explore this very special part of him. She liked the way Ross tasted and the way the velvety skin shifted and slid under her lips. Usually oral sex was awkward for her. She felt clumsy and inept and it made her jaws ache. But not this time.

She just imagined how this might feel to Ross and moved the way she guessed would be good. She glanced up and saw him looking at her with worshipful need. She was doing great.

Soon he was rocking rhythmically into her mouth and she found she could relax her throat and take all of him. He groaned, whispered something, and she quickened her pace, surprising herself with the ease of it all.

And then he went rigid and jerked in her mouth. She felt no urge to pull away, as she had the few times she'd performed this act in the past, and she found her mouth filled with his liquid, which was warm and pleasantly salty.

Gradually he stopped moving. ''That was great. Thanks.'' He yanked his hands out of the ties and pulled her up into his arms.

She laughed, and then he kissed her and it was easy and comfortable…and friendly…and…

Wrong. Kara broke off the kiss and climbed off the bed. The game was over.

''You okay?'' he asked.

''Sure. I'm fine.'' She ducked his gaze, crossing her arms over her breasts. Here they were, Ross and Kara, trapped in the aftermath of their adventure. She had to say something about what they'd done. ''That was…'' What could possibly describe that experiment in trust and control and sensation?

''Yeah,'' he said, ''it was.''

''Exactly,'' she said, glad he understood. ''I'd better get dressed.''

She grabbed her dress and undies from the floor, and rushed into the tiny bathroom. By the time she'd gotten her clothes on, Ross had done the same and was waiting for her at the open door, dressed and holding his backpack.

She stepped under his arm and into the cool spring evening. The green smell of water combined pleasantly with the eucalyptus from the tall trees everywhere, and she could hear the carousel from the kiddieland area. ''Encanto Park. I thought so.''

''Yeah. Bill's cousin works here. He said I could use the place.''

"Nice of him."

Ross looked at her, a long once-over filled with affection. "Feel like some cotton candy? A ride on the merry-go-round?"

"That doesn't sound like kidnapper talk."

"I could tie you to a horse," he said, pulling the end of one of the ties from his backpack.

She shivered with the memory of being bound and in his power. "What, and shock the children? We could scar them for life."

He sighed. "It's just such a nice night. How about paddleboats?"

"Sorry." She shook her head. It had to be over, and they both knew it.

Ross looked away and she watched the breeze lift his hair from his forehead. The lights of the park gave his silhouette a lovely halo.

He turned back to her, a big grin on his face. He'd decided something. "If that's the way it's gonna be—" he poked her shoulder with one finger "—tag! You're it."

"What?"

"Next Saturday. You come up with something."

"You mean, do this again?"

"Something like it. Surprise me."

"I don't know if we should."

"I don't care if we should. You are an incredible partner and I want more." Then he caught himself. "This is practice, remember? And you know what they say about practice."

"It makes perfect?" she asked hopefully.

"Exactly. We'll keep it up until you're perfect. Though that—" he nodded at the cabin "—was damn close."

Practice makes perfect. The flimsiest of excuses, but she *was* learning and her comfort level with sex grew with each encounter. She couldn't argue with that. Even if she should.

7

KARA AWOKE Sunday morning to the sound of someone frantically ringing her doorbell. For a fleeting second, she hoped it was Ross, but she pushed away that dangerous thought and dragged herself to her feet. She was still uneasy with the plan she and Ross had to see each other next Saturday and she had no idea what fantasy experience she could create that would top Love Thief.

Ding-dong. Ding-dong. "Hang on. I'm coming," she called, throwing on her robe. The silk slithered over her skin and made her shiver. These days, every sensation seemed more vivid.

Her caller gave up on the doorbell and started pounding. Had to be Tina. No one else was so impatient. After a confirming glance through the peephole, she opened the door and Tina barged in holding a bakery sack and two pint cartons of milk.

Eight-thirty was way too early for her night owl friend. Something was up.

"I have to talk." Tina dumped her offerings unceremoniously on the kitchen table, then sank into a chair with an exhausted sigh. "I brought breakfast." She fished a squished custard-filled doughnut out of the sack and took a huge bite.

"What happened?" Kara had last seen Tina flirting for Tom's benefit Friday night.

"A mess. I drank too much—I was nervous—and

Tom ended up driving me home and putting me to bed.''

"That doesn't sound so bad."

"Keep listening. I thought he'd left, so I took off some clothes, but he comes back with aspirin and sees me half-naked and nearly runs from the room. Like I had leprosy."

"He was just being a gentleman."

"Then the next morning—yesterday—he shows up with bagels and what he calls his special hangover cure."

"That's sweet."

"Not sweet. An act of pity. He thinks I have an alcohol problem. If I were an alcoholic I'd have known better than to drink a froufrou drink. You know I overdo when I get nervous."

That was true. Tina had problems, but alcohol wasn't one of them.

"So, I tell him, thanks," Tina continued, "but I can handle my own hangover. But he just puts the bagels in the toaster oven and mixes up this concoction like I haven't said a word. And I'm so hung I can't even argue with him. And damned if the drink didn't work. He says it's the Tabasco."

"That all sounds good."

"Hold on. Then after we eat, he opens his backpack and pulls out a textbook and some paper and starts reading and taking notes."

"He what?"

"He's *studying*. At my kitchen table. Can you believe it? The only thing I want to do with a man at my kitchen table is eat and/or screw."

Tina moved onto the second doughnut and guzzled one of the milks. She wiped her mouth. "So, I'm staring at him, you know, like he dropped in from another planet, and he finally looks up and says, 'Take a shower, but keep the water cool. Heat intensifies the effects of the alcohol.'''

"So what did you do?"

"I took a cool shower. And when I come out in my sexiest silk robe, he looks up from the sofa in the living room where he's reading and says, 'You need some sleep,' and pats the spot beside him. So I sit down and he pulls me down so my head is in his lap—sideways, nothing funny—and goes back to studying."

"And then what did you do?"

"I slept. What else? I was tired."

"Wow."

"I know. TWFW. Too Weird For Words. I can't believe I did exactly what he told me to do."

"What happened when you woke up?"

"He wasn't on the couch, so I thought maybe I'd just had a bad dream, but then I smelled something cooking and there he was in the kitchen making grilled cheese sandwiches. He said I needed protein and calcium to settle my stomach."

"What did you do?"

"I ate the sandwich—it was good, too…buttery and light brown, the way I like it—and afterward he said he had to go fix his friend's car." Tina paused, looking worried.

"And then he left?" Kara prompted.

"Yeah. Except first he said he had next Saturday off and would I like to go sailing."

"And you said yes, right? So you got what you wanted—Tom on a date. Your trick worked after all."

"I don't like it. He feels sorry for me. I think he

thinks he's saving me from men or melon liqueur or myself, and it makes me feel…weak, you know?"

"You've dated too many guys who only look out for themselves and their penises. Tom's being nice."

"Well, I'm no sad case. I'm going to tell him to forget it. That I'm busy. That I have to do Jell-O shooters at a biker bar or wash my hair or study for my driver's exam, I don't know."

Kara examined her friend's face. Tina was obsessive about independence, Kara knew, because of her clinging mother and moody father. She'd have to handle this delicately so Tina could get what she really wanted.

"Give the guy a break," she said. "He obviously had to work up the nerve to even talk to you. If you turn him down you'll crush his spirit."

"You think so?"

"Humor him. Go on his sailboat with him. Have pity on the poor guy."

"You think?"

"Yeah. *You* feel sorry for *him.*"

"I could do that. Sure. He was kinda pitiful standing there staring at my breasts like he'd never seen a pair before." Tina munched another doughnut, letting yellow cream slip out of the corner of her mouth—a matter she rectified with a quick swipe of her tongue. "Eew, these are nasty," she said, shoving the last bite into her mouth. "Did you like yours?" She looked at the empty sack. "Uh-oh. Did I eat all three?"

"The milk, too."

"Sorry. Want me to get you some more?"

"That's okay. I'm not really hungry."

Tina studied her. "What's the matter?"

"Nothing. At least I hope nothing. I had another date with Ross."

"No. Another fantasy?"

She nodded.

"Oh. Wow. Tell me *everything*."

"It was kind of bizarre. He pretended to, um, kidnap me."

"Ooh. Wow. Go on."

"He took me to this cottage at Encanto Park and—" The rapt expression on Tina's face made her stop. "I can't tell you everything. It's too personal."

"Personal? This is educational, remember? A learning experience. Dish, girl!"

"It was intense. Let's leave it at that." She kept seeing the look of crazed hunger on Ross's face when she'd teased him with her breasts. She'd felt like some exotic sex goddess—Kara, Mistress of Temptation, not Kara of the Granny Panties. And giving himself over to him that way had been powerful and very sexy. Feelings entirely too intimate to share with Tina.

"Well, I envy you," Tina said. "You're getting handcuffed to beds and tickled with feathers, while I've got Tom asking me to quiz him for his engineering exam. Sheesh." But her eyes were bright with a new light. Tom might be just what Tina needed.

"So, what's the next fantasy?" Tina asked. "Slave and mistress? Headmaster and bad pupil?"

"I don't know. It's my turn. A turn, can you believe it? What if we get carried away?"

"You set up boundaries, right? You don't feel like marrying him, do you?"

"God, no. I just want to jump his bones." *Jump his bones?* That was the kind of thing Tina said. What was happening to her?

"So, you're just infatuated with the fantasies. That's

understandable. Who wouldn't be? A kidnapping…sheesh. You tied each other up, right?''

She nodded. ''He bought silk ties just for that purpose.''

''Nice touch.'' Tina got lost in thought.

Kara didn't like her friend picturing her and Ross in action. ''So, you're advising me to just enjoy the fantasies and keep the ground rules in mind, correct?''

''Huh? What?'' Tina shook the glazed look from her eyes. ''Yeah, right. What you said.''

She hoped Tina was right. She felt good all over, more confident, more like a woman than she'd ever felt before. She'd even stunned Ross, the babe hound. If that didn't put a spring in her feminine step, nothing could. ''Now it's my turn to make up something. What should I do? I have that edible underwear I bought at Naughty and Nice. Strawberry, I think, and grape.''

''And did you get a vibrator?''

She nodded, blushing as she thought of it spilling out of her sack the night she'd run into Ross and they'd launched their plan.

''This'll be fun,'' Tina said, rubbing her hands together. ''And I know this great costume shop. How do you feel about leather?''

''I THINK THIS IS JUST what Emerson Faucets and Stoppers needs,'' Kara said to Baylor Jones, the marketing director of the company, tapping the proposal she'd placed in front of him.

''Blubber to whales,'' he said, smiling at her in an odd way, while the waitress cleared their table from lunch.

''Excuse me?''

"You could sell blubber to whales, Kara," Baylor repeated.

"Just doing my job." She shrugged.

"Something's different about you," he said. "Your hair?"

"Maybe." She'd worn it down every day lately, since she'd noticed that the braid pulled at her scalp. Besides, she liked to run her fingers through her hair, imagining it falling over Ross's face and chest while she rocked on top of him.

Last week she'd been Ross's all-over massage therapist after he suffered some sore muscles skateboarding with the kids at the Boys and Girls Club. She'd worn the edible panties, which he'd made short work of—strawberry was his favorite flavor—then he'd taken his time using the vibrator, proving that gadgets had their place in sexual fun. The memory made her shiver. They'd used copious amounts of almond oil, slithering over each other like seals. This week was Ross's turn.

"Your eyes are different, too," Baylor continued. "I never noticed how blue they are."

His wistful tone snapped her to attention. Oh, my God. He was flirting with her. He'd never given her more than a passing glance before. "Maybe I'm a little different." The new erotic light in her eyes must have snagged his attention.

"I don't know how I missed so much." He held her gaze with warm brown eyes. Baylor Jones was a perfect date prospect, now that she thought about it. Lunch had gone long because they'd strayed easily onto other topics, weaving between work and personal lives in a way that told her they had tons in common. He was smart, funny, ambitious and quite attractive. She'd bet he was decent in bed, too.

"Are you free Saturday night?" Baylor asked.

"Huh?" She set her iced tea glass down on the table with a clunk. He'd asked her out. Just like that. This was what she was working for with Ross, wasn't it? To gain the ability to go out with a guy, sleep with him even, without automatically picturing their initials together on hand towels?

She could test her abilities with Baylor Jones. Saturday night, as a matter of fact. *This* Saturday night.

"I'm asking you on a date," he said, looking amused by her bewildered expression. "Dinner, maybe dancing?"

"Oh, I see. Of course. I knew that." But what about her fantasy date with Ross? He would understand if she canceled, of course. They'd agreed their fantasies wouldn't interfere with real dates. And he'd gone out with that woman from LG Graphics, after all, though that had been a couple weeks back. Ross would be happy for her. Might even want to give her pointers.

She was all set to say yes, even moving her head in an up-and-down direction, when Baylor said, "But you're seeing someone else right now."

She gulped. "I…what? I…um, uh, what makes you think…?"

"It's all over your face," he said with a rueful smile. "You'd like to go out with me, but there's something in the way. Some*one*, I should say."

She sat there with her mouth half-open and finally, miserably, admitted the truth. "There shouldn't be, but there kind of is someone. I'm sorry. Truly."

Baylor sighed, then winked. "Well, let me know when the horizon clears. I'll be around." He had such a nice smile—even when he was being disappointed.

What was the matter with her? Here was her chance

at a sensible relationship that she wouldn't rush to make into something bigger than it should be and she'd turned it down.

For a fantasy.

Was she getting carried away? Making more of the thing with Ross than there was? They had boundaries, right, as Tina had reminded her. She ran through the ground rules in her mind. *Friendship first*...so far, so good on that one. *If it feels weird, we quit*...far from feeling weird, it felt fabulous. *If we're sexually incompatible we quit*...no problem with *that* one.

Stay focused on the goal...teaching her to have fun with sex. They'd done that...in spades. *It can't interfere with dating other people*...bzzt! She'd blown that rule today. *Be honest*...uh-oh. If she were honest with herself, she'd admit they'd reached their goal and it was probably time to quit. Especially now that she'd turned down a real date with a good prospect. A bad sign. She'd have to talk to Ross. After Saturday night. No point in ruining his plans, right? And maybe they'd come up with a new ground rule to fix the problem.

TINA, WHO WAS NOTORIOUS for making men wait, was ready before Tom came to pick her up Saturday afternoon to go sailing. A bad sign. Not only was she ready, but she was watching for him from behind the curtains like a high school girl waiting for her first date.

Why was she acting so weird? Because *he* was acting so weird. She could feel he was attracted to her, but he treated her like a sister or a cousin—friendly, affectionate, but distant. And he kept his hands absolutely to himself.

She heard a car and saw his Volvo roll slowly to a stop right on time. After a few moments, he knocked at her door. She made him wait for a minute's worth of heartbeats before answering—so he wouldn't get the wrong idea about her.

"You ready?" he asked when she opened the door.

"Do I look ready?" She stood on tiptoe, jutting out her breasts, as if to let him better determine the appropriateness of her attire, but really to tantalize him with the innocently sexy tank top she'd chosen to drive him wild.

"You'll need a T-shirt over that," he said. "Even with sunscreen, the glare off the water gives a killer burn."

T-shirt, my ass. Fuming, she stalked into her bedroom for the tightest one she could find.

"Don't forget a swimsuit," he called to her.

Oh, yeah. She had a perfectly scandalous one that would definitely tempt him.

In a few moments, she was ready and they set off. Tom drove silently, just smiling at her now and then. Uncomfortable in the quiet, she started talking. "Is it hard to sail?"

"Hard enough."

"I've seen those sailing races on ESPN and some movies—that one about a catamaran, a while back, and then there's *The Perfect Storm.* Of course, that wasn't a sailboat. Oh, and that one about prep school kids. I've never been on a sailboat really. We used to go waterskiing with some friends. I liked that. It took me a lot of tries to get the single ski thing down. Seems like motorboats are less hassle than sailboats."

"Why do you do that?" he said, glancing at her.

"Do what?"

"Talk about stuff you don't even care about? Silence is fine."

"Excuse me?" She felt slapped and sat up straight, her face hot. "Look, I never pretended to be a quiet little mouse."

"You don't have to be quiet. Just don't work so hard. You're fine the way you are."

"Whatever." She wanted to argue with him, but he must be trying to be nice in his own way, so she watched the desert skim by the window for a while.

"My father taught me to sail," Tom said after a bit.

"Really? That's nice." Her father had taught her to stay clear of him if she wanted to feel good about herself and life in general. "You got along well with your dad growing up?"

"Oh, yeah. Still do." As if everybody did. "How about you?"

"Not exactly."

"What happened?"

"My father was a moody tyrant. I spent a lot of time on tiptoe around him."

"I'm sorry."

"No biggie." She shrugged it off like always. Why complain?

"But it is big when your parents are troubled," Tom said. He turned his face to her. "It must have been hard for you, and sad."

Exactly. He nailed it. And so simply and kindly. She felt validated. Understood. Cared for. A shiver of feeling went through her. Tom Sands was a good man with a big heart. Maybe too good a man and too big a heart for her, a thought that sent an ache straight to her soul.

"I probably take my family for granted," Tom continued. "Like fresh air and good food, you just assume it will always be there. I'm a lucky man."

The conversation flowed easily from there. Tom told

her about his sister and her husband, who lived in Canada, and his parents and their *Leave it to Beaver* devotion to each other and their kids. If Tom wasn't such an open and honest guy, she would have thought he was making it up.

She answered his questions about her own family, explaining the way her mother catered to her father's temper, and how she'd survived by being funny and lively and never letting her father get her down.

She finished just as they pulled into the Lake Pleasant Marina entrance. Tom braked to wait for the van ahead of them to pay the fee, then leaned over and patted her thigh. "Thanks," he said.

"For what?"

"For telling me why." He smiled at her and his eyes were warm and accepting and she felt good. She couldn't remember the last time a man had made her feel just plain good, not horny or challenged, or edgy or hot. Just good.

The feeling stayed with her while she helped him stow the picnic supplies in the small cabin of his boat, arrange the ropes and sails, and motor out of the parking space—a "slip," he called it.

It took Tom forever to get the ropes and sails the way he wanted, and he was right about the sun being relentless, but eventually they were moving across the lake under sail.

"This is nice," she said.

"Huh?" He turned to her, as if called from far away. "Sorry. I get caught up in it all. Sailing's a great escape."

In a few minutes, she understood what he meant and didn't even mind being ignored. The wind seemed to just shove the boat forward with an invisible hand. The gusts were sometimes so big in the sail that the boat tipped partway onto its side, scaring her. But Tom would yank on a rope, crank a handle and shift the wooden tiller until they evened out and skimmed even more swiftly across the water.

She found herself laughing at the feeling, so free and wild yet safe and under control, too. Like nature's own carnival ride.

They scooted over the lake in a zigzag pattern, "tacking," Tom called it, making the boom and big sail flop from one side to the other of the boat to change directions. His serene competence gave her a terrific sexual charge. He let her steer a little, guiding her hand, sitting near enough that she could smell the spicy soap he used and feel his breath on her skin.

When the wind died, they made their way to a cove where Tom dropped an anchor and announced they were going swimming.

"Swimming?" When she'd brought her suit, she hadn't considered getting it *wet.* "The water's cold. It's only April."

"It's brisk, but come on. It'll perk you up." He pulled off his T-shirt, revealing a chest that perked her up plenty.

She figured her bikini would do the same for him, so she changed into it. Easing up the short ladder, she waited for Tom's reaction to the two strips of fabric that had made more than one man slur his words. He glanced at her, frowned, then reached into a compartment on deck for a bottle of sunscreen. "You need this," he said.

Undismayed, she said innocently, "You do my back, okay?"

After a few seconds' hesitation and a hard swallow,

he took the bottle. She turned so he could rub the warm liquid across her shoulder blades, slow and strong. She closed her eyes just thinking about those hands all over her.

"Got it," he said, low, sounding as affected as she was by the sensuality of the moment. She turned so he could do her front. Maybe they'd skip the swimming altogether. He gave her body a gratifying once-over, then he blushed and thrust the sunscreen into her hand. "You finish up."

She smiled and began putting on the lotion—slowly and in his line of sight. He was so *restrained*. That made him practically irresistible. She looked up to see the effect she was having on him just in time to see him jackknife gracefully into the lake. He broke the surface and waved her in.

Damn. She'd have to get wet. She daintily descended the ladder at the back of the boat, dipped a toe into the water and gasped. Cold enough to chill a martini.

"Come on. Don't be a wimp," he teased.

That irked her, so she twisted and dove straight under.

When she came up, holding in her squeal of reaction, he was watching her, looking at her funny.

"What's wrong?" she asked, pushing her hair out of her eyes.

"Nothing. You're beautiful, that's all."

"Oh. Thank you." The compliment shot through her like fire—powerful in its simple honesty.

They swam around the boat a couple of times, and she felt his eyes on her, appreciating her but also making certain she was safe. Kind of sweet. After a bit, they climbed back on board to eat thick ham sandwiches he'd made himself, chips and beer. The swimming had famished her. The food tasted great.

They sailed a little more, and, as the sun began to go down, headed back to the marina. Tina watched Tom's handsome features silhouetted by the gold and orange sunset. All afternoon she'd caught his eyes on her body. In the close quarters of the boat, she'd found ways to lean against him, slide past him, touch his arm or thigh, but he hadn't made a move. Was he shy?

Senses heightened by hours in the sun and wind on the rocking boat looking at Tom's nearly nude body, Tina decided it was time to find out. She tilted her mouth up and kissed him.

At first he was very, very still.

Finally, just before desperation kicked in and she gave up, he kissed her back, as smoothly as he'd handled the sailboat. His tongue didn't push or shove, just tasted, enjoyed her, the way she'd enjoyed the sun and wind and him all afternoon.

When he pulled away, his blue eyes blazed with a deep heat. He cupped her face with both hands and kissed her once more, then pulled back and gave her a look—*there's more where that came from*—before turning to motor them back to their slip.

This would work out just fine, she thought, aroused and pleased with herself for seizing the moment. She could hardly wait to get that big body naked and inside her. If Tom blushed over rubbing lotion around her bikini, think what he'd do when she showed him her sexual stuff. And she would show him her stuff, all right.

Two hours later, they walked up the stairs to her apartment. Tina unlocked the door and turned to kiss him, but he was standing on the first stair step, ready to leave.

"Thanks for coming," he said. "You were a great crew."

"Don't you want to come in? I can fix you a drink or something."

"Not tonight. I've got some studying to do."

"Studying?" She was flabbergasted. She didn't know whether to be hurt or angry. "But I thought we would…"

"We're getting to know each other," he said. "There's no rush." He winked, then turned to take the stairs.

Tina fought the urge to stamp her feet. Of course she could chase him, kiss him senseless, but what if he resisted? She'd feel like a fool.

Forget it, she told herself, shutting the door. Any man who could spend a day with her and not jump into bed if she'd let him was no one she wanted in her life. This wasn't 1950, for God's sake. Men and women knew what they wanted from each other and they went for it. If Tom wanted the *Leave It To Beaver* life his parents had, he was fooling himself. That was a mirage.

But now she was horny. Or, itchy, as Kara would say. She could call one of her regular sex buddies, but the sailing and sun and swimming had worn her out, so she lay down on the sofa and turned on the comedy station.

Even before the comic appeared, her frustration faded to pleasant memories. She could still feel the water's motion in her body, still remember Tom's concentration as he showed her how to hold the tiller—as if everything depended on her enjoying this. One nice thing was that she hadn't had to entertain him. Just being there had seemed to be enough for Tom.

She felt…cared for.

Forget it. June Cleaver, you are not.

She put Tom Sands out of her mind and focused on the comedian who was saying something about airline peanuts.

That had been a great kiss, though, solid and sure and full of promise. Maybe she'd give him one more chance. Just in case.

8

WHERE THE HECK IS ROSS? Kara thought, gulping down her seltzer and lime at Bucky's Barn, the country-western bar Ross had invited her to on her message machine. In a sexy drawl worthy of Clint Eastwood, he'd called himself Mickey Blue from the Rockin' R Ranch, dubbed her Miss Kitty, and asked her to join him so they could "mount up and ride bareback on something wild."

Ever since Thursday, when she'd been unable to make a date with Baylor Jones, she'd struggled with what to say to Ross about quitting. *I'm getting too attached to you.* That should do it. If she knew Ross, he'd leave so fast she'd feel a breeze.

The idea made her sad. Like giving up Christmas. She had a feeling she should talk about it before they started on the fantasy. *Ride bareback on something wild.* How could she pass up *that?* No one had that kind of self-control.

She'd looked up Bucky's in the phone book and arrived just before the designated hour—five o'clock—where she found they were giving free lessons in country swing. Not very sexy, really. Maybe Ross had a private room reserved in the back with one of those mechanical bulls they could set on a slow rock. There might be a lasso involved.

She'd joined the dancing lessons to pass the time until Mickey Blue arrived. By six, she'd worked up an unsexy sweat, had blisters from the cheap cowboy boots she'd had from an old Halloween costume, and there was no sign of her erotic urban wrangler.

By six-thirty she was upset. The Love Thief had been late, but only seventeen minutes. This was an hour and a half. She called Ross's apartment and left a message. On the off chance he'd left her one, she called her machine. "Where are you?" Ross asked impatiently in his message. "We can't ride horses this late and the champagne's getting warm."

Horses? What was he talking about? She borrowed a phone book and discovered there were two Bucky's— one a bar, the other a riding stable on the opposite side of the Valley. Damn. When she brought back the phonebook, the bartender had a call for her. It was Ross, who'd picked up her message.

"I'm sorry," she said.

"No biggie. I was just afraid you'd chickened out on me." He sounded so relieved her heart ached. She *had* chickened out. She just hadn't told him yet. "Come over to my place and we'll go with Plan B."

Plan B. Plan B should be goodbye. The crossed signals were a sign they should stop. By the time Kara got to his apartment, she'd convinced herself. She no longer felt like Miss Kitty, the bareback cowgirl, anyway. She was Kara in too-tight jeans and blisters going to her buddy Ross's apartment.

Ross answered the door in jersey shorts, damp from the shower, his chest sparkling with water drops, his sleek hair smelling of masculine soap and coconut shampoo. Very sexy, but very Ross. His cowboy boots, Stetson, jeans and plaid shirt lay in a pile in the middle of the living room. His Plan B must not involve any lassos or spurs.

"You sh-showered?" she stuttered.

"Had to ditch the horse sweat," he said.

"If it's any consolation, I wouldn't have been any fun. I'm afraid of horses." She had to make this sound less and less desirable—let them both down gently.

"Wouldn't have mattered," Ross said, low and intimate, pulling her close so he could grip her backside and rock her against him. He was already erect. "We were only riding far enough down the trail so they couldn't hear us moan, then we were going to lay out a blanket and drink champagne off our naked bodies."

"Oh," she said. If only she'd gone to the right Bucky's so they could have had that farewell fantasy. *Tell him,* she ordered herself. But he felt so good against her body.

"So, about Plan B," Ross murmured. "You left that almond oil from the massage session here. We could try a little more physical therapy. Every time I smell that stuff I go nuts remembering."

"You do?" she said, desire swamping her good sense.

"Yeah. I rub some on and think of you."

"Really?"

"Oh, yeah," he said, heat flaring in his eyes. "My skin is as soft as a baby's behind. Feel." He took her hand and moved it across his chest, warm and wet, the hair soft. His heart thudded under her hand and his ribs expanded with an unsteady breath. He lowered her hand to his muscled stomach and then pressed it against his erection through his shorts. "But I need you to rub out some, um, kinks."

"M-maybe," she said. What was her plan again?

Before her sluggish brain could rustle it up, Ross's hands had slipped into her jeans and gripped her butt. That pulled the crotch seam tight against her hot spot. If he kept on, she knew she'd melt right here. She went for ground rule number two. "This feels weird," she managed.

"That's because your jeans are so tight. Let's get you out of them and it will feel great."

"That's not what I mean," she said. With aching regret, she reached behind her and extracted his hands from her pants.

"You mean because we've already done the massage thing?" He seemed to be in a sexual haze.

"No. Because we're Ross and Kara in your apartment," she said. "Remember? We tried this before and fell off the couch laughing."

"But things are different now," he said. He reached for her and she couldn't quite pull away.

Things *were* different, all right. Because now she wanted *Ross*. Not Miguel, not Mike, not even Mickey Blue. Ross. As he looked right now, with his hair wet, chest bare, face shining. Everything about him invited her touch, her taste, her nibble.

Danger, danger, a robot voice repeated in her head and she said, "I think we should—"

"What? Get naked? Give me a sec." He started on her blouse buttons. "No bra," he murmured, flinging open her blouse to cup her breasts. She sagged against him and liquid gushed from her. *Touch me down here,* her body was saying. She leaned into him, helpless against the rush of lust. She wasn't addicted. She could quit anytime. Just, please, not now.

Spoken like a true addict. Digging deep where what resolve she had was dissolving, Kara pulled away from those fabulous fingers and croaked out, "We should *stop*."

Ross shook his head, looking confused. "Did you say *stop?*"

She nodded and clutched her blouse closed. "I'm getting addicted to this...to us." *To you.*

"But we're just having fun," he said, his eyes searching her face, looking hopeful.

"And all I think about is having more."

"So let's add Friday nights. Fine with me."

"No. That's a bad sign. Don't you see? Plus, I'm not interested in anyone else but you and this...this...what we're doing," she finished in a rush.

"Oh." Realization dawned on his face, along with alarm. "You mean you're getting serious? Like with one of your squash guys?"

"Close enough." She wasn't window-shopping at bridal stores, exactly, but not wanting Baylor Jones was an indication that she was headed there.

"You're sure?"

"I'm sure." Kind of.

His face just sank and he looked so lost and sad that she almost took it back. But he quickly collected himself—Ross bounced back fast. "Well, it's good you said something. This was an experiment, after all."

"Right. And it worked." *Too well.*

"It was great while it lasted."

"Oh yeah."

They stared at each other for a long moment.

"I should go," she said finally, glancing around Ross's cluttered apartment, her eyes falling on the discarded cowboy clothes. Their last fantasy in a pile of laundry.

When she looked up, she saw Ross was staring at the

clothes, too. "So much for Mickey Blue," he said, shaking his head. "Looks like it's Mickey Blue *balls* tonight."

"What do you mean?"

"I mean I've got a date with Mr. Hand as soon as you leave."

"You'll, uh, touch yourself?"

"Touch? It'll be more like assault. You turned me into rebar."

She thought of his hand on the glorious velvet length of him, stroking himself as he thought of her and ached with arousal. "I've never been able to do that," she said softly.

"Are you kidding? You almost take my head off with your touch."

"No, I mean, um, to myself." Heat rose to her cheeks.

"You can't bring yourself off?"

She shook her head, embarrassed.

"I could help you with that." His eyes twinkled wickedly.

"You could?" She was so swollen she felt as if she held a softball between her legs.

"Yeah. It's a shame we're quitting. That would have been a great date. A few tips from someone who knows what works for you. But..." He let the word hang as an offer.

"But we can't," she finished.

"You're right, I guess." He reached to tenderly cup her cheek. "You are an amazingly sexual woman. I hope you know that now."

"I do. Thanks to you," she said. "You're a great teacher." Her heart ached, remembering everything.

"I didn't teach you anything you didn't already know. I just helped you explore a little."

Emotions crossed Ross's face—softness, regret, affection, desire. She could see herself turning those looks into love and commitment and Sunday mornings reading the paper in bed before they walked their dog and did some work in the garden. Any day now, she'd do her thing to him—make him into her future. Ending it now was best.

"Like when you took over Love Thief," Ross continued wistfully. "I didn't teach you that. When you rubbed me—tortured me, really—with your breasts, I thought I would explode."

"I loved it in the airplane, when you reached under my skirt so fast."

"You were nervous and I thought that might calm you down."

"Calm me down? I almost passed out."

He smiled. "And I loved that."

"And Miguel." She sighed. "Miguel was... *fantástico*."

They laughed lightly at the Spanish word. "Katherine was a dream," Ross said. "Except I was awake. Very awake."

She swayed toward him, feeling fond and nostalgic and itchy. She had to stop before she made that rollercoaster climb of lust and tipped over the top into insanity. "I'd better go."

Ross nodded, then leaned in to kiss her. At the last minute, he sighed and planted his lips on her forehead. "Get out of here before I try to make you my love slave." Then, much softer, "And become yours."

For just a moment, there was nothing in the world she wanted more.

AN HOUR LATER, Kara was in bed, wide-awake, full of regret. Why couldn't they have one last farewell fantasy to memorize? If they knew it was the last one, what could it hurt? They practically owed it to themselves. She reached for the phone, then lost her nerve. Why postpone the inevitable?

Her fingers strayed to the swollen part of her, remembering that Ross had said he'd like to show her how to please herself. She began to stroke the spot, thinking of him. How did he do that thing that was just enough pressure, just enough tickle to make her surge closer to orgasm with each stroke? She moved her finger like he had, then slipped one finger inside herself.

But it wasn't the same without Ross.

She removed her finger and rolled onto her side, determined to fall asleep but throbbing with need. Then she heard a noise from the front of her apartment. Someone was pounding on her door. At ten o'clock at night? Could it be Tina? Or maybe, just maybe, Ross?

She threw on a robe—she'd been sleeping in the nude lately—and ran to the peephole, hoping against hope that her late-night visitor wasn't Tina.

She got her wish. She yanked open the door. "Ross! What are you—?"

"Hear me out," he said, pushing past her. "I know we're stopping, but I think I should show you how to get to climax on your own. So you'll have something for later?" His smile was sheepish with an edge of desperation.

"I don't know…" she said, her body throbbing out Morse code for *Yes, oh yes.*

"One last lesson?" he said. "I'll be your sex therapist. Dr., um, Dr. Michaels. Yeah. Imagine me in a lab coat with a clipboard."

One more lesson? Just one. And she *would* put it to good use after he was gone. She managed a shaky smile and let Ross lead her down the hall to her bedroom.

He stopped in the doorway. "I always thought this room looked like you. Neat and trim and not too girlie."

"I'm glad you approve," she said, trying to sound wry, but she was aroused and nervous and afraid to let one sensible thought escape. "Where do you want me, Dr. Michaels?" she said, trying to get into character.

"There's nowhere I don't want you," he said in his own voice. "On the bed," he added more clinically. "For now." He fluffed two pillows, then braced them against the headboard and motioned for her to recline there. Once she was in position, he sat beside her.

"I understand, Ms. Collier, that you're experiencing some, uh, self-pleasuring dysfunction." A half smile appeared—he'd liked his word choice.

"Um, yes, Dr. Michaels," she said, getting more comfortable in the role, "and it's a persistent problem." She, too, fought a smile.

"Persistent, eh? How fortunate that you called," he said, gently tugging the tie of her robe free. "Persistent problems are my specialty." Slowly he parted her robe, exposing her naked body to his gaze. She felt vulnerable until his ragged breath told her how aroused he was. Her insides liquefied.

"For a persistent problem like this, we'll have to keep trying—" he looked very deliberately at her breasts "—and trying—" then her stomach "—and trying." Then he honed in on the juncture of her thighs so intently she felt as if he'd brushed the thin folds of flesh and teased her at her core. "Until we get it right."

His words and intimate look made her swell so fully

she thought she'd hardly need to touch herself to explode.

"What should I do, Doctor?" she managed to say, her voice shaky.

"What do you want to do?" he murmured.

"I'm not certain." What she wanted was him to touch her, be inside her, all over her.

"If I were you, I'd start here." He cupped one of her hands with his own and placed it on the underside of her right breast. "How does that feel?"

"Soft," she said, loving the fact that his hand guided hers.

"Touch the nipple," he said, and moved one of her index fingers onto the delicate skin there.

"It's like butter," she marveled. She'd had her breasts all her life. Why had she never noticed how great they felt?

"I know. Now watch what happens when you stroke it." He pushed her index finger, then released her hand.

The nipple tightened under her finger, becoming a knot that vibrated with sensation. "Oh," she said as electricity shot from her breast to her core.

"When your nipples get hard, I know I've excited you," Ross murmured. His lust-roughened voice made her other nipple tighten.

"Oh," she said again, the word almost a cry. She made little circles on her nipple. Her clitoris tightened unbearably in response. Ross pushed one of her feet so her knee bent, then slid the bent leg to the side, so she was fully exposed to him. Embarrassment rushed through her and she started to close her leg.

Ross stopped her, held her leg open. "You're beautiful," he said. "I love how you look. And I need to see everything you're doing."

Her awkwardness melted away.

Then he led her other hand to the soft hair between her legs. "Explore," he instructed. "Find out what feels good."

She slid one finger into the cleft and gasped.

"That's the way," he said. "Show me what feels best. Show me how to please you."

She bit her lip, then slid her finger farther between the soft folds of flesh, creating pressure on the aching nub of herself.

"You're making yourself more hot, aren't you?"

She nodded, then closed her eyes to concentrate, focusing on the sound of Ross's voice and the sensations she was giving herself. She moved her finger forward and back, forward and back.

"You're getting more wet, more tight," he said.

"Yes," she whispered, rubbing faster.

"Now, go deep into yourself. The way you like me to be."

She did what he told her, marveling at how she felt inside, strong and ribbed and muscular, warm and smooth and soft.

"Push farther," he said. "Add another finger. Fill yourself up. Give yourself more and more."

"Oh," she said, adding a finger and moving faster. "It's...so...good."

"I know. I can see that in your face. And I can see how wet you are where you're rubbing yourself. Don't forget your nipple. Pinch it. See how that feels."

She did that and felt more tightness. She remembered how in the plane fantasy Ross had put his thumb onto the knot of her clitoris, while still moving his fingers inside her. She did that now and loved the electric jolt it gave her. She kept moving her fingers in and out. She was panting and letting out strange cries and gasps, her mouth open, not caring, only wanting to come, to make it to her goal. Her climax was very close. Her skin began to prickle with heat and urgency.

She was almost there. She couldn't believe it. This was so great.

Then she went numb—she'd scared herself—and the climax slipped away. Panicked, she stopped moving and looked at Ross.

"You can do it. You can bring yourself over the edge. I know you can. Trust yourself."

She started up again. Watching Ross watching her, seeing his faith in her, she stroked herself steadily until the surge struck so abruptly and with such intensity, she cried out and doubled over, writhing and twisting on the sheets.

The spasms hadn't quite subsided when Ross joined her on the bed. "I've got to be in you," he said, kissing her, his hands all over her. He rose up just enough to free himself from his pants, then he pushed into her, full and hard and fast.

She lifted her legs to take more of him, loving the pulling pain of his entrance.

He pushed hard, faster and faster, his face strained and intent, as if he searched for life itself inside her. "You make me crazy," he said, repeating what Miguel had said to her.

She felt crazy, too, and wild for him. She lifted her hips to meet him as he slammed into her, over and over. It felt so right to have him there, craving her, unable to resist her. The pressure began to build in her—and in him, she could tell. Higher, harder, faster.

This was the first time they'd been synchronized like this—two primal animals going for what they needed together in the dark. With a last fierce thrust, Ross's orgasm erupted and hers burst forth with it.

She cried out Ross's name. He hesitated for just a second and she felt the mistake of using his name. So much for Dr. Michaels and his dysfunctional patient, Ms. Collier.

When the spasms ended, Ross left her body and rolled onto his back, his head on her pillow. Side by side, they stared up at the ceiling, breathing hard.

"I guess sex is not a spectator sport for me," he said. "You turn me on too much, Kara."

Kara. He'd called her Kara. Kara and Ross were lying in her bed after making love and the terrible truth was that she was glad. She tried to think up some witty remark, but she couldn't. She was too upset, too confused. "What are we going to do, Ross?"

"I don't know. Let me think." Ross wanted to *think?* Another bad sign.

They kept staring at the ceiling, their chests rising and falling in a gradually steadier way, while Ross thought and Kara worried.

Finally Ross rolled onto his elbow and faced her. "I think I've got it," he said.

"You have?" She turned onto her side, mirroring him.

"You're afraid you're getting too attached, right?"

"Right."

"That you'll start thinking of me in a permanent way, want to get into a relationship, maybe think about getting married, having kids, all that junk?"

All that junk. So Ross. She nodded hesitantly.

"But that's ridiculous, Kara. You're forgetting who you're dealing with here. I'm not one of the Fortune 500 guys you want. I'm Peter Pan, remember? I'll never grow up. If you think about that, how can you possibly get serious about me?''

Good point. He was definitely not her choice for the right man to marry. ''I guess that makes sense.''

''Plus, we're opposites.''

''Yeah, but opposites attract, remember?'' she said, playing devil's advocate.

''Sexually sometimes, but to make a relationship work you have to be the same kind of people.''

''Except you can give a little. Compromise is important.''

''My mother was compromise incarnate. She sacrificed her life for us kids and my dad and she was miserable every minute.''

''But your mother stayed with your father, didn't she? Even after your sisters left for college?''

''True. Hey, whose side are you on? I'm supposed to be proving to you that I'm safe to play with.''

''I know, but I have to be sure,'' she said, staring into those gold-green eyes of his, fighting how wonderful it felt to be inches apart on her pillows like any pair of new lovers exchanging intimate secrets and promises of forever.

''So, yeah, Mom and Dad stayed together, but only out of habit. Like hamsters in a wheel, not realizing there's a big wide world out there if they'd just step off.'' His eyes coaxed her to agree with him. ''The lesson is that you can't give up who you are for someone else. It doesn't work.''

''That's what you really think?'' she said, her heart strangely heavy.

''Oh, yeah. But don't look so sad. You're not me, Kara. You'll find the kind of guy you want. When it's time. And you'll pick a good one, not the losers you've been settling for. That's the point of what we're doing. Getting your head straight about sorting through men to find the right one. When it's time and not just for sex.''

''That's true,'' she said, swallowing a lump of disappointment. ''And who exactly is this guy I want—the one who isn't a loser...in your opinion?''

''I don't know. Someone stable and responsible. Ambitious, but not a jerk. Someone who'll go to movies on Saturday nights and brunches on Sunday mornings. A guy who wants kids and a minivan, who'll take you to Hawaii with his bonus money.''

''You make it sound dull.''

''It's not to you, though, is it?''

''Actually, no.''

''Then it doesn't matter what I think. This is about you and your future Mr. Right. And I'm Mr. Wrong. So how could you fall for me?''

''I guess.'' It was irritating that her jokester of a pal had suddenly gotten wise. ''Well, what do you want? In a woman, I mean. And don't tell me you'll never settle down. Give me a hypothetical.''

''I haven't really thought about it. Someone who won't sweat the small stuff, I guess. Someone who wants to experience life every day. Someone who'll hike the Grand Canyon on the spur of the moment, you know?''

''Yeah.'' Someone the opposite of Kara. A hike down the Canyon sounded like a lot of blisters and misery, and what Ross considered ''small stuff'' were all the little details that added up to life in her mind. ''Sounds like you want your twin.''

He chuckled. ''You said hypothetical. The woman I just described probably doesn't exist. Most women are like you. They want security—or at least someone whose ride has a back seat.''

He gave her an apologetic smile. Pure Ross charm. She knew suddenly why women loved him. Even when he disappointed you, you felt special. He let you in on his failings but asked you if you still wanted to play.

And she did. Definitely. Her body itched to scoot closer and press against him in the warm dark. Her hands ached to slide over his hard muscles and other hard places.

Ross reached out to push her hair gently from her cheek. ''So? Did it work? Have I scared any thought of us in the big R out of your mind?''

''Big R? You mean relationship?''

He nodded.

''You make it sound pretty impossible, all right.''

''I don't want to quit being with you yet,'' he said earnestly. ''There's so much more to explore. Look what you just learned about self-pleasure.'' He ran his hand possessively along the curve of her hip. ''This is good for you.''

''Good for *me?*'' she asked wryly.

''Well, me, too, of course.'' His wicked grin split his face, his teeth white in the dim room. ''This is the hottest sex I've ever had,'' he said, low and hoarse.

''Really?''

''Yeah. You don't realize how amazing you are. I feel sorry for the next guy you take to bed. He won't know what hit him.'' He frowned briefly, as if the idea of the ''next guy'' bothered him. Good. Maybe Ross was more involved than he thought he was. She clutched that idea, dangerous as it was, close to her heart.

''So, are we on?'' he asked, pulling her close, throwing a leg across her thigh in a very intimate gesture. This would be the beginning of slow, personal sex, the kind you had in the big R. Bad idea. Where was the ground rule for this situation? *If we need a new rule, we make one.* Of course.

"On one condition," she said, sitting up. "We make more ground rules."

"More rules?"

"If we want to keep doing this, we have to be more careful."

"Okay, what rules?"

"We set a limit."

"A limit?"

"Yes. Only so many more dates." She had her heart to protect. "Like say four more." That didn't sound like enough.

"Four more? What about all the fantasies we have left? I have lots of new ideas."

"Four more should be plenty," she said sternly, dying to hear what he had in mind.

"How about if we make a list? You tell me yours and I'll tell you mine and we'll see how many weeks we need. Maybe we could even double up and go for two nights a week."

"Stop," she said, loving every word coming out of his mouth. "We're setting a limit, not expanding the action."

"Okay, but I still think a list is a great idea. You know how you love lists. A sex checklist."

"Ross…"

"Okay, okay. We set a limit, but only after we've done our major fantasies. Don't you have fantasies you still want to try?"

"Not really." Her heart began to pound.

"Yes, you do. Come on. You already mentioned doing it in a taxi. We'll put that on the list. What else?"

"I don't know." She flailed about for something. "I guess I like that idea of covering each other in chocolate and, you know..."

"Licking each other clean?" he finished eagerly.

"But maybe that's too clichéd?"

He took her hand and placed it on his penis, hard as stone. "Does this feel like I think it's too clichéd?"

"I guess not," she said on a sharp intake of breath.

He curled her fingers around his shaft and moved her hand slowly up and down. "Imagine we've got chocolate...nice and warm right here, and say I put some all over here." He cupped her breast.

"Oh, please...I...don't..."

"Any Hershey's in the house?"

"There's whipped cream in the fridge." Then she caught herself, released his penis and rolled away from his fingers. "We're finished for tonight. No overtime, no extra innings. That's another new rule. One fantasy a week."

"You sure?"

"Absolutely." If she used control now, she might still have it later—when things got worse, which they just might.

Whatever made her think she could play with this kind of fire and not get burned?

9

Two weeks later, Ross slid into a chair across from Tina for the noon spades game. "Where's Kara?" he asked. His heart got an odd knot in it when he hadn't seen her for a while.

"She had a lunch meeting with the marketing guy at Emerson Faucets and Stoppers. Baylor Jones." Tina shuffled the cards.

Why hadn't Kara told him about this? Ross felt that twinge in his bones, as though he was about to lose something he wanted desperately to keep. *Stop it. You don't own her.*

He studied his hand, not really seeing the cards. "So, what's this Baylor Jones like?" he asked, trying to sound casual. He remembered him as kind of a slick guy. Definitely a squash player.

Tina froze in the act of picking up a card and looked at him with suspicion. "What's he *like?*"

"I mean, will he go along with Kara's campaign ideas?"

"Oh, *that's* what you mean." She grinned—she was on to him, dammit. "You're so dedicated all of a sudden. Sure you're not going for Lancer's job?"

"Forget it. Just prepare to sacrifice your life savings to my superior strategy."

They played the first game in silence. Ross lost, distracted by the thought of Kara aiming her gorgeous eyes at that marketing geek in a dimly lit restaurant, while he tried to impress her with his knowledge of wine. *Forget it, pal. Kara can't be bought off by flashy, materialistic bullsh—*

"Focus here, friend," Tina said, slapping the deck into his hand. His deal. He felt her eyes on him as he shuffled.

"I hear the sex lessons are going well," Tina said.

He nearly shot the cards across the table. "What did Kara tell you?"

"Relax, chief. Not much. Just that she's learning and that you're good."

"That's exactly right. I am good. Tell your friends." The old cocky Ross routine didn't feel right just now, and he wished he hadn't said that.

"I'm a little worried about her," Tina said, unusually thoughtful. "She gives out these daydreamy sighs and practically walks into walls. Slow it down a little, would you?"

"Slow it down? Did she say she wanted that?"

"I mean the shuffling," Tina said, laughter in her voice. "You're practically throwing cards."

"Okay. Sorry." He gathered up the far-flung cards. The week between adventures had become an eternity for him. The minute he had convinced her that the game was safe for her, it started feeling touch-and-go for him. Maybe it was that stupid new rule. *Time limit, my ass.*

They'd been getting together on Thursday nights at his place to talk about things—and for him to create a sex checklist, over her objections. Describing the exotic-dancer-and-kid-from-a-small-town fantasy had gotten them so hot that Kara had just run out the door without saying goodbye, leaving him with a distinctly unsatisfying session with Mr. Hand.

His next assignment was to be a cop arresting her for indecent exposure. Maybe he'd get some handcuffs. Soft ones... His mind drifted.

"Hello in there, Ross," Tina said, calling him back from his plans.

"Yeah. I'm here."

"Are you sure you two know what you're doing?"

"God, yes. Every time I turn around Kara's making a new ground rule. This is just about sex. We're very clear about that." Except even as he'd lain there in Kara's bed and convinced her how different they were, how impossible they'd be together, he'd felt this perverse urge to give it a try. Nothing like being told something wouldn't work to flush out his stubborn streak.

"As long as you're sure, and you're in as much trouble as she is." She smirked at him.

"What's that supposed to mean?"

"Nothing. Enough with the chitchat. I'm going to kick your ass here."

"Not with the king of diamonds and the seven, eight and ten of spades, you're not," he said, throwing down the jack of spades.

"You looked at my cards!"

"You were hanging them in my face," he countered. "What's up with you anyway? You've lost your edge." Tina seemed as distracted as he was.

"I'm preoccupied, I guess." She looked at him speculatively. "Let me ask you something. How long would you wait to have sex with someone?"

"That depends on who."

"A month? Would you wait a month?"

"If she was worth it." For Kara, he'd wait as long as it took.

She looked glum, stared at her hand, then lifted her eyes. "Do you think Tom Sands is gay?"

"Tom from the Upside? Nah. At least he's never slipped me his phone number."

"Pul-eeze. You're not well-groomed enough to be gay. I don't really think he's gay. It's just…hell, I'm giving him one more week."

"Before you jump him?"

"If it comes to that."

"No man is safe when the mighty Miss Tina sets her sights on him."

"Watch it, pal. You're in no position to criticize." She glanced at the clock on the wall. "That's a pretty long lunch Kara's been on with Baylor Jones."

"It's a working lunch," he said, but his gut clenched.

"Sure it is."

Tina was good. She knew just where to poke around to drive him nuts. Why the hell *was* Kara out so long with the guy? He'd love to be a cork crumb in their cabernet right now.

It shouldn't matter, of course. Even if Kara wanted to date the guy, he and she still had their arrangement until they got through his checklist, which he intended to extend as much as possible. This afternoon, he'd find a way to remind her how great this was going, so she'd forget all about Mr. Faucets and Stoppers.

KARA EASED into the conference room for the Plain Jane Bakery meeting twenty minutes late, praying they hadn't started yet, but it was her bad luck to find all eyes tracking her as she scampered to the remaining empty chair, which happened to be across the table from Ross.

"I'm glad you could fit us into your busy schedule,"

Saul Siegel said with his usual gentle sarcasm. Bob and Julie grinned, pleased to see someone else on the hot seat. Tina shot her a questioning look.

"Sorry," she mumbled. She'd had such a pleasant lunch with Baylor that she'd lost track of time. She'd been frankly relieved to find she still found him attractive. The experience had reassured her that she was still okay having sex with Ross on the side. As long as it stayed on the side.

"Okay then. The media buy…" Saul said, evidently picking up where he'd left off when she entered.

Ross caught her gaze. Something about his expression—possessive and demanding—shot her with sexual adrenaline. He slid a piece of paper across the table to her, letting his fingers cover hers for an instant.

She read the note: *I'm undressing you…with my tongue.* She looked up and found him staring at her with naked desire.

A hot knot tightened between her legs.

Tina leaned over and whispered in a singsong. "You're being ob-vious."

As soon as the meeting was over, Ross grabbed her hand and dragged her into the copy room, slamming the door with her body and crushing her into a kiss. "I can't keep my hands off you," he said. One hand pushed up her skirt and reached for her panties, already wet for him, while the other held her tightly to him, as if he owned her. "Wear that blue dress on Saturday. It's hot."

Even as flames licked her insides and she wanted Ross to throw her onto the copy machine and make love to her in its green glow, her mind took charge. They were in the office, for God's sake. Where they *worked.* This was wrong, wrong, wrong.

Someone tried the door from the outside, then exclaimed when it wouldn't open.

Kara slid away from Ross, straightened her skirt and pretended to be checking out the copier, while Ross opened the door. ''Musta stuck,'' he muttered to the secretary, who gave him and Kara a puzzled look. No wonder. The tiny room fairly vibrated with sexual energy. What the hell were they doing?

ON THURSDAY NIGHT, Kara struggled up the stairs to Ross's apartment with the four bags of groceries she'd bought for the dinner she was fixing. There would be no hanky-panky tonight. Just two friends enjoying a meal. They'd confirm a couple of details for their Saturday-night date and that was it for sex talk.

Except, of course, for a sensible review of the ground rules. The incident in the copy room proved they had to take it down a notch.

She also wanted to talk to Ross about applying for Lancer's job. More and more, she'd felt driven to help him. It seemed stupid for him to stall his career. He was more than equipped to take over. If he wouldn't apply for the job, she might just do it for him. As a friend, of course.

Reaching the top of the stairs, she knocked at his door. He called for her to come in and she did, prepared to start her lecture. Except he was playing his guitar on the sofa, wearing the Love Thief's tight black jeans with just a black leather vest over his bare chest. He looked so good with his muscular arm over the guitar, his skilled fingers on the strings, that she stood there, bags dangling, her speech stuck in her throat.

''What's in the bags?'' he asked softly, his magical fingers still working the strings.

"Stir-fry," she choked out, mesmerized. "What's with the outfit?" If he was planning a swooning groupie fantasy, she was *there*. Let the bok choy wilt on the terrace.

"I have to pretend to be a rock star for Lionel and Lucy's daughter Abby. She's turning five and having a little birthday party. It'll just take a few minutes. Mind coming with?"

"Not at all." Anywhere, anytime.

The more time Kara spent with Ross, the more she saw of his thoughtful side. She knew he picked up groceries and took out trash for the elderly couple two doors down—he claimed it was so they wouldn't call the cops when he played his stereo loud, but she knew he was just concerned about them. And he did minor electrical repairs for the landlords and painted all their signage. And here he was serving as entertainment for their daughter's birthday. Things about Ross sneaked up on you.

Ross helped her bring the bags into the kitchen, then she followed his rock-star-caliber butt down the stairs. Outside the landlord's door, he started in on a popular rock song.

The door flew open and a little squirt with bright red hair chirped, "You came!" then threw her arms around his knees.

"I couldn't miss the big five, could I, buckaroo?" he said. He squatted down to her level. "You've grown up since yesterday—a whole year's worth, I think." He pretended to measure her with his hand.

"I told my friends all about you," Abby said. "Will you play…" She rattled off a list of songs, to which he nodded, then they all went inside.

Six little girls sat in a rapt circle around Ross while

he played and sang, making eye contact with each of them in turn. Kara could practically see the crushes developing on their little faces. She felt a tightness in her chest and realized she had a bit of a crush, too. Temporary, of course, and lust inspired, no doubt.

When Ross finished, Lucy brought out a homemade cake with a lopsided top layer and erratic frosting.

Abby proudly presented two pieces to Ross and Kara.

"You make this yourself?" Ross asked, taking a bite of his.

"Just the frosting."

"That's the best part," he whispered. "But don't tell your mom I said that. Might hurt her feelings."

Abby just beamed, then ran off with her friends to play games. Her mother hugged Ross. "She'll be talking about this for weeks," she said, then turned to Kara. "I hope you know how special this guy is."

"I think I do." The more special he seemed, the more trouble she was in.

"Just trying to rise to the company I keep," Ross said, grinning at Lucy, then Kara. God, he made her feel good.

They headed up to the apartment and Kara's thoughts turned to The Talk—no more hot looks at work and Ross ought to get serious about going for the creative department manager's job.

Ross put his guitar in his bedroom and she was dismayed to see he didn't put a shirt on under that damnable leather vest. Her attraction was a low-level hum of electricity, sparking now and then when he looked at her or their bodies accidentally brushed.

He helped her unload the bags—a monstrous pile of food—bok choy, green onions, cabbage, peppers in three colors, cherry tomatoes along with peanuts, hot Thai peppers—and a brand-new wok with utensils.

"You bought a wok?" Ross asked.

"You like Asian food. I'll show you how to use it and you can do some cooking for yourself instead of takeout all the time. Better for you."

"I'll pay you for it."

"It's a gift—from a friend." His bewildered gratitude embarrassed her. Was she doing too much?

Now was the time to talk about being civilized at work, but she just didn't feel ready. Instead, she opened a cupboard to see what he had in the way of dishes. Just some souvenir Arizona Diamondbacks glasses, a few coffee mugs and three stoneware plates, all chipped. "Is this all you have?"

"Plenty for me."

"I just bought a new set of dinnerware. I'll bring you my old stuff."

"Not necessary."

"I'd rather give them to you than have you buy them from Goodwill later."

"Okay," he said, puzzled by her generosity. "You're doing too much for me."

She was just making his place more homey and complete. Right? Something about her motives bothered her, but she ignored it.

"Check these out," Ross said, opening a cupboard to reveal shelves crammed with mugs and tumblers of cartoon characters, comic book superheroes and movie stars. "Now these are worth something." He held out two mugs with the Three Stooges garishly shaped into their surfaces. "I'll trade these for your plates."

"No thanks. You keep them. Drinking out of Curly's nostril kind of kills my appetite," she said. She thrust a bag of celery at him. "Clean and chop the vegetables, okay? I'll work on the meat. That's assuming you have decent knives." She pulled open a drawer that should have held silverware, but instead contained watercolor paints and felt markers.

"To the left," he said.

She opened the drawer he'd indicated and lifted out a huge wrench. "You have tools in here? Next to eating utensils?"

"What do you want? They're in separate compartments."

"I'm scrubbing everything. And you need a new drawer organizer. Look at all these crumbs." She removed the plastic tray and began taking out the utensils, relieved for an excuse to delay The Talk.

Then Ross's warm hand stopped her. "Kara," he said softly, taking the silverware organizer out of her hands and putting it on the counter. "What's the matter?"

"Nothing. I'm just fixing dinner and getting you organized."

"Kara."

"Okay. I just...I think... We need to be careful at work, Ross."

"This is about slamming you against the door at S&S yesterday, right? I know. Something came over me. It won't happen again." His eyes held hers. "I swear."

"Okay," she said, relieved that they could keep their little boat afloat a while longer.

"So no more critiquing the natural habitat," he said. "Deal?"

She nodded, waiting to scrub the knife blade until he left to put on some music.

Heated blues filled the air and Ross came back whistling along. His meltingly tuneful whistle reminded her of how good he'd sounded at the birthday party. "You played really well for Abby and her friends."

"Hell, they'd have been happy with the Barney song," he said, chopping away on the bok choy.

"No, I mean it. You're very good. Your voice is nice and your guitar work is...subtle. Have you ever considered being in a band?"

"I sit in with friends on some gigs. But just for fun. I don't need to make money at something for it to be worthwhile."

"I'm not saying that. It's just that if you performed in public, then other people could enjoy you, too. Like I do."

He turned to her in the warm glow of the stove light. "You always want to push, don't you? Raise the bar? If you're good, be better?" He gave her that look—as if he thought she was crazy but liked her anyway.

"Why not? And, while we're on the subject, I've been thinking about you and Lancer's job, Ross."

"Not that again." He whacked at a celery stalk.

"You'd be great. I saw how you steered Julie away from that extreme design for Plain Jane without wounding her. Not to mention the overlapping deadlines with Rich in production. He gets testy on a dime, and you manage him so well."

"I appreciate your concern, big sis, but I don't want the job—and you're turning that stir-fry into frappé."

She looked down and saw she'd whipped the vegetables into a froth of oil. Pure frustration. Why wouldn't Ross even *try?* He was letting everyone down.

Why does this matter so much? It's his life, not yours. She took a calming breath and focused on the way the steam rose around them, aromatic with garlic, peanuts and onions. Their easy teamwork felt nice. At least that. And she hardly felt sexual at all.

Before long, the food was ready and they sat at the table set with the chipped plates and the Three Stooges mugs, into which Ross had poured her pricey chardonnay. At least the wine could breathe in the huge mugs. The still-sizzling wok rested on a towel between them— Ross didn't even have hot pads—and they were face-to-face, sharing a cozy meal for two in an uneasily domestic scene.

Through the window behind Ross, the sky was a gorgeous backdrop of sunset streamers in pink, gold and purple.

"Well, let's dig in," she said briskly, dishing out rice, then adding mounds of stir-fried chicken and vegetables.

Ross scooped a forkful into his mouth. "Mmm," he said, chewing slowly, oil glazing his lips like an invitation. "This is great. You can do this anytime you want."

How about every night for the rest of our lives? She pushed away that thought. She was skating on the thin ice of her resolve again. Imagining something permanent with Mr. Fleeting. And it had only been two weeks since they'd lain in her bed and agreed that Ross was absolutely wrong for her—out of the question as a relationship prospect, perfectly safe for sex alone.

But coming to his house the past two Thursdays had intensified her feelings for him, especially as she saw more of his lovable side. He'd been so good with Abby tonight. What a great father he'd make.

Stop! What was she doing? Even worse, she could feel herself making a little shopping list—new shower curtain, dish drainer, hot pads, toilet seat cover, maybe some inexpensive bookshelves…oh, and bring over the vacuum.…

"So," Ross said, calling her away from her dangerous plans, "I talked to my friend with the cab. He's off a week from Saturday, so taxi-driver-and-fare is a go."

Ross had been more than willing to hail a cab and just go at it to fulfill her cab sex fantasy, but she was too embarrassed to make love with a real cabbie watching them in the rearview, so they'd compromised—Ross would borrow the taxi and pretend to be the driver and they'd go at it in private.

"Good. That should be fun."

"Fun? I hope it will be sexy as hell," he said.

She gave a nervous laugh. At least they were talking about this in a civilized way—over the dinner table and far from the couch, where they'd nearly lost it last week.

"And here's my next one," Ross continued. "Virgin cheerleader with the football captain. What do you think?"

"I *think* that's the last one. Didn't we agree?"

He shrugged. He always had a new idea. Too bad they were such good ones. "Here's how it goes," he continued. "I checked out the high school and no one's around after about ten. Say the cheerleader's practicing her cheer and the football star comes out to run the field and he seduces her on the goal line. Sound good?"

"I don't know," she said, feeling a little rush as she imagined making love outside under the stars. "Do I have to be a cheerleader? That's a little too rah-rah for me."

"Okay, let's see. What I like about that one is the virgin part. The first time…going very slow, very gentle, savoring every little movement."

She felt the tingle in her belly start up. "That could be nice."

"You always respond so intensely—like it's the first time every time." His voice reminded her of his fingers under her flight attendant uniform stroking her into heat.

"Oh," she said, trying to clear her head.

"So, how about a virgin on her wedding night? We rent a tux and a gown—all that tight, gauzy stuff to peel off. What do you think?"

"I can't," she said, abruptly snatched from her haze by the picture he'd painted. "Not a bride. It's too..."

"What? Expensive?"

"Swear you won't laugh?"

He crossed his heart.

"It's too symbolic. A wedding dress means two people promising their lives to each other, taking that huge leap of faith." She swallowed hard. "I just think that the wedding moment means something. Sorry."

"Sure. I get it. Forget that one," he said, looking extremely uncomfortable. He played with his food a moment, then looked up, cheerful again. "How about the virgin brainiac and the jock failing chemistry? You can be my tutor. Or I could be the virgin. That might be even hotter."

"Possible," she said, hiding an unexpected and stupid sting of disappointment. What did she think he'd say? *I understand completely. Maybe someday we'll wear that tux and gown for real?* Absolutely crazy. She was definitely losing control of her attitude.

"This Saturday is the indecent exposure arrest, right?" Ross said. "Will you wear that black dress from the Hyatt?"

"I think it should be something new," she said, fighting away her worries.

"Okay, but make sure it's easy to get out of. Something in silk, maybe? Actually, what I'd really like is just you. Naked."

"Naked?" she said, her pulse quickening. Instantly the tension that always hummed between them crackled to hot life.

"Oh, yeah. The hottest thing we've done so far was that time on your bed."

"You mean when I..."

"Touched yourself? Yeah. Showing yourself to me the whole time, letting me watch you doing what I told you." His voice grew husky. "You were nervous, but still brave, opening yourself to me, trusting me."

"You liked that?" She held her fork poised, her hand shaking, heat popping inside her like bursts of fireworks.

"It made me crazy. I was dying to put my hands on you, in you, and my tongue, too. I wanted to taste you."

"Oh."

"And when you came, you looked so incredible—innocent and wild and caught off guard. I nearly lost it just watching."

"Really?" she said, vaguely aware of something falling onto her plate. In a daze, she brought her fork to her mouth, but there was nothing on it.

"Really." Ross scooped up her dropped food with his own fork and leaned nearer. "Open up," he said softly.

She wanted to open up, all right—her clothes, her mouth, her legs—and bring him inside to take care of the ache between her legs, the burn in her heart. Right here on the kitchen table. So much for a civilized dinner. There was nothing civilized about this feeling roaring through her.

She shoved the fork out of his hand, spraying rice across the table, lunged forward and kissed him. She was vaguely aware that she'd dipped her chest into the rice bowl, but she didn't give a damn.

Ross grabbed her cheeks, and she his. Holding each other's faces, devouring each other's mouths, they rose to their feet.

"Whoo-hoo." The muffled call came through the window.

They froze and looked out. Lionel was grinning at them, giving them a thumbs-up.

Ross smiled sheepishly, and Lionel walked on.

"This is bad," Kara said, panting for air. "We can't let things fall apart like this."

"Fall apart? I'd say they're coming together. How about lonely waiter at a Chinese restaurant and his last customer?"

"If we can't control this, Ross, we have to stop it."

"Are you sure?" he said, begging her to change her mind.

"Yes. Absolutely." He had no idea how close she was to haunting bridal fairs.

They stood there panting at each other for a long minute.

"I should go home," she said finally.

"Stay for the game."

"What?"

"Suns versus Lakers?"

"I don't know...."

"Come on. Friends watch games together. Let's just use a little self-control," he said, smoothing her hair, patting her cheek. "Ross and Kara will watch a game together tonight just like old times. No contact. No hot looks. Just friends enjoying some b-ball. I can do that. Can you?"

Numbly she nodded, though they'd never watched sports together, even before they started having wild sex. She didn't know a thing about basketball, nor care, but she forced herself to concentrate on the scramble of giant players racing back and forth across the TV screen, determined to memorize the rules, learn all about the players—anything to keep from climbing all over Ross and ruining everything.

"WOW, DID YOU SEE THAT?" Ross looked at Kara for her reaction to the amazing basket the Suns had just made. But Kara's eyes were shut and her mouth hung open sweetly in sleep. Her breathing was soft and deep, making him want to cuddle up around her. But then he'd want to be inside her. What a horn dog. This was *Kara* dozing on his couch, not Katherine or Angel or any of the other fantasy women.

She'd stayed, even though she didn't care about basketball, because they were friends. The truth was that he just wanted her around. More and more, he liked having her in his line of sight, liked hearing her views on things—crazy though they were. He liked how she really listened before she started arguing with him.

He loved showing her his projects, the new music he bought. He found himself saving up witty things to say just to bring that sunny smile to her serious face, that light to her sober blue eyes.

He hated when she started fussing at him, though, like about that damn management job. She wouldn't let up about that. He liked his life just fine. Why upset a good, smooth thing? Besides, he might lose interest in design, decide to pursue music. He had to keep his options open. Kara thought the only move was up. Ross knew you could move out, move around, move on.

He noticed there was a Nerf dart hanging from Kara's hair. They'd had fun shooting at each other during half-time. He squatted down to lift the spongy toy from a strand of her hair, then stopped to stroke the silky curve of it. He liked it loose around her shoulders. She'd been wearing it that way almost every day lately. She had a new light in her eye, a nice sensuous swing to her step. All because of their sex game.

That was important. That was worth it, even if they were on an uncertain footing lately, with emotions slipping between their fingers every time they turned around.

He noticed that the angle of her head would mean a definite neck kink. She needed some sleep, he knew, because she had a presentation tomorrow morning. He'd put her in his bed. Gently, very gently, he reached under her legs and shoulders and lifted her into his arms.

"Whaaa?" she said, still asleep.

"It's okay. I'm taking you to bed."

"Wonderful," she murmured, cuddling against his chest. If only she meant that the way it sounded. He carried her into his room and laid her on his bed.

She looked so perfect in his room, surrounded by the piles of his clothes and shoes, his weight bench and bicycle and stacks of magazines and pizza boxes. She was a sweet, serene center of the confusion that was his life. And he felt drawn in, pulled to her, wanting to lie there beside her just to be near her.

Uh-oh. His heart swelled with a feeling bigger than lust. The kind of feeling that made you hold a woman all night and not notice morning breath because you cared so much about her.

This was more than sex. Way more. This was love. He was falling in love with Kara.

Could he handle it? Maybe. But what about Kara? If she felt this way about him, would she get hurt when things changed? Because with him they always did. And he'd sworn he'd never hurt her. He felt sick inside. Maybe Kara had been right about stopping. This could get complicated. It might already be.

But if he just kept quiet about it, his feelings might settle down. If he didn't tell her, she'd never know. Plus, they had all those ground rules to protect them.

He backed away now, to let her sleep, his last sight the strip of moonlight shining silver on her hair. He grabbed a couple of sheets from the laundry basket and tried to get comfortable on the sofa, gripping the cushions to keep himself from lunging back into that room and going for it.

Exactly what he'd be going for, he was afraid to figure out.

KARA OPENED HER EYES with a start, unsure where she was. In the gloom, she made out a tangle of sheets, then propped herself on her elbows. The weight bench and bicycle told her she was in Ross's bedroom. The last thing she remembered was watching basketball and nodding off. Ross must have carried her here. She looked at his Roy Rogers clock—three o'clock.

God. She had a presentation at nine. She'd be exhausted. She climbed out of bed and found Ross on the sofa lying on his back, his head kinked sideways against the corner of the sofa, feet dangling off the end. Poor thing.

She watched his chest rise and fall and felt a wash of desire. He was gorgeous, of course, but in sleep, she could see his softness. She felt emotions rise in her—affection, tenderness...and something more.

This is Ross, remember? Peter Pan? Mr. Playful? The guy with a black book so big it's cross-indexed? But he'd carried her to his bed and slept out here, inviting neck injury rather than send her out into the night or risk their friendship by climbing into bed with her.

He was so much more mature than he believed he was. He was capable of a solid relationship. He'd described her Mr. Right in materialistic terms—minivans and timeshares—but what was important was the foundation of love and partnership beneath those things. It wasn't the Sunday brunches and Saturday movies, it was the companionship and intimacy of spending time together. And Ross was capable of all that—and more.

Or maybe she was just trying to make him into Mr. Right. That was a scary thought. She shook her head. It was too late and she was too foggy for this kind of analysis. She needed sleep. So did Ross.

She squatted so she was level with his face, fought the urge to kiss him, and whispered, "You can go to bed now."

"Hmm?" He turned toward her and his eyes flew open. "Kara. You're still here," he said. He smiled in soft pleasure and he touched her cheek.

"But I'm going home now." She cupped his hand with hers, a loving gesture she couldn't resist. "Go to bed before you hurt yourself."

"Oh," he said fuzzily.

"And thank you," she said.

They looked at each other. *I wanted to,* he was telling her.

"I know," she said out loud, and backed away. She felt the warmth of his hand on her cheek all the way out to her car.

10

THIS WAS IT, Tina decided. When Tom came over to study on Saturday, they were going to make love. She'd been patient. She'd gone along with his go-slow approach. Enough already. Saturday night would either be her Waterloo or her *Love Connection*. She almost didn't care which. She was sick to death of waiting and aching and wondering just how much he really wanted her.

Was there someone else? A past heartbreak? A dead girlfriend? A problem with premature ejaculation? Impotence?

Or, worse, was it something about her that made him withhold sex? What? What? What?

Tonight she would know for sure, one way or the other.

They knew each other plenty well—so well it made her uneasy. She liked how he listened hard to her, then nodded, considering, as if he had to store away what she told him for a later exam. It was nice, but it made her nervous, as if he was poking around where he didn't belong. She wanted him inside her pants, not her heart.

She wasn't going to assault him or anything. He'd want to be in the driver's seat. She was secure enough about her sexuality that she could let him steer for a while until he got tired. Then she would take over.

She wore a deep-veed, clingy T-shirt with shredded sleeves and tight, high-cut shorts, her reddest lipstick,

tallest sandals and most seductive scent. She was a for-
midable sex object. If she were a superhero, she'd be
Sexual Woman.

She'd placed candles in strategic locations, including
a bank around her bed, lit some jasmine incense, and
turned on jazz lush enough to lead any warm human to
sexual thoughts.

Tom hit the bell right on time, wearing the usual
stonewashed jeans and a plain white T-shirt, carrying a
book and a notebook under his arm. He had no idea he
was soon going to be whipping out of those clothes and
flinging those books aside to screw his brains out—or
rather let her do it for him.

"Hey," she said in the doorway.

His gaze raked over her body and he licked his lips.
This wasn't unusual. He had more and more been giving her those looks—like a kid with no money looking
in a candy-store window—but this once-over was more
like a four-over. Maybe five. "You look…great," he
said. "What's the occasion?"

"No occasion. I just felt like this." She took a deep
breath of his wake. She loved the spicy soap he used.
Simple, but it smelled like Tom to her. "Lots of studying to do?" she asked innocently.

"Some. I have an exam on Monday, but I'm mostly
ready."

Good, because she didn't want to feel guilty about
him failing an exam because she'd kept him busy all
weekend.

He paused in the doorway and sniffed the air.
"What's burning?"

"Jasmine incense."

"Nice," he said, but she could tell he was just being
polite. "Nice music, too," he said.

"I thought it would be relaxing," she said. "Can I get you a beer?"

"After I finish studying."

"Come on. It will calm your mind."

He looked at her, his eyes flaring with hunger. "Give me two hours and I'll be all yours. We can go out then if you want. I know you like to dance."

"Okay." But she wasn't waiting any two hours. This was it. She sat close to him on the sofa and looked over his shoulder, pretending to examine his book when she really was giving him a chance to check out her cleavage, which he did. At length. "Whatcha studying?"

"Geometry," he said huskily.

"I see," she said, letting her hair fall forward to brush his cheek. "I was always good with shapes." She traced a parabolic figure in his textbook with a red nail.

"I'll bet," he said wryly.

"Well, I guess I'll let you get to it," she said.

"Just a couple hours," he said, looking at her with longing. She headed for the kitchen, her hips swinging provocatively. "Maybe less," he added faintly.

Yep, this would work out just fine.

She returned with nail polish and sat in the chair to his right, resting a freshly shaved and lotion-smooth leg on the edge of the table and began to paint her toes red. This position put her cleavage at exactly the right angle and the sensuous task was something she knew he couldn't ignore.

Sure enough, Tom's eyes flickered to her, then back to his book, to her toes, her breasts, back to his book. He shifted in his seat, then looked at her breasts, toes, breasts, book, breasts, breasts, then finally said, "Could you not do that?"

"Is the smell bothering you?" she asked innocently.

"You know what's bothering me."

"I'm almost done," she said, slowly covering her last two toes. She leaned over to suggestively blow the polish dry, then she said, "I'm hungry. How about a snack?"

"No thanks," he muttered. She could feel him fighting the urge to watch her sway out of the room.

She went to the kitchen and fetched a tall cherry Popsicle from the collection she kept for the neighbor's little girls who liked to hang with her. She returned to the chair, flung one leg over the side, revealing exactly how high up her shorts were cut, then pushed the icy treat slowly into her mouth and pulled it out equally slowly. "Mmm," she said, closing her eyes. "Delicious."

Tom's eyes zeroed in on her mouth, his lip tugging upward. "Don't tell me...your favorite flavor."

"How did you know?"

"Call it male intuition. Look—" he leaned forward and gripped her kneecap, a sensation as erotic as if he'd touched her breast "—I don't know what you're cooking up, but I've got to study."

"Your choice," she said, holding the Popsicle sideways and running the point of her tongue down it and then onward to lick a thin stream of cherry juice that trailed her forearm. Out of one eye, she saw a shudder run through Tom's big bear of a body.

Tonight was the night, all right. No way could he hold out.

Ten minutes later, however, her mouth was numb and her lips tingly and a sliver of wood had poked her tongue from the stick, and Tom was still glued to that damn geometry book. *Enough.* She tossed the red-stained stick onto the end table and moved to the sofa again. "You look all knotted up," she said, and squeezed his shoulder muscles with her fingers. "Let me give you a rubdown." She kneeled beside him.

"Okay," he said hesitantly, shifting so his back was within her reach.

She pressed her breasts against his back as if to get more leverage and dug in.

"You're very good," he said hoarsely, relaxing under her fingers.

"I could do even better if you took off your shirt."

He whipped it off.

God, he was well put together. Tan and buff, but not overly so. "You're real knotted up here," she said, rubbing the shoulder blades area. Her arms were beginning to ache from trying to make headway with all that tight muscle. Her lips were still numb from the Popsicle and now her hands were going that way. She had never had to work this hard to get laid before. Tom just let her rub away, letting out an occasional groan. She worked her way lower to his waist, slipping her fingers under his waistband from the back.

He took a sharp breath. She slid slightly forward onto his abdomen, her heart racing. She moved closer to his penis, desperate to know he was erect, but he scooted forward and away from her fingers.

"I think you got it," he said. "Thanks. I have to read a couple more pages here." He bent forward to dig into his book, which would have infuriated her, except she saw that the book was upside down and Tom was breathing very hard. She grinned and gently took the book from his hands. "I think it's time to study something new, Tom." She tossed the text across the room and straddled his lap.

Tom looked scared and delighted and full of dread—

like an obsessive gambler who had just hit a jackpot and knew he was hooked for the night.

"How about studying this?" She grabbed the hem of her shirt with crossed arms, tore it over her head and flung it after the geometry book. She was naked to the waist.

Tom groaned deeply, as if he faced a great temptation. "I don't think we should do this, Tina," he said, his eyes full of anguish.

"Sure, we should." She took his hands and put them gently on her breasts. "Study away. If you get lost, I'll help you find the right place."

He didn't answer, but he didn't remove his hands.

"We've waited a long, long time," she murmured, and kissed those lips she'd been dying for since their sailing day a month ago. She reached for his penis through his jeans. It was all that she'd hoped for—thick and sturdy and very interested.

Tom gave a great growl of frustration and pushed her gently off his lap. "Not like this," he said.

"What's the problem?" she said, aching and irritated. "We waited. We got to know each other. So now let's have sex."

"I don't work that way, Tina," he said, his blue eyes going indigo with the storm inside him.

"You seem to be working fine to me," she said, staring boldly at the bulge in his jeans.

"I don't want to be just another man you sleep with." He picked her T-shirt off the floor and held it over her breasts, as if to hide them from him.

"You think I'm a slut? Because I sleep with more than one man?" She scrambled to her feet, then furiously yanked her T-shirt over her head. "Men who sleep around are studs, but let a woman have a healthy sex life and she's scum!"

"That's backward," he said.

"Bull. You're the one who's backward. Get with the times."

"I mean your shirt," he said softly. "And it's inside out, too."

She looked down and saw he was right. "Don't change the subject. Sex is a perfectly healthy thing two people can share. If I'd known you were so uptight about it, I wouldn't have ever—"

"I want more than sex with you, Tina." He stood and moved close to her.

"You what?"

"You heard me."

"You mean...an exclusive relationship?"

"More." He looked at her steadily.

"I can't promise more, Tom. You can't either, really. We could have something great—great sex, great times—but, beyond that, there's too much pressure, too many expectations."

He looked at her for a long moment, then sighed. "I was afraid you'd say that." He picked up his own shirt and put it on. She was gratified to see it, too, was inside out.

"What? You're just giving up?" she said.

"What else can I do?" He stared at her. *Change your mind,* he seemed to be saying.

"Why does everything have to be your way?" she said, glaring at him. *Why do you want so much from me? And exactly what I can't give.*

"What are you afraid of?" he said, still holding her gaze.

"I'm not afraid. I'm realistic. And you're dreaming."

She turned her back on him. He had some ideal of a woman in his mind and she'd never live up to it. She wasn't even going to try.

When she turned back, Tom had picked his book up from the floor, grabbed his notebook and was heading for the door. Leaving. Walking out. Her heart lurched. She would see him at the Upside after this. He'd serve her Stingers and Cosmopolitans and Wallbangers, but there would be no light in his eyes when he looked at her, no secret smile, no soft pat of encouragement on her hand.

When he reached the door, she called out, "Tom," sounding completely pathetic.

He stopped moving and when he turned, his face was full of agony—an agony she recognized, because she was feeling it, too. She was so relieved she ran to him. He grabbed her into his arms and lifted her off her feet to kiss her. "Okay," he breathed in her ear, crushing her to him. "You win."

Thank God. He'd given in. And before she'd had a chance to say she'd try it his way—a thing she'd surely fail at. Joy rushed through her.

He kissed her again, holding her tightly against his chest, so broad, so sure, like home. His hands slid to her waist and squeezed. They were so big they almost touched in the middle of her back, then they swept lower to press her butt against him.

Lust scorched her insides. Maybe she was extra horny because she hadn't slept with anyone since she'd started seeing Tom. Or maybe it was because she'd had to work so hard to get him. It didn't matter. All she knew was Tom was rubbing himself against her stomach—big and thick and eager—and she was so excited she thought she might faint.

I've waited for you, his body seemed to be telling her. *All this time.* Then his hands came forward and pushed under her T-shirt to grasp her breasts, holding them securely, his fingers soft on the tips.

"Tina," he breathed. Then he released her. She had only a second of empty loneliness before he drew her into his arms and carried her down the hall to her bedroom, his face so full of hunger she felt herself melting. She reminded herself to stay focused. Her job was to make sure he had no regrets about giving in. She would show him how wonderful sex-and-sex-alone could be.

When they got to the bedroom and he lowered her to the bed, she popped up and pushed him to a sit at the end of the bed so she could undress for him. She tugged her T-shirt off again—for good, this time—then slowly unfastened her shorts and slid them down, revealing transparent white undies.

Tom's eyes widened with appreciation.

She reached down to caress his erection through his clothes. He quaked for a second, then gripped her by the hips and pulled her belly to his face, kissing her through her panties, practically cutting off her circulation, holding on as if her body were a precious thing. She felt herself go liquid.

It was kind of worshipful and that was dangerous, but it was so Tom and so nice, she just let it be. She locked her fingers into his dear hair and let him desire her.

Then his fingers slid under the bottom edge of her panties and gently touched her. Flames flew along her nerves and seemed to shoot out her fingertips.

Oh. She rubbed against his hand, really getting into it, until she remembered her purpose was to give him pleasure first. She pushed him onto his back on the bed and slithered down so she could tug at his belt. He lifted his butt so she could push off his pants and briefs. Then she took his swollen penis—as big and beautiful as the rest of him—into her hand and slid her fingers up and down its length, cupping his testicles with her other hand.

He quivered and exhaled in a whoosh. She tightened her fingers and kept moving up and down, feeling his flesh slide the way it soon would inside her body. He groaned, pushing into her hand. Then he found his way under her panties again. He surprised her with a finger inside her.

Electricity shot through her. She lost awareness. *Focus*, she told herself. She had a goal here, but Tom kept sidetracking her with amazingly perfect things. While his forefinger performed magic, his mouth found her nipple and his teeth closed on its edges with a gentle tightness that was perfect. She was pinned by sensation—a wire from where he tantalized her nipple to where his fingers explored her most intimate spot.

Her vision faded again. He was so sure and so good with his fingers and mouth. Her self-control was shot and she jerked and quivered and moaned like a teen with her first experienced lover.

"Is that good?" he breathed. "I want you to like it."

"Oh, yes. I like it. Like it lots," she said. "It's good…good…good-good." She didn't know what she was saying anymore.

"I can't believe I'm touching you like this," he said. "You are so perfect."

She looked into his eyes and saw danger. Lust and desire and yearning and caring. She wanted to melt into that look, but she knew its dark side—demands and expectations and inevitable disappointment. With all her might, she pulled herself away from his pleasuring hand and mouth, yanked her panties off, and deliberately impaled herself on his uplifted penis.

"Wait," he gasped, trying to stop her hips. "I have...condoms."

"I'm on the Pill. No diseases. You?"

"None," he groaned out.

She shoved past his resistance until her parts reached his belly, glorying in the wonder of being filled by him. His delicious length reached all the way to her cervix and tried to push beyond. *Let me in. I want in,* it seemed to say. He looked up at her in wonder and his hands grasped her hips possessively.

She lifted and lowered herself rapidly several times, knowing he would love the friction. He did. His eyes closed and his face contorted with pleasure.

She arched herself at him. Her breasts ached for his mouth, her clit begged for his touch.

As if he'd read her mind, he pulled a nipple deeply into his mouth. More electricity, like a line of lightning to her throbbing sex, which his other thumb abruptly and perfectly found.

And, then, despite all her efforts to put his pleasure first, she held still while, with a few gentle strokes, he propelled her into an orgasm that rocked her to her soul. Impaled on his penis, she writhed and twisted, shuddered and bucked helplessly, all the while making choked sounds.

She vaguely heard him breathe, "Yes. That's right. Come on, baby. Go, beautiful."

As the orgasm began to fade, she became aware that Tom's penis was pounding into her. He gripped her hips as if to squeeze the life from her, then climaxed with a great surge. He'd waited to see her safely to her release before he allowed himself his own. The chivalry of that gesture electrified her, shoving her up the hill and over, catching the tail end of his orgasm with a powerful one of her own.

What a dear man. She felt strange, almost homesick. As if she'd been missing something all her life that this old-fashioned guy had just offered up as sweet and easy as breathing. She clutched him, feeling their hearts pound out messages to each other, their lungs expand and contract for air they couldn't seem to get enough of, and tried not to scare herself. The first time was always special, she told herself. And she'd worked hard for this one. That had to explain this power, this amazing connection.

The night passed in a blur of sensations—strokes and kisses, gasps and cries, rocking and sweating and groaning out loud. A whirl of pleasure and passion.

Late, late into the night, when Tina was still panting from the orgasm Tom had brought her to from behind, she felt his body go heavy, and his hardworking penis twitch lazily inside her. He'd fallen asleep.

She liked men to leave when the action was over for the night. She liked the bed to herself for sleep. But she knew she couldn't ask Tom to go. It would hurt his feelings. And she didn't want to do anything that would keep her from more sex with him. A lot more sex. The rest of it she wouldn't think about.

Tom's heavy arm found its way to her breast, and even though she felt smothered and crowded and nervous as hell, his steady breath soothed her fears. For now.

11

"I DID IT," Tina crowed, standing on Kara's porch on Sunday morning with a McDonald's sack—another breakfast Kara wouldn't get to eat, she was sure. Luckily, she'd already had some yogurt and granola.

"Did what?" Kara asked wearily. She'd gotten home late from the arrest fantasy with Ross, which had been more erotic than either of them had expected. Ross had found some toy handcuffs and they'd sort of added some elements of the Love Thief to remarkable effect. The end result was sore muscles, sated body and a very late night.

"I slept with Tom," Tina said, marching into the apartment. She dropped the sack on the table. "Food."

"You've sunk to McDonald's? What happened to Karsh's Bakery?" She'd rather *almost* get to eat quality pastries than fast-food ones.

Tina shrugged and pulled out two orange juices and three plastic-wrapped Danishes. "I was distracted and drove past the bakery."

To pass up her pastry shrine, she must have been in a trance. "So, you slept with Tom. You make it sound like you just climbed Mt. Everest."

"Oh, yeah. He was huge."

"You don't mean that." The light in Tina's eyes was too strong to be based only on Tom's physical prowess.

There was more to this than a Tina sexploit. She was actually blushing.

"So what happened?"

Tina dished the details of her seduction by shoulder rub and erotic Popsicle licking, and Tom's caving in on his ultimatum. When she finished, Kara said, "But it was more than sex, right?"

"What?" Tina gave her a sharp look.

"I can tell by your face. You're involved." Tina hadn't even cracked an orange juice and the Danish rested untouched on the table.

"No." Tina shook her head violently.

Kara picked up a Danish. "Mind if I have one?"

"No, no. Help yourself," she said distractedly.

Too bad it wasn't the usual fabulous baked goods, since Kara was actually going to get to taste some this time. She peeled the wrapping from one and handed it to Tina before opening her own.

Tina held the Danish but didn't take a bite. "I did let him spend the night. You think he'll think that means I'm giving in?"

The pastry wasn't half-bad, Kara noticed, finishing it in quick bites. She took the one she'd given Tina and bit off a chunk before she answered. "Would that be so terrible? You like him, he likes you. Maybe you're ready to settle down."

"No way. I take care of myself. I'm not like my mom, tiptoeing around an awful man because I'm afraid to be alone."

"You're not that much like your mother."

"I work at it, too." Tina stared into space, scared to death, Kara could tell. "Even if I wanted to get serious—and I'm not saying I do, because I don't—it would never be with Tom. He's studying to be an engineer, for God's sake. His idea of an exciting evening is watching a PBS special on the insect world. That's not me. That's boring.''

''You didn't seem bored when you were scheming to snare him.''

''That's the point. Now that I have him, I'll lose interest. After a while anyway. After a lot of fabulous, mind-bending sex.''

''Maybe you're just afraid to be hurt. Maybe you're rejecting him before he can reject you.''

Tina's face went stony. ''Don't psychoanalyze me, Kara. You're my friend, not my shrink.''

''Sorry. I just want you to be happy.''

''I am happy. For now. And that's all anyone gets— right now. Beyond that it's wishful thinking. And I made that clear to Tom before we went at it.'' She looked more worried than happy, Kara saw.

Kara opened another Danish and dug in. ''You know, this isn't half-bad. How are their apple pies?''

Tina drummed her polished nails on the table. ''Could I get some focus here.''

''Sure, sure,'' she said, chagrined. She'd been so busy eating, she'd forgotten Tina's problem for a second. Plus she saw she was eating the last Danish. She was turning into Tina.

''I just want things to stay like this for a while, you know?'' Tina said.

''Maybe it will work out,'' she said, pressing her fingertip to a large crumb of Danish and eating it.

''Why does this have to be so hard?'' Tina sighed. ''Tell me about you and Ross. At least that's working out.''

''Working out?'' Kara's Danish-filled stomach lurched at the thought. ''I'm kind of worried actually.

The other night I fell asleep at his place and he put me to bed.''

"Really?" She leaned forward. "What was the fantasy? Midnight intruder?"

"That's the problem. It was no fantasy. It was very real. And I woke up at three in the morning feeling so happy to be in his bedroom with all his junk. He was sleeping on the sofa, being a gentleman, and he looked so sweet I just wanted to drag him into bed and cuddle all night."

"You wanted to cuddle? Uh-uh-uh. That's a bad sign."

"Don't you think I know that?" she said sharply. Tina's alarm confirmed her own fears. She couldn't shake the comfort of being around Ross, the pleasure of his company, even watching stupid basketball. "I'm afraid I'm doing it again, Tina. Confusing lust with love."

"But Ross is completely wrong for you."

"But he doesn't seem quite so wrong anymore. He's sweet and loyal and loving and responsible."

"And an overgrown kid with a million women on a string and no intention of changing that."

"I know," she almost sobbed. "That's what's killing me."

"Damn. This was supposed to cure you of falling in love, not send you over the cliff."

"What should I do?"

But Tina was frowning at the pile of torn cellophane and empty juice containers on the table. "You ate everything."

"Sorry. I've got granola and yogurt."

She scrunched up her nose. "Any Ho-Hos or Twinkies?"

Kara just looked at her.

"Right. No junk food here." She made a cross with her fingers. "I just thought with Ross around you might have branched out into some red dye and preservatives." She got up and started rummaging in Kara's refrigerator, emerging with the aerosol can of whipped cream, bottle of chocolate syrup, and bowl of strawberries left over from Ross and Kara's body-dessert fantasy.

Tina sat down with her bounty. "Are you *sure* you're screwing up?" she asked, lacing a strawberry with syrup. She topped the berry with whipped cream and bit it from its stem.

"Pretty sure. Baylor Jones asked me out and I had no interest."

"Baylor Jones? He's cute. And not a tight-ass like Scott. He'd be perfect for you. That *is* bad." Tina leaned her head back and squirted whipped cream into her mouth.

"And I've been kind of fixing up Ross's apartment like I'm thinking about living there." She swallowed hard. "I had a fleeting thought of him in a tux and me in a wedding dress."

"Whaa—?" Tina's head snapped forward, her mouth wide with fluffy cream before she slowly closed down on it.

"We were talking about a virgin bride fantasy, but still…"

"It's obvious what you have to do," Tina said firmly, squirting cream into her mouth from the side.

"What?"

Tina gulped down the cloud of foam. "Go out with Baylor."

"What?"

"The only cure for a bad man is a new man. Trust me, I know these things. Quit with Ross and start with Baylor."

She did like Baylor. She had to do something to break the bad cycle. And he'd said he'd be around. "Okay," she said slowly. "I'll, um, do that. One of these days."

"Not one of these days. This Saturday." Tina pointed a strawberry at Kara for emphasis before slathering it with whipped cream.

"This Saturday? But Ross has something set up and—"

"Kara," Tina thrust the white-topped strawberry under her nose. "Tell Ross it's over."

Tina was right. She'd been fooling herself that things weren't so bad. "All right," she said, accepting the lush fruit, inhaling its sweet smell. Mmm. Ross had fed her these as part of their body tasting.

"Kara," Tina said, seeming to read her mind. "Do it. You have to."

"I know," she said, and put down the tempting strawberry. If only Ross were as easy to resist.

ON SATURDAY NIGHT, Kara stood on the corner in drizzling rain waiting for Ross. He was late, which was nothing new, but the rain made it annoying. Plus it gave her time to regret not breaking things off on Thursday.

She'd had every opportunity during dinner at his apartment, but he'd been so excited about an antique blues album he'd spent a fortune on, she couldn't bring it up. That very purchase was an example of why she had no business thinking of a relationship with the man. He didn't even own a car, but he spent thousands of dollars on old music. Lately, for every thing she dug up that they had in common—a sense of humor, a good imagination—she tripped over three more they disagreed about. Big ones, too, like finances, work, the future.

Then he'd brought out a Victoria's Secret catalogue and showed her what he'd ordered for her, so she couldn't bring herself to ruin the moment by telling him it was over.

She had managed to keep him from adding new fantasies to the list he'd insisted they make by starting a debate about his algae-laden Charlie's Angels' shower curtain. She wanted to replace it for the sake of science—there were probably cures for six diseases growing there—and he insisted on keeping it for sentimental reasons. He'd bought it in mint condition at a nostalgia shop and it was exactly like the one he'd lusted over during the onset of puberty.

In the end, she just left with everything unsaid. The taxi fantasy was too exciting, anyway. Now she was waiting for Ross and the taxi and worrying about breaking it off. Water dripped off her nose. Why did he have to be late all the time?

Finally she spotted a beat-up white car with a taxi sign on top approaching. It rattled up to her, some metal part scraping the road and rumbling so loudly the muffler must be gone, then squealed to a halt.

Ross lunged out and loped to her side of the car. "Sorry I'm late," he said. He even wore a chauffeur's cap. "The thing was junked up inside so I took it to a car wash, but the vacuum wasn't working, so I had to go to another one." He paused, zeroed in on her chest. "The stuff came," he said in a dazed Ross voice.

She looked down and saw the new Victoria's Secret teddy was visible through her soaked silk blouse.

"Yes, it did," she whispered, loving the lust on his

face. If they quit now, Ross wouldn't see the rest of the new lingerie. That gave her heart a pang. Maybe they'd keep on long enough to sample the new outfits—plus, she still had the body paints from the Naughty and Nice lingerie store. *No, no. This has to stop.*

"Hop in," Ross said, doffing his cap. "I know just the place to take you."

"I'm sure you do," she said. And she *was* sure, from oh, so many nights with him. She sat, keeping her legs apart so her skirt rode high on her thigh to tantalize him.

Ross made an appreciative noise, then leaned in to help her with the seat belt, deliberately sliding the back of his hands across her breasts and stomach as he adjusted the strap. The sensation set her on fire, as she knew he knew it would.

Ross closed his eyes, obviously trying to gather himself to keep from falling on her.

"I know," she whispered. She wanted to grab him by his T-shirt and pull him onto her. Why waste time driving when he'd only borrowed the cab for three hours?

But Ross stood with a sigh. "Hang on. We'll get there soon enough, miss." He tipped his hat again and went to the driver's seat.

She noticed that the dusty, musty, motor-oil smell of most cabs had been masked by car freshener. Ross had been late trying to make their fantasy lovelier. *See how thoughtful he is.*

But it has to stop, she reminded herself. No more after this.

They set off, the rain tapping cozily on the roof of the cab, the wipers swishing rhythmically—at least *they* worked. Ross pointed out landmarks and historical places, giving everything a colorful flair.

She recognized the information from an ad campaign they'd done for the city's visitors' bureau, though she was surprised at how much Ross had retained. He acted as if he didn't care about anything but the art of a project, but he absorbed all the nuances. She'd been right to put the bug in Siegel's ear about him taking over the creative department manager's job.

She'd done that yesterday over Tina's objections. *What are you doing? Giving Ross a makeover? Turning him into someone you could fall in love with?* If only Tina would pull her punches a little. Kara was just helping Ross. The fact she was about to end their game proved it.

She hadn't mentioned it to Ross yet, knowing he'd bristle. She'd let Siegel talk to him first, though she had put together a quick résumé to remind Saul of all Ross had to offer S&S.

She leaned against the back of the cab seat to soak up the precious moments of the last fantasy. The rain-polished streets seemed magical, with taillights and streetlights glowing red, green, yellow in smeared haloes of color like a holiday display. Ross spun his web of Phoenix tales, letting her see things through his eyes, making ordinary places seem mysterious, fascinating, fresh.

The windows hummed open. ''The desert offers a lot,'' Ross said, ''but it's subtle and full of surprises. Take rain. It can be a soft sun shower or a fierce flash flood that tears through washes like a burst dam. Breathe it in.''

She inhaled deeply, loving the way the air was thick with moisture. She'd been so annoyed with Ross's lateness that she'd forgotten how much she loved rain—so rare in the Valley that each shower was an occasion to celebrate.

"That spicy smell is creosote," Ross explained, "otherwise known as greasewood. Practical and magical. Used as a sealant, in cosmetics and herbal remedies. Some herbalists consider it to have mystical properties."

"So lovely," she said on a sigh. Little flicks of rain struck her like wet sparks.

She saw they were near Papago Park, driving past the smooth red stones with their Swiss-cheese caves and holes.

"That's the Tovrea Castle," Ross said, pointing out the mansion on a hill, built deliberately to look like a birthday cake with saguaro cactus on terraced landscaping as the candles. "They say if you wish on the castle at sundown, your wish will come true twice over."

"Really?" she asked.

"And what would you wish for, miss?"

That this would never end. That they could just keep driving their taxi around forever. "I don't know," she lied.

He was quiet for a long moment. "Maybe we both have the same wish." Had he read her mind? Did he want to work out a way to keep on? "Sometimes two strangers and their secret wishes can be…intimate."

Right. He was talking about their game, not their future. Good reminder. She leaned back and watched the scenery go by, wistful but relaxed, loving the flick of rain on her cheek.

They headed across the Tempe Bridge, its looping white lights making it seem like an entrance to a fairyland, then backtracked under the bridge to a deserted stretch of road where Ross parked on the shoulder.

She was almost sorry they'd stopped. She was so happy riding with Ross in the rain, talking about the town they both loved, letting him open her eyes to the subtle things she often missed but he never did.

But when Ross climbed into the back seat with her, bringing in the smell of rain and creosote, and her heart started pounding in that familiar way, she was glad they'd pulled over.

Ross tossed his cap onto the front seat and looked at her. "You're so pretty."

"Is my mascara all over?" She rubbed under one eye, but he stopped her hand.

"You're beautiful. How many times do I have to say that?"

"You make me feel that way," she said, cupping his jaw with both hands, her chest tight with emotion.

"I just say what I see. You know that."

She did. She loved his honesty.

He cupped her face, too, and they just looked at each other, breathing each other's breath in the dark, warm cocoon of the cab. The rain tapped gently on the roof and moist air billowed in from the open windows. An occasional raindrop touched Kara's skin, giving cool delight. Over Ross's shoulder, the lights from the bridge winked and gleamed, their reflections softly brilliant on the wet tarmac.

They should be exchanging fake names and talking through her fantasy, but tonight was their last time, so Kara was in no hurry to get into the game. Ross seemed okay with the delay. It was almost as if he knew tonight was different.

"Do you know your wish?" Ross asked, speaking in character.

You forever, she wanted to say, not as a lonely cab fare, but as Kara, rain-damp and full of feelings that had nothing to do with a sexual fantasy and everything to do with the tender, amazing man holding her face in his hands.

She couldn't do that, so she kissed him, reminding them both why they were here. Ross caught on. Fast. She welcomed his mouth, like the desert welcomed this rare rain, and lost herself in sensation.

Ross slid his hand under her skirt and traced the line of the teddy the way that always set her on fire.

"Oh," she rasped, loving the flames licking through her on familiar pathways.

"Is this your wish?" he asked. "That I touch you here?"

"Oh, yes."

He tugged at the snaps, which he knew were there since he'd picked out the item, and then his fingers found their way to the warm wet place they belonged. "I know you like that," he murmured, "because of the way you're breathing now, and you always turn red right here." He kissed her neck on the spot.

She should remind him that they were supposed to be strangers to each other—a cabdriver and his world-weary passenger—but his intimate knowledge of what aroused her was too wonderful. She no longer cared about protecting the game or obeying the rules. She wanted to hear every precious word he said, to memorize every look, every intimate glance so she could remember later when she was alone and lonely.

"And right before you come, your eyes go cloudy, the tip of your tongue sticks out just a little, and your face gets this amazing light, like you've never had anything this wonderful happen to you before.''

"I never have," she murmured.

"Then I know it's time to do this." He made a quick circular stroke.

"Oh. Oh. Oh." It was starting now. She'd climax too soon. She stopped his hand.

He chuckled softly. "I know. You want to come with me inside you. Don't worry."

She didn't worry at all. She knew everything would work perfectly, the way it always did.

She reached to unzip his pants. These were the jeans with the zipper that stalled a little. She bent it to the left and eased the tab down. There was Ross—warm and velvet and hard as steel. She gripped him the way he loved, squeezing and sliding with the pressure that made him groan and push into her.

"You know me so well," he said, letting her stroke him, while he watched. Then he slid a hand under her blouse to tease her nipple. Her hand on him stilled as she was swept away for a bit. But he always catered to her. This time—this last time—she would focus on him first.

"I want to taste you," she said, and maneuvered herself into the space between the seats to take him into her mouth.

He grasped her hair and whispered words of pleasure.

She slid her lips up and down, loving the delicious blend of rain-wet air and his salty taste and the soft-hard length of him. She listened to his breathing, its fits and starts telling her what felt best, though she already knew it by heart.

When he was close, she redoubled her efforts, but he

lifted her up to kiss her mouth. "I want to watch you come," he said.

"You first," she said, trying to return to him.

"Stay up here," he said, his eyes teasing, even as he held her firmly by the shoulder.

"Uh-uh," she said, laughing but trying to wrestle out of his grip. "Ouch." She banged her shoulder on the back of the driver's seat.

"Get up here, woman," he commanded.

"No!" she said, almost laughing as they wrestled for dominance in the who-climaxes-first struggle. "Ouch. That hurts." Her skin had gotten pinched between his elbow and the seat.

"Hold it right there!" An official male voice commanded from outside the window.

Kara yelped and they both froze and looked up. A police officer sheathed in a raincoat was looking in the window from a few feet away.

Ross couldn't believe this was happening. He made sure Kara was covered before he saw to his zipper. "What is it, Officer? Am I parked illegally?" He hoped that was the only unlawful thing they'd been doing.

"Keep your hands where I can see them and step out of the car," the cop said.

Ross did as he'd been told, holding his hands out, open-palmed, feeling like a criminal. This was surreal. Like their arrest fantasy, only not at all fun. He took a fleeting look around to see if, by chance, they were being videotaped for some reality cop show, but the only person in sight was this stern-looking patrolman, who motioned him away from the car and, keeping one eye on him, spoke through the open door to Kara. "Are you all right, miss?"

"I'm fine, Officer. We're both fine." Kara scrambled out of the car. "Is there a problem?"

The cop looked from her to him, assessing their honesty, then frowned at Ross. "Let me see your license, registration and proof of insurance, please."

"Sure, sure, no problem," Ross said. He fumbled around in the cab until he found where Roger kept the official papers and handed them with his driver's license to the policeman.

The cop examined his license. "Are you Ross Gabriel?"

"In the flesh," he said, hoping humor would lighten the moment. It didn't.

"This is a Class A license, Mr. Gabriel. You need a chauffeur's license to drive a cab."

"It's my friend's cab, actually, and—"

"This is my fault," Kara said, stepping protectively between Ross and the officer. "I asked him to borrow the cab so we could, um, drive around. I have a thing for taxis."

Ross watched blush shoot up Kara's face to her scalp. She was embarrassing herself to get him out of trouble. His heart warmed. The rain had flattened her hair so she looked sleek as a seal and her face gleamed in the reflection of the bridge lights. They should make love in the shower next, all wet and slippery....

"Did this man threaten you in any way?" the cop demanded of Kara.

"Oh, heaven's no. He's my boyfriend." She put her arm around Ross's waist, stood on her tiptoes and kissed him on the cheek, her lips tense with anxiety.

He's my boyfriend. Ross felt himself grin like a loon at the cop. "That's right, Officer. She's my girlfriend. I'm her boyfriend. We're boyfriend and girl-friend. Absolutely.''

The cop stared at him for a few beats, then turned to Kara. ''You're telling me that your boyfriend here bor-rowed a cab because you have a thing for them? What kind of thing? Never mind...I don't want to know.''

''It was completely my idea,'' Kara continued.

''And he wasn't forcing himself on you?''

''No. Not at all. We were changing positions—'' She stopped speaking, her eyes wide at how that sounded. ''I mean getting more comfortable...I mean...''

The cop shook his head, completely disgusted.

''If we were doing anything illegal we didn't realize it,'' she continued.

''Ignorance of the law—''

''Is no excuse,'' Ross chimed in. ''We know.''

The cop frowned. Uh-oh, he'd stepped on the guy's line. Was he looking to get arrested?

The cop sighed wearily. ''Wait here.'' He walked toward his cruiser, probably to see if Ross was wanted in another state for taxi crimes. What was he going to do if they got arrested? He wouldn't let Kara go to jail, that's for sure. But he wasn't looking forward to fight-ing off a boyfriend for himself, either.

Kara gripped him tightly around the waist. ''I'm so sorry. This is my fault. I'll pay the ticket,'' she said.

The ticket? How would she feel about posting his bond? ''I'll take care of this. Don't worry.''

''I mean it. This was my fantasy and if I hadn't been so noisy...''

''I love when you're noisy. And I was the one who opened the windows.'' He kissed her, loving the feel of her mouth. He should be freaked. He might spend a night in jail—standing up with his back against the wall—or at least get slapped with a huge ticket and maybe get Roger into a legal hassle, but all he could think about was the fact that Kara had said he was her boyfriend and he didn't feel like taking a plane to Canada.

He actually liked the idea. Wanted her to say it again, in fact. He was still pondering what that meant when the cop swaggered back to them.

"Here's how it's going to go down," he said. "I'm going to give you a break on the lewd and lascivious behavior, since you obviously chose this spot for privacy," he said, giving Kara a look. "And I'll let the parking in a no-parking zone go, too."

"Thank you so much, Officer Reynolds," Kara said, reading his badge quickly. "That means a lot to us."

"Yeah. Thanks for the break," Ross added, starting to walk Kara to her side of the car.

"Hold on now," the cop said. "We're not done here."

So Ross stood in the rain while the cop wrote up a ticket for expired plates and handed Ross his copy. The ticket would be voided once the plates were renewed, but Roger wouldn't be happy about the required trip to the DMV.

"My advice to you," the cop said, leaning in the window to speak to Kara, "is to be more careful about the games you play." Then he stood and spoke to Ross, "And, for God's sake, keep it off the streets."

"You got it," Ross said, and climbed into the driver's seat. The rain had freshened the subtle scent Kara wore and he was figuring out where they could go to make love when Officer Reynolds spoke again. "You're not planning to drive this vehicle, are you?"

"Excuse me?" Ross said.

"This car doesn't move until the registration is up-to-date. And then it will be driven by a driver with the appropriate license."

"Are you kidding me?"

"Ross," Kara said firmly, leaning across him. "We understand, Officer Reynolds. We'll just call someone to come and get us."

The officer gave her a half smile. "A difficulty in the law. I'll be driving off now. I advise you to take care of this situation immediately."

"Certainly. Thank you." After the policeman turned away, she said, "We just have to wait until he's gone and then take the cab back. He's giving us a break."

"Right. A break." Ross shook his head, but he knew she was right. They sat in the cab, the rain tiptoeing on the roof, and watched the officer climb into his car, spin it around and roar away. Probably to harass other lovers with expired plates.

"Here's how it's going to go down," Ross imitated in an officious growl. "That guy watches too much TV."

They both laughed.

"Can you believe that?" Kara said. "We almost got three tickets!"

"Tickets? We could have been arrested."

"No!"

"Oh, yeah."

She kept talking about Roger's registration, but he'd lost interest. He was too busy noticing how beautiful she was in the rain-misty light, her eyes sparkling with laughter. His heart filled with warmth and he remembered what she'd said that first made him feel this way.

"You told the cop I was your boyfriend," he said, leading up to it slowly.

She laughed. "I know. Sorry. I completely freaked. And then you go and babble, 'Oh, yes, Officer. We're boyfriend and girlfriend. Absolutely,' making it sound like a complete lie." She laughed again.

"Yeah," he said. *What if it isn't a lie?* He started to say that, but she kept talking.

"I had to say something to make sure he knew you weren't forcing me or anything." She hesitated. Something flickered in her eyes. "That was all I could think of. Boyfriend and girlfriend...sheesh..." Her voice trailed off uncertainly.

Here was his chance. *How about if we try it? Be a couple?* But it sounded lame all of a sudden. Maybe he'd just had some weird feelings there for a second, what with the trauma of nearly being arrested and all.

They decided to drop Kara off at her apartment before he took the cab back to Roger and returned to her place, since Kara stubbornly refused to ride his motorcycle. He didn't have a helmet for her, anyway, so he agreed.

They made small talk on the way, but it was strained. Kara seemed preoccupied, too, as if there was something she needed to say. *I completely freaked,* she'd said, like them being a couple was so out there. That made him feel strangely empty.

Why not kick it up a notch? Kara was smart and had a great sense of humor. The sex had loosened her up. And maybe the fantasies were the secret to keeping him interested. There was so much more they could explore.

The problem with Kara and men in the past—besides the fact they were dweebs—was that she was the one who fell in love first. Not this time. He was right there with her on the love thing.

If he told her all this, they could make love in her

bed. For real. No roles or costumes. Kara and Ross unplugged. That picture pushed him past any doubts that remained. His heart began to rattle in his chest, more noisy to his ears than the cab's engine.

When Ross pulled up to her apartment, the cab rumbling loudly enough to wake everyone in her complex, Kara swallowed hard. She knew what she had to do. The near arrest had been a big symbolic exclamation point to her decision. *Boyfriend and girlfriend.* Saying that out loud had shot such a rush of longing through her she'd hardly been able to speak.

This was it. If they stopped tonight, let her inappropriate feelings subside, they could preserve their friendship, which they both agreed was more important than this sexual adventure.

Before long she'd be hanging at Ross's place, regaling him with stories about her dates—with Baylor, probably—and he'd be doing the same for her. Just like the old days. The thought turned her heart into a solid rock of pain, but she turned to Ross. "We need to talk."

"Exactly what I was going to say."

That was odd. *We need to talk* were the four words men dreaded most. "I've had a wonderful time these weeks with you," she continued, "but—"

"Me, too," he interrupted. "It's been incredible."

"But the cop incident made me think…"

"Me, too."

"Oh, good. Then we agree? We have to stop?"

"We what? Oh." He looked confused.

"I mean, if we keep this up," she said, "someone's going to get hurt." *Me.*

Ross didn't speak.

"I know I've said this before, but this time is definite. From here on it will just get too complicated."

"You're sure?" he said hollowly.

She nodded.

He seemed to be considering her words. "One more time for the road? We still have the virgin thing, you know."

"Not a good idea." She had to go cold turkey. No last, lingering fantasy, where real feelings might spill out like champagne poured too fast into a flute. "We have to remember what we agreed when we started. We agreed that—"

"Don't," he said, cutting her off. "If you recite a ground rule I'll bust this window with my head."

She paused, surprised at his intensity. "Are you okay, Ross?"

"I'm fine. You're right." He sighed again. "I just…it's a shame about all that Victoria's Secret stuff." His sorrowful expression didn't match his wry words.

"Yeah," she said. "When I wear them, I'll think of you." She'd aimed for humor, too, but it came out wrong.

"Do me a favor and don't, okay?" He seemed hurt.

"I don't want you to think this is easy for me, Ross. It's very hard. All that we've done has been amazing and so good for me. You've taught me so much." She looked into his eyes, glanced at the mouth she loved. She'd never taste it again. She looked at his hands, which were gripping his thighs as if for life itself. Those fingers would never touch her intimately again. Tears welled in her eyes and she wanted to fall into his arms and take it all back.

But she had to stay strong. She whispered, "Better get the taxi back," gave him a quick peck on the cheek, inhaling his smell one last time, like a secret vice, and got out of the cab. "Drive carefully," she said. "Watch out for Officer Reynolds." She turned to run up the walk, blinking back tears, feeling as if her heart was leaking all over her insides.

Behind her, the battered cab rattled away. She turned to watch it go, standing there for a long, long time. She took a deep breath and squared her shoulders. This was for the best. She'd call Baylor first thing Monday morning and ask him out—for Saturday night if possible, so she wouldn't be tempted to call Ross and recant.

Already her body ached everywhere, as though she'd fallen down stairs and gotten bruised head to toe. But she was still on her feet. Not desperate. Determined to move on. Not even crying—though her eyes were a little watery. She'd caught it in time.

12

HE WOULD HAVE BEEN OKAY, if it hadn't been for Baylor Jones, Ross thought on the following Saturday afternoon, staring at his phone. Breaking it off had made sense when Kara explained it last week in the cab. Their friendship was number one, after all.

Kara had high standards, he knew, and he wasn't *that* confident of his feelings. He couldn't stand disappointing her. The idea of sex as themselves, not as characters in a fantasy, had enticed him into wanting to go for something more. Dangerous.

As if to prove the rightness of the decision, he'd gotten home to four phone messages from women wondering where he'd disappeared to, asking if he was interested in "getting together"—code for no-strings sex. When he returned those calls, he'd have a delicious month of romps to look forward to. It didn't get much better than that.

Then Monday at work, Kara had announced she had a date with Baylor Jones. *Our plan worked,* she'd said, all cheerful and bouncy. *You showed me how sex can be fun without getting uptight and planning the future. I can date Baylor with open eyes now. Isn't that great?*

Yeah. Just great.

He stared at his phone. He'd picked it up three times, each time barely keeping his itchy finger from speed-dial one—Kara's spot. What was he going to say to her—*Don't go out with that dweeb. I've got a whole new list of fantasies we can act out?*

Then he looked at the message machine where the women's messages still waited. He should make a date. Get started on life without Kara. He pushed *play* and picked up a pen to write down the numbers. Except then he hit *delete*, erasing each sweet offer, one by one. He didn't want a month of sexual romps. He wanted Kara.

He knew where he could find her tonight. Jones was taking her to a trendy wine bar and then to dinner at a restaurant where you turned over your Gold Card when you walked in and they handed it back to you maxed out. The guy was pulling out all the stops just to get in Kara's pants, no doubt.

Don't let him, Kara. Don't let him touch you.

Every time he thought about it, his vision faded to gray and he wanted to hit something. He *had* hit something, as a matter of fact—the wall a couple of times— and now it hurt to play his guitar, which he'd been doing between aborted calls…lonely blues so fierce the whine of the strings made his ears ache. He was an idiot.

Why hadn't he just told her he wanted to try the big R? Because it sounded feeble, that's why. Kara needed a rock, and he wasn't sure he was that solid. How could he ask her to risk it when he couldn't promise anything?

He watched the clock tick. She'd be in the shower now, washing those gorgeous breasts, that flat stomach, those great thighs. Washing herself for Baylor Jones. What kind of a name was Baylor? You named a suit Baylor Jones, not a man. *Baylor, Baylor, Bo Baylor, banana fanana fo failer.* Baylor the Failer. Not a man for his Kara.

Now she was drying off. He saw the towel brush

between her legs, that place he loved, so delicate, so responsive, and he got hard. The thought of Baylor touching her there, hearing those breathless sounds she made, made him sick. The guy wouldn't think to find that place on her thigh that, when Ross stroked it just so, made her rigid with pleasure. Hell, the guy probably wouldn't even care if she climaxed.

He shouldn't be thinking like this. This was damaging. But he kept it up and an hour later, he found himself roaring on his bike to that chichi wine bar to get Kara. *I love you. I want to be with you. No more games.*

He kept the ferocious hunger for her at the front of his mind, blocking out the fact that he was operating on undiluted testosterone, and if he'd just kick back with a beer or take his board to a skate park and take a few blows to the head, he'd get over it.

But here he was, standing in the door to the bar, running his fingers through his hair so he looked good for Kara. He blinked to adjust his eyes to the expensive Pinot-Noir light of the place, then zeroed in on Kara like a homing signal. She was sitting on a love seat leaning toward a guy—Baylor the Failer, no doubt—smiling, now laughing, at something he was saying.

Ross strode across the room, feeling like John Wayne in a bad Western—*Take yer hands off my woman.* He didn't give a damn how stupid he looked.

The place was crowded with people sitting at the bar and standing in clumps, all trying to look New York. By the time he'd woven his way to where Kara and her date sat, Jones was gone. He caught the guy's retreating back heading toward the john alcove. Good. He could talk to her alone.

Extravagantly bowled wineglasses sat on the tiny table in front of Kara and there was a wedge of cheese they'd been nibbling on. Everything so tasteful and elegant. Until Ross crashed in. He was an idiot, but it was too late for second thoughts because her name was on his lips.

"Kara," he said from behind her.

She turned in the love seat and looked up at him. "Ross?" She blanched, but then he saw what he'd needed to see on her face. Delight. Relief. Joy.

"Come here." He took her arm and guided her to her feet. She rose willingly, if a little confused, then he crushed her into his arms over the back of the sofa—a move straight out of a movie, except this was real, as real as the strawberry flavor of her lips, the sweet flower of her perfume, the shaky breath from her dear lungs—all of it sending life into him. He'd been dead, he realized, except for longing, since he'd dropped her off after the interrupted cab sex and she'd told him it was over.

She sagged in his arms, then managed to pull away. "Stop it," she said, her mouth bruised looking from his kiss. "No more games. I'm on a date. And we never planned 'jealous boyfriend,' anyway."

"I'm not playing, Kara. This is real."

"What are you saying?" She searched his face.

"I'm saying I...I love you, Kara."

Her eyes went wide with surprise. Before she could say anything that made him doubt his own words, he pulled her tight and kissed her again, this time with more tenderness than he thought he had in him.

Kara couldn't believe what was happening. Ross had appeared and declared his love and now he was kissing her and it was wonderful and amazing and heavenly and....

A man cleared his throat. She jerked back to the reality of Baylor at her elbow. "One visit to the rest room and the world turns over," he said.

"Baylor," Kara said, hazy with enchantment. "This is so rude. I'm so sorry. I didn't realize this would happen."

"I guess I'm not surprised," Baylor said.

She could see he was hurt and she didn't blame him. He was a nice guy and the drink they'd shared had only made her like him more. And want to sleep with him less.

"Rebounds are risky, but you seemed worth it, Kara. I hope you know what you're doing." He gave Ross a once-over of disapproval. Ross did look out of place in the toney crowd in his red Keds, T-shirt and jeans, but Kara didn't care. She was so happy to see him he could have appeared in a gorilla suit and she'd have been delighted.

She watched Baylor leave, feeling Ross's eyes on her, burning a hole into her. She turned to him.

"I couldn't stand the idea of you being with that guy," Ross said. "Or any other guy. You belong with me." He cupped her face in his hands. "We belong together."

Her heart rose in her throat, pounding and pounding so she could hardly think. All she could do was look into his hazel eyes, dark with emotion and desire. "Ross, I don't know…I don't think…"

"Tell me you don't feel the same way."

She couldn't make the words come out. "I feel that way, I guess. I'm just scared."

"Me, too, but let's go for it." He grinned and grabbed her by the elbow, and before she knew it he'd hustled her out to the parking lot and straight to his motorcycle, which gleamed a menacing, daredevil black and silver. She stopped short. "I can't ride this."

"Sure you can. Here." He handed her a helmet.

"It's too dangerous."

"Not as dangerous as taking a cab. The driver would get one hell of an eyeful. I'll drive carefully. I promise."

Weakened by his kiss and in a haze, she hiked up her dress, threw a leg over the saddle and wrapped herself around Ross's warm body.

Ross backed up the bike, kicked it to life and they roared off. Kara gasped in terror, plastered her face to Ross's back as best she could with the helmet in the way, closed her eyes and held on with a death grip. If she was going to die, she'd rather do it with Ross.

After a few minutes, when she realized they were still upright and the wind wouldn't blow her off, she opened her eyes to look.

And found it amazing. Ross steered the bike evenly on the road and she could tell he was deliberately going slow. It was startling to be part of the scenery, to be close to the cars driving beside them, music drifting from open windows, touched by the spring air, open to the scent of orange blossoms, mesquite-grilled food from restaurants they passed, seeing pedestrians, neon signs in complete detail, not blurred or smeared by window glass. She felt Ross's heart pounding against her palm. He was here—solid and sure—and he wouldn't let her get hurt. And she realized she wasn't scared of the bike. Or anything right now. Adrenaline and love made her feel invulnerable. Ross loved her. And they were going to make love to each other—for real and for the first time ever.

What are you doing? her sensible side demanded.

This is some fantasy-induced drama. Ross is just jealous of Baylor. Men get like that. You're doing it again, falling in love too soon.

This wasn't the same old pattern. This was different. Ross loved her. She knew him better than the men in her failed relationships. This was new. Better. Right.

All the same, she closed her mind and just held on to Ross all the way to his apartment.

Once inside his place, Ross cupped her cheeks and searched her face. "I want to make love to Kara. Not Katherine or Angel. To you."

"I want that, too." Words failed her, so she kissed him with her whole heart. The kiss was full of the discoveries of the first one—*so this is how you taste, how your breath moves, how your lips feel*—but deeply familiar, too, like coming home from a long, dangerous journey, safe and sound.

They broke apart and began to undress without saying a word. The moment felt almost sacred, as if they were offering themselves to each other, open and honest and completely there.

Kara let her dress drop to her feet. She'd worn plain white underwear tonight because she had no intention of sleeping with Baylor, but Ross's eyes gleamed with the same look as Miguel's that first night when she'd worn the sexy black-lace teddy.

Ross whipped off his T-shirt and tossed it to the side, then removed his pants to stand before her, his erection prominent and proud.

Kara unhooked her bra and let it drop, then slid out of her panties. She felt no embarrassment, no shyness, just pleasure and pride.

"Look at you," Ross said.

"Look at us," she answered.

They smiled at each other in wonder, like Adam and Eve discovering their sexuality. Then Ross took her hand and they walked to his bedroom, where they went to separate sides of the bed.

Kara slid under the sheet, but before she could pull it up, Ross yanked it completely off the bed. ''I want to see everything,'' he said, reminding her of Dr. Michaels, the sex therapist. He climbed onto the mattress beside her, examining her with adoration, treasuring her. He cupped one breast the way Miguel had.

She touched him, too, feeling the swell of his pectorals, the flatness of his stomach, the muscles jumping under her fingers. He held still, watching her, as he had when she'd overpowered him as the Love Thief. When she reached his velvety penis, he closed his eyes. She curled her fingers around the shaft and slid upward to end in a gentle touch at the head.

He groaned. ''You know me so well,'' he said, words he'd used as the cabdriver. He cupped her with his palm and slid two fingers gently between her folds to the live wire of her body hidden there. That reminded her of Mike reaching under her flight attendant uniform, riveting her in place with his fingers.

She rolled from her side to her back.

''I want you to feel everything,'' he said, the Love Thief again. All the lovers were coming back, combining together into Ross. ''I want to make love to you,'' he said.

Make love. Not have sex. Ross and Kara would be making love. Just the two of them. No roles, no games. For real, this time.

Kara realized she'd wanted this, longed for it, fought it since the adventure began. At last it was all right. She loved him and, best of all, he loved her.

She spread her legs, open to Ross, open to anything he wanted to do to her, aching for him to fill her, to go deep, as far as he could go. He stayed poised at her entrance for a moment, then he whispered, "I love you, Kara," and pushed into her.

She gasped, the pleasure of his entry, the relief of it, and the joy of hearing his words all equal in her heart.

"I feel right when I'm inside you," Ross said, his face full of love. "Like I belong here."

"You do belong here. Exactly here." She bent her knees, lifting her hips, bringing him in deeper.

He pulled out and thrust in, hard, then out and in again and again. There was no playful teasing in their lovemaking this time. The bed banged against the wall with the force of their movements. They worked hungrily toward climax, moving as one, laying claim to each other, body and soul. Ross was inside her, part of her. He was in love with her, feeling what she felt.

Ross thrust again and again. Kara lifted her hips to get every bit of him, to give him all of her. She felt her orgasm approach, sensed his in the quickening of his thrusts.

Once more and they were swept away on the wave, calling each other's names. That sounded so right, she thought as she felt the sparks and stabs of utter pleasure. The orgasm seemed to go on forever, as if her spasms added to his and his to hers, making both bigger and longer.

Finally, finally, they shuddered to rest, panting, wearing sweat like a glove. Staying inside her, Ross rolled to the side, holding her tightly against him, something he'd never done before. Their fantasies hadn't allowed for cuddling, or whispering things: *I love you. You make me so happy. I think of you every minute. I can't stand to be away from you.* So these were the things they said to each other as their breathing slowed and settled and their hearts stopped pounding.

Then they changed positions, spooning—her back to his front. After a few peaceful minutes of murmurs and squeezes, Kara felt Ross's breathing deepen into sleep. She wanted to move, so they could both sleep more comfortably, but if she so much as twitched, Ross grabbed her against him hard. She smiled and snuggled in for the night.

This was the right thing to do. It had to be. How could she feel this good otherwise? This was different than with any other man. She felt connected to Ross. And Ross wanted it, too. That was what had been missing in all the other relationships—a matching love. This time it was real, not wishful thinking on her part.

What would they do now, though? Live together? Get married? That seemed impossible, but Ross had said they belonged together. What else could he mean?

Doubts lifted fingers of warning from where she'd submerged them—what if this was just the game intensified to a dangerous level? What if Ross is wrong for you?—but she absolutely would not spoil the moment. This was real and Ross was changing. He was about to get the new job, for one thing. That would ease her worries about his stability. Just a few adjustments and this would all work out fine.

She tugged Ross's hand more firmly onto her breast. He squeezed gently, as if he were testing an avocado for ripeness rather than reassuring the woman he loved. So perfectly Ross.

13

SEVEN O'CLOCK on a Monday morning and Ross was awake. Bizarre. He rarely came to consciousness before nine-thirty on a weekday, and after nonstop lovemaking all weekend, he should be sleeping like the dead. But he was wide-awake—and happy as hell because Kara was in his bed. Of course he could roll over for more z's, but he'd rather watch her sleep, her face relaxed, a half smile on her lips, a love bite on her neck.

He was so glad he'd gone and ripped her away from Baylor the Failer and told her he loved her.

He was supposed to be the sexual expert, but Kara had taught him things about sex he didn't know he didn't know.

Sex had always been fun, freeing, relaxing and healthy. But now he saw it could be the uniting of two souls, two people striving for a shared pleasure, glorying in this high moment of being human. Far from the French *la petite mort, the little death,* this was a declaration of *life*. Life in all its preciousness shared with the woman he loved.

He'd been going through the motions with other women. Everything changed with someone you truly cared about, someone whose feelings meant more than your own, whose pain was your agony, whose pleasure was your highest goal.

Jeez. He was getting carried away. Uncertainty tightened his gut. He had no track record with love. He'd loved Beth, after all, and look how that had ended—boredom for him and pain for her. But he hadn't felt like this about Beth even at the beginning. Surely, this was different. This would last.

He pushed aside his doubts. He'd taken the plunge and he wasn't backing out now. Kara was counting on him. They wouldn't rush into anything irreversible. Like marriage. That made him break out in a sweat. Maybe, after a while, they'd try living together. There was a chance this could just run a natural course. *Take it one day at a time.*

Right now he was up early, so he would make love to Kara, start their new life together right. He kissed the sweet spot on her neck, where he'd given her that hickey. He loved that—making her his own, giving her proof of his passion to look at all day at work.

"Mmm," she said, turning lazily toward him, sliding against him, tangling her legs with his. Then she opened her eyes. Alert, she jerked to a sit. "What time is it?" Her gaze flew around the room.

He lifted his Roy Rogers clock and held it close to her face. "Early. Only seven. We have plenty of time."

"Seven? Oh, no!" She leaped out of bed. "I've got to get going."

"I thought we'd have some start-the-week-right nookie."

"God, no. By now I should be done with yoga. I still have to shower, have breakfast and fix my lunch. Plus I have no clothes." She was talking as she galloped around the room picking up underwear and her dress. They'd only gotten dressed once to hit a restaurant, then hurried back, ripping things off as they headed for bed.

Ross rolled to a sit, shaken by this early morning

ruckus. He liked to kick off slowly from the sleep pool and gradually get his day legs under him. Kara was rattling the early morning molecules and it made his head hurt. "I've got Cap'n Crunch," he managed. "Except the milk might be bad."

"I don't do sugar cereals. Thank you, anyway. I've gotta get home, Ross. I'll see you at work."

He looked at her from bed, scratching his head, feeling foggy. "What's your hurry? Siegel and Sampson never show up until ten on Mondays."

"I don't care about them. I have work to do," she said, clip-clopping on one shoe to his chair, then bending to look under it.

"On the weight bench." He'd had to move it out from under him when he'd leaned back on the bench so she could get at him better from her position kneeling between his legs.

"Oh." She stood bolt upright and stared at him, remembering.

Amazingly enough, sex without games was proving to be even hotter than the fantasy stuff. Maybe because they'd become vulnerable to each other emotionally as well as sexually. He was proud of himself for realizing that. Kara was teaching him things. Maybe he could teach her something, too. Something about how much better the day went when you started off with a breakfast boff. He crooked a finger at her.

She rushed to him and leaned down for a kiss. "I don't want to go, Ross," she moaned. "This has been so...so..."

"Repeatable," he said. "Come here and I'll show you," he said, trying to pull her into the bed.

She stayed back. "I have to go. Tonight will be great, though." Then she galloped out of his apartment before he even had a chance to suggest a personal day. She'd never fake a sick day. Not that he made a habit of it, but a mental health day now and then kept his creative juices flowing and made him feel less like a wage-slave.

He felt a flicker of distress at how weird it would be to live around Kara and her work style. They might be like twins in the sack, but they were opposites in the workplace—and life.

He used strawberry Quick in his Cap'n Crunch, since the milk was bad, took a quick shower and moseyed into work. First stop, Kara's office. She was keyboarding like mad, the phone tucked at her ear, nodding her head at the caller's words.

He caught her eye, blew her a kiss.

She looked queasy, then waved him away, as if he were distracting her from something important. *Lighten up,* he thought.

"Gabriel?" Uh-oh. Siegel. Not a good start to the week.

"Hey, Saul," he said, turning.

"Step into my office, would you?"

"Now?" Ross thought back to see if he owed the man any work. Nothing that he could remember. In fact, Saul had seemed quite pleased with the extra stuff he'd done because Lancer was tanking it.

"Please," Saul said, motioning toward his door.

He followed Siegel into his chichi digs—all black leather, expensive wood and original oils—and sat on the edge of a spongy glove-leather chair across from Saul's desk.

Saul shut the door. Closed door meeting. Not good. Ross was not interested in overtime, not with Kara in his life and all those new sexual things to explore. Saul smiled at him. He definitely wanted something.

"So what's up?" Ross asked.

"I thought we'd talk about Lancer's job."

"Excuse me?"

"I understand you're interested."

"Where did you get that idea?"

Saul leveled his gaze at him, as if he thought he was being coy. "Let's just say a little bird told me."

Kara. Had to be Kara. What the hell was she pulling here? "I like my job fine, Saul. I wouldn't turn down a raise, of course, but everything else is copacetic."

"Your résumé looks good, Ross. I'd forgotten you won those Plus One Advertising awards, and you handled the office well when Lancer had that little incident in Las Vegas."

"What résumé?"

Siegel frowned, then opened a folder and pulled out a piece of paper, which he slid across the desk to him.

Businesslike formatting. Card stock paper. Definitely Kara's work. "The little bird was misinformed. I don't want the job." He shoved the paper back across the desk.

"Don't be modest. The starving artist routine gets old. Ambition is a good thing. Trust me on this."

Ross just stared at him. "No, thanks."

Saul stared back. "If you mean that, we've got a problem. I haven't put out feelers or placed ads, figuring I'd promote from within—good for morale and all."

"The problem's yours, Saul, not mine."

Siegel leaned closer across his desk. "I like you, Ross. You've got good ideas. I can see you've been getting more serious, not watching the clock or playing chicken with morning meetings, letting Kara cover for you."

He flinched. He didn't think the partners were wise to his bad habits.

"Maybe it's time you looked to the future," Saul continued. "Got some savings going. This means a definite salary boost. Full benefits. A real office. Nameplate and all."

"I like my job, Saul, and I'm not interested in headaches. I've seen you with the Mylanta cocktail three times a day."

Siegel looked annoyed. "I have acid reflux and I'd have it on a yacht in Bimini. It's physiology, not stress." He tapped Ross's résumé. "The job's yours anyway, at least until we can post the position. Lancer's a cardboard cutout right now. There are some timing problems with the New Mirage tourism campaign and I need someone to step in before we start a downward service spiral."

"You're telling me I *have* to do the job? Against my will?"

"Calm down. This is an honor, not a punishment, my friend. We're putting our faith and trust in you, our loyal, hardworking employee." Siegel smirked. Ross liked his wit. If it weren't a matter of principle, he'd probably laugh. Besides, it wasn't Siegel he was angry at. It was Kara—the woman he loved. And that was definitely not good.

She's just trying to help you. But an ache in his gut told him it wasn't that simple. Kara wanted to fix him. Like she'd been fixing his apartment. She'd made no secret of the fact that she wanted a man who was going places. Now that they were together, she was trying to jump-start him into a career—whether he liked it or not.

Next she'd attack his wardrobe. Instead of the surf shop where he bought thick cotton T-shirts and tough-wearing pants and shorts, she'd drag him to Macy's men's department with its endless racks of this season's green, where the only way to distinguish one corporate soldier from the next were the designs on their jewel-toned ties. Before long, she'd have him signing up for a time-share in Aspen.

Kara, don't do this to me.

He started down the hall to her office to confront her, but realized he should wait until he was calm enough to be gentle.

But then he got busy. Julie and Bob weren't speaking, which was why the Stone Pony Mineral Baths account had two different logos. Instead of cooking up ideas for a logo for a skateboard club wanting to go national, he spent two hours finessing things between Julie and Bob, then talking to the account exec, even ending up on a conference call with the Stone Pony CEO, gritting his teeth the whole time.

He was still grouchy when he ran into Kara in the lunchroom.

"How's it going?" she said sweetly, stars in her eyes.

"How do you think it's going?" he snapped. "It started out with a meeting with Siegel, where, evidently somebody's been playing fairy godmother."

"You met with Saul?" she said. "How'd it go?"

"Why did you tell him I wanted that job?"

"You already do the job, so you might as well get the money and prestige that go with it." She came close to him and touched his arm, but he pulled away. He would not be distracted by her touch.

"It's a moot point now. Siegel strong-armed me into it until he can hire someone."

"That's wonderful," she said. "I knew you could do it."

"Aren't you listening to me? I told him no. I don't want the job. I never did." And then he added fiercely, "Don't try to change me, Kara."

"I'm helping you get what you want."

"What *you* want, you mean. If you really want a house in the suburbs and a membership in the country club, go after someone who'll get that for you. Because it's not me. Where the hell did you get the idea it was?"

"Why are you attacking me? I was just helping."

They locked gazes. She was hurt. Not fair. He was the injured party here. "I'm just upset," he said. "Forget it."

"I understand," she said shakily. "I guess I should have checked with you, but I didn't want you to say no before you heard what Saul had to say."

"It's okay." But it wasn't and that familiar feeling rose in him—the desire to shake off the sticky webs of obligation, to break free, be himself, ready to take off if he needed to, with no one he could hurt or disappoint.

"WHOSE TURN IS IT?" Kara asked, staring blindly at her spades hand.

"Huh?" Tina said, bringing her gaze back to the card game. No one seemed interested in the game today, but at least Tina was happy—she was in a lovestruck haze over Tom. Kara and Ross smiled at each other, but tension buzzed between them.

She'd never forget the look on his face—*how could you do this to me?* Like she was his mother making him eat Brussels sprouts or do his homework.

What had she done that was so wrong? She'd been helping him as a friend. In fact, when she'd spoken to

Siegel they'd still been only friends. He'd accused her of trying to change him. Not fair at all.

They planned to meet at Ross's place for dinner after work. They'd get past this awkwardness, she was certain. Make-up sex was supposed to be the best.

FIVE HOURS LATER, Kara stood on the terrace outside Ross's apartment and watched rain drip off the eaves to form puddles at her feet. Here she was, waiting for Ross in the rain—just like the night of the cab sex. He was an hour late. Where could he be? They'd left the office at the same time.

The landlords weren't home or she'd have waited with them. She could go to her own apartment, but she kept thinking Ross would be here any minute. How had it all gone so wrong? The weekend had been so perfect—they'd been best friends in love. She'd thought they had it all—sharing love and work and life.

But since the argument, it was as if the filter over a lens had popped off and everything that had been soft and hazy and pink and pretty now looked hard and clear and flawed. She'd always promised herself she'd choose her man carefully and with her future in mind. How could she have chosen Ross?

He was always late, even now when they were both on their best behavior. Was he doing it on purpose? At work, he'd seemed to *want* to be angry at her about the job. Almost as if he'd been looking for an excuse.

The rain poured down, increasing her gloom. During their cab fantasy, the rain had been mysterious and sensuous and romantic. Now it was just wet and irritating. Where was Ross? Was he ducking her? Was this some passive-aggressive way to show his anger?

He was on a motorcycle, she remembered abruptly.

Dangerous in the rain. She pictured the bike sliding on a greasy puddle, his poor body tossed onto the street. Oh, God.

She was about to bang on a neighbor's door to start calling hospitals when she saw Ross's motorcycle pull into a parking spot. He bounced off the bike and strolled across the lot, taking his time, as though she hadn't been waiting for him for an hour, terrified for his life.

He looked up at her from the parking lot. "Kara!" he said, his face pure delight.

She would not smile, much as his expression warmed her. They had to reach an understanding about this. When he'd bounded up the stairs to her, she said, "Where have you been?"

"I'll show you." He opened his backpack and pulled out a dozen bedraggled daisies, which he presented triumphantly to her. "For what happened today."

"Thank you," she said, taking the flowers. He was trying, at least. "I've been waiting and waiting, worried sick."

"Why would you worry? I picked up dinner and it took longer than I expected to get the Peking duck." He held his open backpack under her nose, showing her the white sack, grease spotted, emitting the enticing scent of sesame oil and garlic.

"That's great," she said, trying to calm down. "Next time, call me. What if you'd been hurt? I was about to call hospitals."

His open expression closed up. "I wasn't hurt, Kara. I was getting our dinner—and flowers for you." Again she felt like his mother, or his jailer, and she hated it. "I just forgot you don't have a key yet."

"I'm sorry. You're right. I just...I just worry." That wasn't a helpful thing to say, but the day's frustrations and her fear about their relationship and his possible death by rain-wobbly motorcycle had just balled up into a panic.

"I know you do," he said with a weary sigh, the kind of sigh you gave your parents when they reported you missing after midnight or something equally over-reactive. "I'll get a key made. Relax." He reached past her and unlocked the door, shaking his head as though she was neurotic.

She wanted to apologize for her outburst, to explain her tension and the newness of everything, but instead she joked. "I guess we're having our first fight."

But he only frowned. "We're not fighting." As if a fight meant something terrible, instead of just part of a relationship.

They laid out the food—an activity usually filled with jokes and pokes with chopsticks—in near silence, then sat down to eat. Even the tattered daisies didn't lighten the mood.

Ross took a bite of beef broccoli, frowned, then examined one of the small containers. "This is the wrong sauce," he said, his jaw muscle ticking. He picked up a bite of duck with his chopsticks, chewed, then stopped. "Is yours cold?" he demanded.

"It's okay," she said, though the meat was icy.

"No, it isn't. It's cold. I'll get them to deliver something better." She knew Ross didn't care about things like this. He patronized the mediocre restaurant because the owner was a friend. He didn't care about the food, just the gesture. He was worrying about it because of her.

She dropped her chopsticks and felt tears slide down her cheeks. "This isn't right, Ross. You're acting strange."

"I'm doing my best. What do you want from me?"

"I want you to be yourself, except…" Better? Was she trying to improve him? "I just don't know how to do this—this relationship thing."

"Neither do I," he said, taking another bite of the cold food. They chewed in silence for a minute. Then he looked up at her. "I know I love you," he said hopefully.

"Me, too," she said. But that obviously didn't solve the problem. Wanting it to work wasn't enough. You could shave the corners off a square peg, but it would always be a squeeze into that round hole. "Maybe we can't do this," she whispered, voicing her worst fears.

"Sure we can," he said stubbornly. "You didn't mean anything about the job. You were trying to help me." But that didn't make him feel any better, she could see in his face.

"You got so angry with me. If we'd still been just friends, you would have shrugged it off."

"If we were friends you wouldn't have pushed."

"Maybe this is a mistake," she blurted.

"No, it's not. We should give ourselves a chance," he said, but his expression said *yeah, BIG mistake*.

"Maybe we just got carried away with the fantasy," she said slowly, her throat so dry and tight she could hardly squeeze out the words. *Please argue.*

"Do you think so?" he asked carefully.

"What do you think?" *Last chance, Ross. Tell me I'm wrong.*

"We might have done that," he said. "It happened fast. I saw you with that guy and knew I didn't want to lose you."

No. Had it just been jealousy that made him say he loved her? It couldn't be just that, could it? She wanted to erase those words, take back today, try again fresh. "I'm sorry about Saul and about getting mad about your being late," she said, tears sliding down her cheeks.

"I'm making you cry," he said, leaning forward to wipe her face with a napkin. "That sucks."

"It's okay," she said, sniffing. "It's not you. It's me."

"Hey, now. You're stealing my clichés."

She tried to laugh, but the sound jammed in her throat. "Have we ruined things between us?"

"I don't think so," he said slowly.

Relief filled her. They'd just overreacted and assumed the worst. They had to give each other some slack, get used to this new thing between them.

"Ground rule number one, remember?" Ross said. "You're my best friend, Kara. I don't want to lose that. No matter what. The most important thing that's happened these past weeks is that we've gotten closer as friends."

She looked at him, stunned, while the world tilted on its axis. He was worried about ruining their *friendship*, not their *relationship*.

"The sex has been amazing," he continued. "Beyond words—really—and I don't want to give that up." His eyes flared with heat for a moment. "But even that isn't worth it if it ruins our friendship."

"What about—" she gulped "—the love part?"

"I know." He frowned. "I guess love brings out the worst in us. You're acting neurotic and demanding and I'm—"

"Neurotic and demanding? Because I thought you might have been killed in the rain? Because I don't like waiting for an hour?"

"Let me finish. Jeez. I was about to add that I'm

acting flaky and belligerent. See what I mean? We're so uptight about this we're picking fights. We're trying too hard.''

You can't give up who you are for someone else. That was what he'd said when he was trying to convince her how wrong he was for her.

If not for the amazing sex, Ross was the last man she would choose for herself. But there was so much more she'd felt and wanted and believed possible. Her tears poured down in earnest.

"Hey, hey," he said. "You're turning your Kung-Pao chicken into Kung-Pao soup."

She swiped her cheeks.

"We have to hang on to the best of what we have," he said. "Our friendship. That's always worked."

She nodded.

He leaned forward and kissed her.

Despite her misery, she felt the sizzle, the race of electricity along her nerves, and she wanted to forget everything they'd said and just fall into bed with him.

Ross broke off the kiss. "I want to make love to you so bad.''

"Me, too," she said, fighting tears and lust and heart-break. He would do it, too. He would try to have friend-ship and sex. It was love that was the problem—love and the commitment and adjustments that went with it. "I can't do that," she said. "It hurts too much."

"I figured," he said sadly.

Relationships were hard enough with both people pulling in the same direction, hoping and loving and compromising away. But Ross was uncertain and she was scared. They were too different. Being opposites struck great sparks for sex but made for a destructive blaze everywhere else.

''You want to stay for the basketball game?'' he asked.

She looked around the apartment. Everywhere were touches she'd put there—a bookcase for his video games, stripe marks on the carpet where she'd vacuumed. He had a dish drainer now and hot pads and kitchen scrubbers, even a toilet seat cover—a non-girlie one. She couldn't stay. Not in this nest she'd been fixing up for the two of them.

''Too soon,'' she choked out. She needed to go home and sob.

''Later then. When we're feeling more normal.''

''Right.'' Normal? She'd fallen in love with her best friend. How would she ever feel normal again?

14

"I TOLD YOU I'd meet you at your place when I got off," Tom said crossly to Tina, leaning across the bar.

"I was bored," Tina said. "I wanted to get out. Let's go dancing at that after-hours place."

"I have to study tomorrow," he said.

"You always have to study. We never do anything fun." She knew she sounded bitchy, but she felt that way. Ever since last week when Tom had convinced her to go to his parents' house for dinner. She'd seen the nervous looks his parents had exchanged over Tom's head. *What trouble has our poor son gotten into?* Tom insisted they were just protective of him, but she could tell they saw her as a slut who was taking their precious darling for a ride. That made her blood boil. To make a nice impression, she'd worn a modest dress and very little cosmetics. It hadn't helped a bit. She was who she was and it showed.

Since the dinner, she'd taken a good hard look at what had been happening between Tom and her and hadn't liked what she'd seen. She'd been changing herself to please Tom. She'd cut down on her makeup—he'd convinced her she looked better without it—started reading while he studied and keeping hours that were compatible with his class schedule. She'd even tried to learn to cook for him, though he hadn't asked and seemed perfectly willing to prepare all the meals.

The capper had been letting him talk her into the family visit. She'd actually been nervous about what they would think of her, hence the conservative dress. On top of it, Tom had taken her for granted while they were there, leaving her to help his mother clean up the dishes, while he worked on his dad's engine with him.

Things had changed between them without her noticing. The night they'd first had sex, when Tom had been in agony over her, he'd agreed to do it her way—sex only. But he'd gradually pressured her into becoming the kind of woman he wanted.

He hadn't *forced* her really, just seduced her with his adoration. But it wasn't adoration, she knew. It was sexual fascination. She'd seen it before, but this was the first time she'd succumbed to it. In his heart of hearts, Tom disapproved of her as much as his parents did. Once he stopped being obsessed with her body and the remarkable sex they had, that disapproval would bloom big time. So, she'd started forcing the issue, even while a secret, weak part of her prayed she was wrong.

"We do plenty of fun things," Tom said patiently. "We went sailing on Saturday and to a movie after the dinner at my parents. What are you doing, Tina?" He said the last words low.

"I'm being me. That's not acceptable?"

"Stop it."

"Stop being me? Sorry, no can do. I'd like a drink, please. Martini. Shaken, not stirred." She lifted her chin at a hell-raising angle.

Tom blew out a breath and went to mix her drink, but he looked puzzled, frustrated and worried. For a second, she felt awful to be hurting him, but she couldn't seem to stop. She seemed to want to show him her worst self, to get her cards on the table and see if he could take it.

Tom brought her the martini. "Don't overdo it," he said wearily.

"I can handle my liquor," she said, deciding to dump this martini into her water glass when he wasn't looking and order another one.

"If you say so."

"You poor, poor dear," she said. "I make you suffer so."

To his credit, Tom resisted her gibe and went back to work.

Tina turned to the three men standing nearby. "So, what business are you guys in?"

It turned out to be insurance—some tedious kind— so she drank a second martini and disposed of two more in her water glass when Tom wasn't looking, all the while pretending to be fascinated by the Three Bland Men who lived and breathed the nuances of premiums and underwriting.

Tom was stewing behind the bar, shooting her glares. Good. He was mad. Now she'd force him to say what he really thought of her.

She had just asked one guy about collision deductibles when a hand gripped her elbow. "I'm taking you home," Tom growled in her ear.

"I'm not going home," she said, pulling her arm away. "Your shift's not even over."

"Jane's covering for me." He tugged at her.

She let him walk her out the door and across the parking lot, striding so fast she could hardly keep up on her short legs. She'd never seen him angry before. They would fight now and probably end it tonight. Part of her felt sick with sadness at the thought.

To fix that, when they reached the car she yanked her arm away. "Quit dragging me around like property. You don't own me."

"I'm trying to take care of you."

"I can take care of myself. I'm getting sick of this he-man act. And just because you're a stick-in-the-mud doesn't mean I have to turn into one."

He stared at her for an angry minute, then shut her door and went to his side and got in. "Why are you making this into an issue?"

"Because it *is* an issue."

He rolled his eyes and started the car.

"You always do that. Dismiss my concerns like you're above them. Like you're above me."

"We have a nice relationship. Why are you trying to wreck it?"

"I was just having a drink with some friends. Do you have a problem with me talking to other men?"

He glared at her. "I don't give a damn who you talk to unless you're doing it to hurt me."

"You knew I was a flirt when you met me."

"You put on that act because you're insecure."

"Oh, ho. Aren't you the shrink? Listening to a bunch of drunks' woes does not make you a psychologist, Tom Sands."

"I'm just being honest, which is something you can't seem to be—even with yourself."

Tears stung her eyes. Why was she letting him get to her? "I can't argue when I'm drunk," she said, though she wasn't even tipsy. She leaned her head on the back of the seat and felt tears slide into her ears. Now she was crying? She'd really lost her edge these past weeks. Her self-control had gotten downright flabby.

Tom didn't speak the rest of the way to her house.

She didn't either, contenting herself with dark thoughts and an occasional glance at his profile to be sure the muscle still danced angrily in his cheek.

When they got to her apartment, Tom came to open her door, but she was already out. He took her by the arm, as if to steady her. She could have shaken him off, but since she was pretending to be drunk, she decided to let it be. This might be the last time he held on to her, and it was so nice, leaning on him like this.

He walked her into her apartment and straight to her bedroom, where he pulled back the covers for her. She lay down and allowed him to take off her shoes and dress, revealing his favorite bra and panty set. He looked longingly at her, wanting her, but he covered her with the sheet, keeping his face neutral, just like the days before they'd slept together.

He disappeared and she could hear him in the kitchen pouring water. He brought back a glass and two aspirin. "Take these," he said grumpily.

She did.

He turned to go and panic shot through her. She didn't want him to leave. She'd accomplished her goal—gotten him mad—but it felt like someone had turned off the sun, and left her in the deep, cold darkness, all alone. "Don't go," she said humbly. "Let's talk."

With his back to her, he sighed and dropped his head. Without turning, he said, "I thought you didn't want to talk when you were drunk."

"I'm not that drunk," she said.

He turned to her with a brief smile. "Yeah, I got a whiff of your water glass." He returned to her bed and sat beside her.

"I'm sorry I've been mean," she said, embarrassed

that fat tears were sliding down her cheeks. "I just feel really bad. Your parents don't like me and I—"

"They don't *know* you. And you didn't help, saying things just to shock them. Why did you tell my mother you consider Madonna a role model?"

The truth was his mother had complimented her dress, adding that it was nice when women didn't have to show everything they had all the time. That pissed her off. She liked showing what she had. "Because Madonna's message is be who you are, and too bad if people can't take it. Your mother can't take who I am."

Tom was silent for a moment. "My parents might be old-fashioned, but they'd like you fine if you'd be yourself instead of trying to be outrageous every second."

"Outrageous? You think I'm outrageous? You're just like your parents. You despise me, too."

"I love you, Tina."

His words closed down her throat. "But I'll make you miserable," she blurted, forcing out sound. New tears surged out. That was what was really bothering her. She sat up and took his arms, her lips trembling. "Don't you see? You're pretending I'm someone I'm not. You don't know me."

"I do know you. The real you—the one you hide from everyone."

Not true. Couldn't be true. Tom was telling himself some hero myth. Since she'd met him he'd been happiest when he thought he was rescuing her, whether from melon martinis or overbearing barflies or her own boo-boos.

Tom leaned in to kiss her and she wanted to melt into his embrace, pull him into bed and forget all this relationship insanity. But something in her wouldn't give up. She'd realized she'd been pretending to be the woman Tom wanted, just as her mother had molded herself to please her temperamental father all those miserable years. And now that she knew the truth, she couldn't go back to before.

She would not turn out like her mother. Not even to have Tom's big hand to lead her up the walk, his broad shoulders to lean on, his big bear body to make love with. Not even for that.

"I'm not who you want me to be and I never will be." She stiffened her arms to hold him away.

"You're more than you think you are, Tina."

He wanted her to be more. He wanted too much. And she knew as sure as she was sitting here in her underwear that she couldn't be more. She had to break things off. Now. Say what she had to say to end it. "The real problem is that I'm getting bored." She swallowed hard because her next words, a terrible lie, would do the trick—get him to leave her alone, to stop looking at her with all that longing and trust and love in his eyes. "I don't love you, Tom. I'm sorry, but I don't."

"You don't mean that."

"Yes, I do. That's why I've been so awful to you lately. It's over."

"You're serious about this? You don't...love me?" He looked slapped and pale as a ghost.

She nodded, shaking a tear to her cheek.

He was silent for a long time, his breathing ragged, his face filled with anguish. "Okay, then. I won't beat my head against the wall. I don't want that pain. I did that once. I quit school over a woman. Set my life back too far."

"So it's good you know now before it gets worse."

He gave a humorless laugh. "What makes you think

it can get any worse?'' His blue eyes sparkled with hurt, then he pushed to his feet and headed to the door.

Everything inside her wanted to leap out of bed and fling herself at him. *Don't go. Don't give up. I'm bluffing.* But Tom was a decent, sensible guy, and he knew when enough was enough. That was part of him she craved—that rock-solid stability—and it was what allowed him to do the right thing. Walk out of her life forever.

Tom turned at the door. ''Take care of yourself, Tina. I'd like to say I'll be here if you change your mind, but I don't think I'm strong enough.''

And then he was gone.

Pain coursed through her in waves. The joke was on her. Somehow, Tom Sands, with his study sessions and sailing lessons and golden-brown cheese sandwiches had burned through the Teflon coating of her heart and made it ache. It would take a long, long time to heal, and she was scared to death she'd never be the same again.

''WHO DIED?'' Saul Siegel said, looking from person to person around the conference table. He tossed a Nerf ball at Tina. ''You look like something the cat couldn't bring itself to drag in, and what we have here—'' he indicated Kara ''—is the empty-eyed husk of our Kara. Where's the marketing plan? The projections? The timeline?''

''The CEO didn't get back to me yet,'' Kara mumbled.

''Since when does Kara the Dogged meekly accept delays? Go out there, wrestle him to the ground if you have to.''

Tina didn't even jump to Kara's defense with a smart

remark. Something bad had happened with Tom the night before and they hadn't been able to talk about it—or about her breakup with Ross. They would talk tonight over drinks. Many drinks.

"Ross, you're handling the art department so well, why don't you see what you can do with these two?" Saul finally said.

"I'll give 'em all she's got, Cap'n," Ross said in a halfhearted Scotty-from-*Star-Trek* voice. He shot Kara a sheepish smile.

They'd managed to stay genial, but she could hardly bear to be around him. The sound of his voice made her shake; brushing past him in the hall made her pulse pound; eye contact was like a match in kindling. She ached for what they'd lost, relived every moment of that glorious weekend of love, when she thought they had it all. If she'd known how quickly it would end, she'd have focused more on the details, taken notes, maybe videotaped it like Tina had once jokingly suggested when it was just a game.

She tried to stay busy and keep positive. Her goal now was to hang on to her friendship with Ross. But how could they stay friends after what they'd shared? The thought of Ross sleeping with another woman—which he soon would, if she knew him—felt like touching a hot stove. She'd broken all the ground rules, one by one, saving the best for last—friendship first. She wanted Ross in her life, but there was no longer a place for him there.

"WHAT SHOULD I HAVE?" Kara asked Tom at the Upside after work that evening. Tina hadn't yet arrived. Kara had offered to meet somewhere else, but Tina had declared she wasn't going to let a breakup scare her away from her favorite bar.

"Hell if I know," Tom said, his face drawn, dark circles under his eyes. Kara had a pretty good idea it was Tina who had made him look so wretched.

"I'm sorry things didn't work out," she said.

Tom shrugged, but he looked like a lost little boy. "I don't get it. I did everything I could. And she was happy. I know she was."

"I'm sorry," she repeated, not knowing what else to say. She'd tried to find out what had happened, but Tina had put her off until tonight.

"I would never hurt her," Tom continued, misery in his voice. "I care about her. I..." He hesitated. "I love her."

"I know. It's hard." It disturbed her to see such a big, serene man hunched over in pain, blurting his private sorrow to someone he barely knew. *Give her time,* she wanted to say, but she had no idea whether Tina would ever come around.

Kara and Tom were still looking gloomily at each other when Tina entered the Upside. Kara watched her march in, head held high, until she caught sight of Tom. Then she faltered, snatched her lip between her teeth and blurted, "Let's sit here." She nodded at a high cocktail table to her left and away from the bar.

"Sure," Kara said with a last, commiserating look at Tom before she joined her friend. Tina sat with her back to the bar and Kara saw she was trembling. "Why don't you talk to him? He loves you," Kara said.

"But I don't love him. It's as simple as that."

"I don't think it's simple at all."

"Please." She shot Kara a glare with tear-filled eyes.

"No lectures. I can't talk about it. Let's just be friends and drink."

Kara decided for once Tina was right. She surely didn't want Tina's opinions about the Ross situation. When the waitress brought their drinks, Tina held up her Harvey Wallbanger to click against Kara's. "What a mess we're in," she said. "I should never have started all this—hitting on Tom and getting you mixed up with Ross. If I ever again suggest you try it my way, smack me."

"Live and learn, right?" Kara sounded way more philosophical than she felt.

"Here's to the G-Spot Pleasure Wand," Tina said, raising her glass. "Sex in all its battery-operated glory. A mechanical solution to a biological problem. Get another person involved and it gets all messy."

"Here, here." Kara clicked her glass against Tina's so hard their drinks sloshed.

They nursed their drinks and danced around their respective heartbreaks. After a while, Kara noticed they'd slowly shifted their chairs until Tina faced the bar and was following Tom's every move, while Kara watched the door for Ross to rush in, admit the error of his ways and demand they live happily ever after.

"This is fun, huh?" Tina said hopefully. "Talking this all through—woman to woman?"

"A blast," Kara answered, trying to smile.

"I know." Tina slumped. "I'm miserable, too."

Kara held out her glass for Tina to tap. "To misery," she said.

"And company," Tina added.

Not long after that, they gave up and headed home.

"ROSS, HONEY, what brings you here?" Ross's mother said, looking completely baffled at his presence on her doorstep. "The girls won't be home till June." He felt guilty that she thought he only came to Tucson to see his sisters, who were both in college. It was true that without his siblings as buffers, he avoided his parents, who spent too much time harassing him about where his career was headed and hinting about grandkids.

"Can't I just visit my folks?" Since Kara and he had broken up three weeks ago, everything in his world had gone gray and he'd felt the need to go somewhere he felt loved—hounded, but loved. And maybe he'd get some perspective on relationships from the source of his first lessons on the subject.

"Of course you can. Come here, you." His mother pulled him into a tight hug. "Jaaake," his mother shouted down the stairs to the basement, blasting Ross's ears. "Ross is here!"

"Hey, Ross!" his father called up.

Ross answered him.

"Your father thinks he's antiquing the dining-room chairs," his mother said. "I'm shopping for a new set, just in case. Come help me with the egg salad. When your father gets done destroying the furniture, he'll be starving for some bad cholesterol." She shook her head in dismay.

Had his parents stayed together out of habit like he thought? They hadn't divorced when his sisters left for school, as Kara had pointed out, but he hadn't thought about the significance of that. The truth was he'd never spent any time thinking about his parents as people. They were just…parents.

Ross followed his mother into the warm and sunny kitchen, which hadn't changed since he'd left home. He found the eggs in the same copper-bottomed pot his mother always used, soaking in cold water in the sink. He drained the eggs and began cracking and peeling, while his mother removed ingredients from the refrigerator.

"How are you liking your new job?" she asked.

Here we go. "It's not a new job, Mom. I'm just filling in until they get somebody to take over."

She turned to him, cutting board in hand. "Why would they want anyone else when they have you?"

They didn't, actually. Saul kept telling him how great he was doing. And, the truth was that after what happened with Kara it was a relief to stay busy with absorbing work. "I don't know. We'll see."

His mother put down the cutting board and began chopping celery. "Your father and I are very proud of you. You're coming into your own. Now all you have to do is find that special someone."

He felt kicked in the gut. *But I already found her. And lost her.* Or rather, *gave her up.* He couldn't talk about Kara with his mother. It was too new, too raw, so he turned the tables on her. "Are you and Dad happy?"

"What?" She looked startled. "Are we happy?" She blinked, then turned back to her work. "Sure. We have a fine life."

"But you used to say that if it weren't for us kids, you'd travel, see places, meet people."

She laughed softly. "When did I say that? Probably when you kids were fighting or your father was hiding behind the newspaper, right?"

"I don't know."

"I was young. People say things when they're young. You used to tell me you were catching a bus for New York every time we made you do your homework."

"Maybe." But he'd seen the longing in her eyes, her frustration and disappointment.

Even now, she was staring out the window, lost in thought. "I've felt restless at times," she said finally, handing him a knife to cut up the eggs he'd peeled. "But I settled down."

Or just plain settled. Maybe his father and he and his sisters had worn her down, trapped her in this hamster wheel of a life.

"Don't worry," she said, smiling at him. She reached up and messed his hair the way she used to when he was a kid. "It's good that you waited until you were old enough to know what you want."

But did he know? He'd thought he wanted Kara, but had he really? Maybe he had the same restless soul his mother did. He loved Kara now, but how long would it last?

"Where's that son of mine?" his father hollered from the basement. "Get down here and give your old man a hand."

"Go on, dear. I'll finish up. Bring him up in fifteen minutes for lunch, and tell me how many chairs he's ruined."

Ross put down the knife, wiped his hands dry and headed downstairs.

"Good to see you, son." His father hugged him and slapped him on the back so hard it stung. "You need money?"

"I'm fine."

"Of course you're fine. You're a big deal manager now." His father surveyed him with pride in his eyes.

"Only on an interim basis. Until they hire someone else."

His father shrugged, handed him a brush and pointed

at a chair. Judging from the unevenness, drips and streaks on the other ones, his mother would be buying that new dining-room set for sure.

"Tell me about this interim job," his father said.

Ross started talking and before he knew it his mother was shouting down at them that lunch was ready, and he realized he'd been going nonstop for twenty minutes.

"A shame the job's only temporary," his dad said, not looking at him. "Since you like it so much."

"I don't like it," he said, pausing. "I don't hate it. I mean, I *like* it, but that doesn't mean I *want* it." He thought about yesterday, when he'd been so immersed in planning the production schedule that he hadn't looked up until after six and hadn't thought twice about missing his usual pickup game of b-ball. "It's not that bad a job. It's interesting and all."

"Give it time. You'll grow into it," his father said. "Nothing good comes easy."

"I guess." Maybe he would talk to Saul about trying it for a few more months. At the very least, the work was helping him get over Kara. And he needed something for that. Whenever he thought of her, his heart got a little smaller and tighter. Right now it was a pea-sized knot rattling around in his chest. He frowned and dipped into the stain so hard some slopped over the sides.

"Pretty soon you'll be buying your own place, finding a nice girl and making a home together," his father mused. "Your mother would love some grandkids to spoil."

Now his dad was on him, too. Harassment and love—the double-edged sword of being home.

"Did things turn out the way you expected, Dad?"

he asked abruptly. "I mean with Mom and the marriage."

His father stopped misapplying the stain and turned to him. "Nothing's ever quite what you expect, Ross, but your mother and I made a nice life."

"Come on up, boys." His mother's voice drifted down to them.

"What about Mom?" Ross said, putting the brush in the can of turpentine. "She always said the family tied her down."

His father chuckled, putting his brush away, too. "You don't understand your mother, Ross. Complaining is her way." His father studied his face. "You don't believe me? I'll let you in on a secret. Your mother left us once."

"What?"

"Remember when she went to help her sister in Austin?"

"Vaguely."

"You were too young to grasp much, thank goodness. It was a trial separation. Really threw me for a loop. But she came back after only a month. She didn't talk about it and I never pressed her, but I know that your mother realized she was happier here with me and you kids and all the hassles that went with us than off on her own."

"Are you sure?"

"Let me show you something." His father led the way upstairs and pointed to the wall of family photos—shots of him and his sisters in the yard, at their cabin on Oak Creek, in the hotel they used to go to in Flagstaff for a taste of snow each winter, picnics at Encanto Park, Thanksgiving dinners, trips to Disneyland.

"Now these are from the last three years since the

girls went off to school.'' His father pointed at a display beside the grandfather clock that featured the Oak Creek cabin, Flagstaff, even Disneyland. Except these photos held just his parents.

''You kids are gone and aren't we the world travelers?'' his father said, his eyes twinkling. ''So much for Europe and China and the Peace Corps, like your mother always said she wanted.''

''Why don't you go?''

''I'm game. But your mom likes our life. That's what I'm telling you. With your mother, complaining is a habit. She saw herself as giving up her freedom, but she really got what she wanted. Kind of like you with that new job of yours, eh?'' His dad winked and jabbed him in the ribs with a sharp elbow.

The elbow wasn't the only jab Ross felt.

Was complaining just a habit with him, too? To keep from admitting the truth—that he liked his new job? ''So, you and Mom are happy?'' he asked his dad.

''Deliriously. But don't tell your mother. You'll upset her.'' Again his father winked. Then he looked serious, his eyes intent. ''It's sad, though, that she's scared of her own happiness—like it'll disappear if she admits she feels it.'' He shook his head, held his son's gaze. ''Don't be like that, Ross. Don't be afraid to be happy. Trust your heart.''

Emotion clogged Ross's throat. For a second, he wanted his dad to give him another one of those painful bear hugs, but he'd already headed into the kitchen. Ross followed him, arriving in time to see his father lean in to kiss his mother.

''You reek of turpentine,'' she said, scrunching her nose. But she kissed him and then looked into his eyes, and for the first time in his life, Ross saw how much his parents cared for each other. They'd stayed together not because of him and his sisters or any hamster wheel of habit, but because they loved each other. Deeply.

Watching them embrace, Ross flashed on a picture of him with Kara in a house they might share—with his art and her kitchenware, his turntable and her big firm bed. Why couldn't they be like his parents, who were different but found a way to be together? A way based on love.

Maybe he had been limiting himself. Telling himself he couldn't commit to a job or a person just as his mother had told herself she was trapped by the family she loved. She'd been foolish, wasted time, made her children feel insecure and her husband uncertain. Ross didn't want to do that.

I just don't want to see you lose out because of a false view of yourself. That's what Kara had said about the job she'd shoved him into. Maybe she'd been right. Now he was doing the job, which he'd been half-afraid he couldn't handle, and now enjoyed. As much of a pain in the ass as Kara's pushing could be, it might be exactly what he needed.

Don't be afraid to be happy, his father had said. *Trust your heart.* And his heart told him he needed Kara—to challenge him, to push him, to love him. And, for the first time, he knew he wouldn't let her down.

She, on the other hand, might not be so sure of that. He'd have to show her. He'd start by doing something about this job. First thing Monday morning, he'd talk to Siegel about it. He'd maybe even go into Macy's and check out one of those suits, though that made him shudder. A minor problem, really. If Kara and he worked together, surely they could be happy without getting trapped in any hamster wheel. It wouldn't be easy, but, like his dad said, what good thing was?

15

SIX IN THE MORNING and someone was at Kara's door. That was entirely too early for visitors.

"Come in," Kara said to Tina, fuzzy brained from lying awake all night thinking about Ross. Again. Going on three weeks and she didn't feel a bit better.

"I need to talk," Tina said, pushing inside the apartment, holding a paper sack and an opened pack of Twinkies, which she thrust at Kara. One of the Twinkies was gone and the other had a bite out of it.

"This is too much," Kara said. "You're coming earlier and earlier and the breakfasts you're bringing are getting worse and worse."

"Sorry. I couldn't find much I liked at the 7-Eleven." She rummaged in the sack and came up with a long skinny sausage stick. "Slim Jim? It's protein."

"No thanks." Kara followed Tina to the kitchen table.

"I'm going crazy," Tina said. "Yesterday I caught myself working problems on one of Tom's study sheets I found under the couch cushion. For fun!"

"You miss Tom. It's a way to feel close to him."

"No, something's really wrong. Last night I got dressed up to tear up the town—dancing, partying. I had a new dress, new shoes, new hair. Except I fell asleep in the chair before nine." She took a tug of the Slim Jim. "It's like I'm turning into Tom."

Kara started to speak, but Tina kept going. "I eat at the same places he likes. I forget to wear makeup—he liked me like that, can you believe it? And you know where I'm going from here? To the boat store. Just to look at stuff. I'm even thinking of taking a sailing class."

"You told me you liked sailing."

"Am I depressed? Schizoid? What?"

Kara looked into her friend's lovesick face. "Maybe you're changing. Did you think of that?"

"Changing?"

"Yeah. Maybe you're developing new interests. You thought Tom was making you change, but maybe you were doing it on your own."

"That's too easy. I must just be in one of the stages of grief."

"How do you feel about the new things you're doing—wearing less makeup, not partying, learning about sailing?"

Tina's gaze was anxious, confused and a little hopeful. "How do I *feel* about them? Well, I don't mind, really. It made me nervous when I was with Tom—like I was giving in, you know?"

"But you're still living like that."

"Yeah. I am. Hmm." She kept chewing the sausage stick, but her face began to brighten like a dimmer switch flaring toward full power. "So maybe this is the way I really am? And it's not just for him?"

"Sounds reasonable." She had to be very, very careful or she'd scare skittish Tina away from what she wanted.

Then Tina dropped the Slim Jim and put her head in her hands. "Who am I kidding? I miss him so much I want to die." She raised tear-filled eyes. "I miss the way he really listened to me. Even when I was such a bitch to him, he said he loved me—the real me. What if it's true? What if he does love me? Just the way I am?"

"Then you'd be a fool to let him go," Kara said, her own voice shaking with emotion. "Talk to him. Be honest with him."

"I can't." Huge tears rolled down Tina's cheeks.

"Yes, you can. You have to." How could Tina be so stubborn?

"But I don't deserve him." The words came out raw, as if torn from her throat.

"Oh, Tina." Kara got out of her chair and went to hug her.

Her usually bristly friend accepted the embrace with both arms. "I'm so scared," she said into Kara's shoulder.

"Of course you're good enough for him," Kara said, leaning back to look in Tina's face. "You're a fabulous, kick-ass, smart, funny, sexy woman and Tom's lucky to have your love."

"You think?" She searched Kara's face. For once, she was really listening.

"I know. Talk to Tom. Tell him what you told me. Trust him with the truth."

Tina gave her a watery smile. "You're a good friend, Kara. I don't deserve you, either."

"Sure you do. But you are going to have to do something about the bad breakfasts you've been bringing."

In a moment, Tina collected herself. She took a deep breath, wiped her face and squared her shoulders, as if preparing for battle, and set off...to *think* about talking to Tom.

Kara gnawed absently on the remains of Tina's Slim Jim, her own words haunting her. *Trust him.*

That was great advice for Tina, but what about for her? Did she trust Ross?

Obviously not, since she'd given up at the first roadblock. In the work world, she'd fought her way to success time after time, but at the first hint of trouble with love, she'd let it drop like an overheated sweet roll. She'd had no faith in him at all. Or her own choices. Ross had seemed wrong in so many ways. He didn't even have a good job.

But Ross was fine with his job. He and Tina were right. She had been trying to change him so he would seem more like the right man for her.

But that was wrong. When you loved someone, you believed in him, whether he pumped gas, made art or trimmed palm trees. You loved him whoever he was. You gave your heart freely, committed yourself, for better or worse. You had faith in him. In your love.

And she did love Ross for who he was—for his humor, his kindness, his laid-back style, his sexy confidence, maybe even for his Charlie's Angels' shower curtain. But she'd told herself that wasn't enough. She'd given herself a ground rule and ignored her heart.

If Ross didn't want a more responsible job, that was his business. She took another bite of Tina's Slim Jim. Mmm. She looked at it. How low had she sunk? She should be eating carrot sticks and low-fat yogurt.

But she was sick of that stuff. She wanted something wicked and sinful and spicy like Slim Jims. And Ross. What a boring life she'd had before he came into the Hyatt dressed like Miguel. She loved Ross, but she also needed him, for exactly the reasons he'd seemed wrong for her. He kept her eyes open, kept her jumping, tipped her out of her safe little Tupperware tub into his unpredictable world of delights.

She jumped to her feet, her heart pounding. She had to talk to Ross, tell him she had faith in him—in them—and that she loved him no matter what job he had.

Showing him would be better. What would work? And then she knew exactly what to do. All she needed was the costume.

TINA PUSHED HER WAY into the Upside, her heart in her throat. This was it, for all the marbles. There was Tom, dear Tom, the love of her life, working away, his big body, solid and sure, filling the space behind the bar, just the way he filled her heart.

So what if he'd rather serve drinks than chitchat? So what if he liked to be in bed at nine? She didn't mind if she was in that bed with him, naked and in his arms.

Tom loved her. That was what mattered. More importantly, he believed in her—the inner Tina, the soft, shaky woman she guarded from everyone but just might be able to trust to him.

But what if he'd given up on her? She faltered for a second. Maybe she should come back another time or call him tomorrow.

As if by radar, Tom looked up and caught sight of her. His face filled with such joy that she found the courage to head for the bar, holding his gaze, not caring a bit about the men watching her pass.

She stopped in front of him.

"What can I get you?" Tom asked, his eyes bright with…could it be *hope?*

You. For the rest of my life. She felt tongue-tied. "I'm not sure exactly what I want."

Tom watched her, wary, but he absorbed everything

about her face, every curve, every wrinkle she hid with makeup, every fear she hid with bravado, and beyond, to her hopeful soul.

She couldn't make a word come out, so she reached across the bar, grabbed Tom by his shirt and kissed him. Her whole heart was in that kiss. It was big.

Distantly she heard the dull crack of thick glass breaking. Careful Tom had let a mug crash to the floor, then he grabbed her up and hefted her over the bar and into his arms. "Let's make that a double," he said, and kissed her again, and it was warm and wonderful and safe…and scary.

"Champagne on the house!" he shouted to the crowd, more exuberant than she'd ever seen him.

"Not so fast," she said, yanking him down to her eye level. "We have to talk about this." The entire bar was silently watching, so she lowered her voice. "I'm still me. I'm not perfect. I get wild and bitchy and insecure. I'll make you angry and I'll let you down."

"Don't you think I know that?" he said softly, kissing her on the forehead. "And I've been an ass. I was afraid you'd run away, so I hung on too tight. Be whoever you want to be. Party all night if you want. Just come home to me."

Amazingly enough, the moment he gave her that freedom, she no longer needed it. "I love you, Tom," she said, her eyes watery with tears. "So much."

Tom lifted her off her feet for another kiss. The bar crowd cheered. Maybe they just wanted free drinks or maybe they knew true love when they saw it.

They weren't out of the woods, Tina knew. They would struggle and argue and complain and adjust. And they would go really, really slowly. But when she looked into Tom's eyes, as deep and blue as the lake they'd sailed, she had the feeling they might just make it.

EARLY MONDAY EVENING, Kara stood on Ross's doorstep, her heart in her throat. He'd wanted to talk to her, too. Something about a new plan. Ross talking about a *plan*—now that was a good sign.

She sniffed the rose bouquet, taking the sweet musk deep into her lungs for courage, and pushed the prickly netting away from her face. It wasn't just the tight costume that was cutting off her breathing. Her whole future was at stake here.

If Ross went pale and shut the door in her face, she'd be devastated. But she hoped he'd hold out his arms and accept the whole package. Just as she was ready to do.

She rang the doorbell. No answer. Come on, Ross. Surely he wasn't still in the shower, though it would be just like him to be late for his own fantasy wedding. That wasn't fair, since he had no way to know there was a miniskirted bride hopping from foot to nervous foot on his terrace.

"You look pretty." Abby, the little girl from downstairs, said, craning her neck to look up at Kara. "Can I smell?"

Kara bent down so Abby could get a sniff of her bouquet. Something ripped on her dress in the back. Uh-oh.

Abby's inhale drew a red petal into her nostril for an instant. "Mmm," she said, stepping back to examine Kara in wonder. "When I get married I hope I look just like you."

"When you get married, I hope you *feel* just like

me,'' she said. ''Feeling is the most important part of a wedding.''

Abby looked at her seriously, as if she'd absorbed this wisdom deep in her heart. What a mature little girl, Kara thought, until Abby said, ''Do you have any candy on you?''

''Excuse me?''

''At my cousin's wedding there were white and pink mints. I got sick and threw up in the bathroom.''

''I see. No. No candy right now, but if we have a wedding, I'm sure there will at least be cake.''

''Oh, okay. But not lemon. I hate lemon cake.'' Abby bounded away just as the door flew open and Kara looked up to see Ross standing there in a dress suit. For a second, she almost thought he'd read her mind and was dressed for her bridal fantasy. It wasn't a tux, but it would have looked perfect on top of a wedding cake, even down to the funky retro tie with hula dancers that was so very Ross. Was it one of the Love Thief restraints?

He helped her to her feet, looking at her with the same wide-eyed wonder she knew her face wore. ''You look…amazing,'' he said, pulling her inside.

''This is for that fantasy you always wanted…the virgin bride,'' Kara said, suddenly embarrassed about the speech she'd planned. ''It's a costume. I mean, we're not going to really get married or anything. It's just symbolic, you know? Like I said before? Remember?''

He just stared at her.

''I'm wearing it because I want you to know I have faith in you—in us. No matter what you decide to do with your life—become a creative director or a comic book collector.''

''Well, I think—''

She rushed on, wanting to get it all out before he could argue. "I realized that love doesn't come in a neat package with everything all figured out. You have to open yourself up and love who you love, accept him for who he is and let that be enough because...because it will be plenty...."

"You're absolutely right. And I—"

"Plus, you're good for me. You keep me alive and open. You help me slow down and smell the desert rain. Maybe I can't hike the Grand Canyon on a whim, but I want to explore life—with you, anyway—and if we practiced hiking a little at a time, I could maybe work up to it, and—"

Ross shut her up with a kiss, and she melted and the world tilted and spun until she thought she might faint with happiness.

Ross broke off the kiss. "You don't have to hike the Grand Canyon as long as I never, never have to buy a minivan, no matter how many kids we have."

"Kids? What are you...? Isn't that rushing things?"

"Not the way I feel right now," he said softly. "You make me want everything, Kara. Kids and a house and a dog and a future. You're good for me. I figured out I kind of need to be pushed."

"You do?"

"But only in the direction I really want to go," he warned.

"Of course."

"And I kind of like knowing where my video games are and having hot pads so I don't burn my hands...and I took the job."

"You what?"

"Yeah. Meet the new manager of the creative department. Even Peter Pan has to grow up some time. I talked to Siegel today and as long as I can keep some clients of my own—to keep up my artistic chops—I'll do it.''

"Ross, that's wonderful!'' she said, then moderated her tone. ''But only if it's what you want. Because there was nothing wrong with your life the way it was.''

"Except it didn't have you in it,'' he said, and his face went soft with love. ''Thank you for believing in me, Kara, even when I wasn't ready to believe in myself.''

"I believe in us together, too. And thank you for keeping my life fresh. Thanks for giving me taxi rides in the rain and chocolate-covered strawberries and sexy lingerie and…Slim Jims.''

"What?''

"Never mind. You make my life sparkle.''

"And you make my life solid. And worth something.''

And then their lips met in a kiss sweet with forever.

After a long, long while, Ross ran his hands down the back of her dress. ''So this is for the virgin bride fantasy, huh?''

"Yeah,'' she murmured in his ear, nibbling his lobe. ''The one you always wanted.''

"Sounds great. For now. Until we wear this stuff for real.'' Kara couldn't believe her ears. What had seemed a foolish fantasy—Kara and Ross as bride and groom—would one day happen. She felt she was floating a few inches above the ground.

Until Ross started kissing her neck and working on the row of tiny buttons at the back of her dress. Then she landed firmly on the ground to enjoy every second of this.

Struggling with the buttons, Ross groaned. ''I thought

it would be fun to get you out of all this, but I want you *now*."

"Not a problem," she said. She stepped away from him, grabbed the hidden seam between her breasts and yanked the sides apart, revealing the fact that she wore nothing underneath.

"Ooh, baby," Ross said, his eyes full of lust and love. "No underwear. Kara Collier, you're my type after all."

"And you're mine," she said, tugging him closer by his belt. She'd fallen for the absolute wrong man and it had turned out absolutely right.

Is your man too good to be true?

Hot, gorgeous AND romantic?
If so, he could be a Harlequin® Blaze™ series cover model!

Our grand-prize winners will receive a trip for two to New York City to
shoot the cover of a Blaze novel, and will stay at the luxurious Plaza Hotel.
Plus, they'll receive $500 U.S. spending money!
The runner-up winners will receive $200 U.S.
to spend on a romantic dinner for two.

It's easy to enter!

In 100 words or less, tell us what makes your boyfriend or spouse a true romantic
and the perfect candidate for the cover of a Blaze novel, and include in your submission
two photos of this potential cover model.

All entries must include the written submission of the contest entrant, two photographs of the model
candidate and the Official Entry Form and Publicity Release forms completed in full and signed by
both the model candidate and the contest entrant. Harlequin, along with the experts at
Elite Model Management, will select a winner.

For photo and complete Contest details, please refer to the Official Rules on the next page. All entries
will become the property of Harlequin Enterprises Ltd. and are not returnable.

Please visit www.blazecovermodel.com **to download a copy of the Official Entry Form and
Publicity Release Form or send a request to one of the addresses below.**

Please mail your entry to: **Harlequin Blaze Cover Model Search**

In U.S.A.
P.O. Box 9069
Buffalo, NY
14269-9069

In Canada
P.O. Box 637
Fort Erie, ON
L2A 5X3

No purchase necessary. Contest open to Canadian and U.S. residents who are 18 and over.
Void where prohibited. Contest closes September 30, 2003.

HARLEQUIN® *Blaze*™

HBCVRMODEL1

HARLEQUIN BLAZE COVER MODEL SEARCH CONTEST 3569 OFFICIAL RULES
NO PURCHASE NECESSARY TO ENTER

1. To enter, submit two (2) 4" x 6" photographs of a boyfriend or spouse (who must be 18 years of age or older) taken no later than three (3) months from the time of entry: a close-up, waist up, shirtless photograph; and a fully clothed, full-length photograph, then, tell us, in 100 words or fewer, why he should be a Harlequin Blaze cover model and how he is romantic. Your complete "entry" must include: (i) your essay, (ii) the Official Entry Form and Publicity Release Form printed below completed and signed by you (as "Entrant"), (iii) the photographs (with your hand-written name, address and phone number, and your model's name, address and phone number on the back of each photograph), and (iv) the Publicity Release Form and Photograph Representation Form printed below completed and signed by your model (as "Model"), and should be sent via first-class mail to either: Harlequin Blaze Cover Model Search Contest 3569, P.O. Box 9069, Buffalo, NY, 14269-9069, or Harlequin Blaze Cover Model Search Contest 3569, P.O. Box 637, Fort Erie, Ontario L2A 5X3. All submissions must be in English and be received no later than September 30, 2003. Limit: one entry per person, household or organization. Purchase or acceptance of a product offer does not improve your chances of winning. All entry requirements must be strictly adhered to for eligibility and to ensure fairness among entries.

2. Ten (10) Finalist submissions (photographs and essays) will be selected by a panel of judges consisting of members of the Harlequin editorial, marketing and public relations staff, as well as a representative from Elite Model Management (Toronto) Inc., based on the following criteria:

Aptness/Appropriateness of submitted photographs for a Harlequin Blaze cover—70%
Originality of Essay—20%
Sincerity of Essay—10%

In the event of a tie, duplicate finalists will be selected. The photographs submitted by finalists will be posted on the Harlequin website no later than November 15, 2003 (at www.blazecovermodel.com), and viewers may vote, in rank order, on their favorite(s) to assist in the panel of judges' final determination of the Grand Prize and Runner-up winning entries based on the above judging criteria. All decisions of the judges are final.

3. All entries become the property of Harlequin Enterprises Ltd. and none will be returned. Any entry may be used for future promotional purposes. Elite Model Management (Toronto) Inc. and/or its partners, subsidiaries and affiliates operating as "Elite Model Management" will have access to all entries including all personal information, and may contact any Entrant and/or Model in its sole discretion for their own business purposes. Harlequin and Elite Model Management (Toronto) Inc. are separate entities with no legal association or partnership whatsoever having no power to bind or obligate the other or create any expressed or implied obligation or responsibility on behalf of the other, such that Harlequin shall not be responsible in any way for any acts or omissions of Elite Model Management (Toronto) Inc. or its partners, subsidiaries and affiliates in connection with the Contest or otherwise and Elite Model Management shall not be responsible in any way for any acts or omissions of Harlequin or its partners, subsidiaries and affiliates in connection with the contest or otherwise.

4. All Entrants and Models must be residents of the U.S. or Canada, be 18 years of age or older, and have no prior criminal convictions. The contest is not open to any Model that is a professional model and/or actor in any capacity at the time of the entry. Contest void wherever prohibited by law; all applicable laws and regulations apply. Any litigation within the Province of Quebec regarding the conduct or organization of a publicity contest may be submitted to the Régie des alcools, des courses et des jeux for a ruling, and any litigation regarding the awarding of a prize may be submitted to the Régie only for the purpose of helping the parties reach a settlement. Employees and immediate family members of Harlequin Enterprises Ltd., D.L. Blair, Inc., Elite Model Management (Toronto) Inc. and their parents, affiliates, subsidiaries and all other agencies, entities and persons connected with the use, marketing or conduct of this Contest are not eligible to enter. Acceptance of any prize offered constitutes permission to use Entrants' and Models' names, essay submissions, photographs or other likenesses for the purposes of advertising, trade, publication and promotion on behalf of Harlequin Enterprises Ltd., its parent, affiliates, subsidiaries, assigns and other authorized entities involved in the judging and promotion of the contest without further compensation to any Entrant or Model, unless prohibited by law.

5. Finalists will be determined no later than October 30, 2003. Prize Winners will be determined no later than January 31, 2004. Grand Prize Winners (consisting of winning Entrant and Model) will be required to sign and return Affidavit of Eligibility/Release of Liability and Model Release forms within thirty (30) days of notification. Non-compliance with this requirement and within the specified time period will result in disqualification and an alternate will be selected. Any prize notification returned as undeliverable will result in the awarding of the prize to an alternate set of winners. All travelers (or parent/legal guardian of a minor) must execute the Affidavit of Eligibility/Release of Liability prior to ticketing and must possess required travel documents (e.g. valid photo ID) where applicable. Travel dates specified by Sponsor but no later than May 30, 2004.

6. Prizes: One (1) Grand Prize—the opportunity for the Model to appear on the cover of a paperback book from the Harlequin Blaze series, and a 3 day/2 night trip for two (Entrant and Model) to New York, NY for the photo shoot of Model which includes round-trip coach air transportation from the commercial airport nearest the winning Entrant's home to New York, NY, (or, in lieu of air transportation, $100 cash payable to Entrant and Model, if the winning Entrant's home is within 250 miles of New York, NY), hotel accommodations (double occupancy) at the Plaza Hotel and $500 cash spending money payable to Entrant and Model, (approximate prize value: $8,000), and one (1) Runner-up Prize of $200 cash payable to Entrant and Model for a romantic dinner for two (approximate prize value: $200). Prizes are valued in U.S. currency. Prizes consist of only those items listed as part of the prize. No substitution of prize(s) permitted by winners. All prizes are awarded jointly to the Entrant and Model of the winning entries, and are not severable - prizes and obligations may not be assigned or transferred. Any change to the Entrant and/or Model of the winning entries will result in disqualification and an alternate will be selected. Taxes on prize are the sole responsibility of winners. Any and all expenses and/or items not specifically described as part of the prize are the sole responsibility of winners. Harlequin Enterprises Ltd. and D.L. Blair, Inc., their parents, affiliates, and subsidiaries are not responsible for errors in printing of Contest entries and/or game pieces. No responsibility is assumed for lost, stolen, late, illegible, incomplete, inaccurate, non-delivered, postage due or misdirected mail or entries. In the event of printing or other errors which may result in unintended prize values or duplication of prizes, all affected game pieces or entries shall be null and void.

7. Winners will be notified by mail. For winners' list (available after March 31, 2004), send a self-addressed, stamped envelope to: Harlequin Blaze Cover Model Search Contest 3569 Winners, P.O. Box 4200, Blair, NE 68009-4200, or refer to the Harlequin website (at www.blazecovermodel.com).

Contest sponsored by Harlequin Enterprises Ltd., P.O. Box 9042, Buffalo, NY 14269-9042.

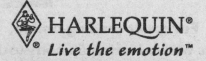

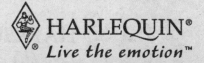

Blaze™

HARLEQUIN® *Blaze*™

Rory Carmichael is a good girl, trying to survive the suburbs.
Micki Carmichael is a bad girl, trying to survive the streets.
Both are about to receive an invitation
they won't be able to refuse....

INVITATIONS TO SEDUCTION

Enjoy this Blazing duo by fan favorite
Julie Elizabeth Leto:

#92—LOOKING FOR TROUBLE
June 2003

#100—UP TO NO GOOD
August 2003

And don't forget to pick up

INVITATIONS TO SEDUCTION
the 2003 Blaze collection
by Vicki Lewis Thompson,
Carly Phillips and Janelle Denison
Available July 2003

Summers can't get any hotter than this!

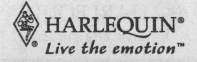

HARLEQUIN®
Live the emotion™

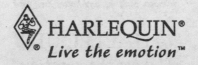